WE NEVER SAID GOODBYE

We Never Said Goodbye

First published in 2017 by Fridhem Publishing

1 2 3 4 5 6 7 8 9 10

Copyright © Hélene Fermont 2017

A CIP catalogue record for this book is available from the British Library.

Paperback ISBN 978-0-9954907-2-7

E book ISBN 978-0-9954907-3-4

Typeset by Elipsis Digital Limited, Glasgow
Printed and bound in Great Britain by Clays Limited, Bungay, Suffolk

www.fridhempublishing.com

For everyone who saw me through the hardest of times.
You know who you are.
May your lives be blessed with love, laughter and joy.
H.

CHAPTER ONE

June 2014

"WHERE IS HE? Mike's never late. Perhaps he forgot today's our wedding anniversary?"

Louise looked around at her spacious kitchen, with its new wallpaper in a pale shade of blue, the rustic old table and chairs. Smiling, she reached for the mobile on a shelf above the stove. *He's probably booked a table in some fancy restaurant, I bet it's the new French bistro in the high street,* she thought, slumping down in a chair and stretching her long, shapely legs. She couldn't avoid seeing her own reflection in the glass cupboard next to the sink.

Big blue eyes, small, slightly upturned nose and short, thick blonde hair – Louise's mind drifted off to when she used to be a model. She'd long since stopped thinking about it, until now.

She missed the glitz and fun back then. In particular, the sense of belonging and making new friends, both in her hometown of Malmö, and overseas. Not forgetting the lovely clothes, especially those she had been allowed to keep from Chanel, Lagerfeld and Yves Saint Laurent.

All of it seemed so long ago now. Almost as if none of it took place; a figment of her imagination.

She'd made an extra effort to look her best that morning,

hoping Mike would appreciate it. She'd even gone as far as applying false eyelashes and the shade of lipstick he preferred. At forty-five, Louise dreaded signs of age on her face, making her feel less attractive and not as young as she used to be. *Perhaps the time has come when I will have to consider a nip and tuck here and there?* she pondered, chewing her lip. The years passed so quickly; nearly everyone she knew from her modelling days had since succumbed to Botox and plastic surgery.

After her retirement, Louise felt bereft and at a loss as to what to do with her life. Eventually, she and her best friend, a fellow model, decided to venture into business together. Trine Larsen had been a permanent fixture in Louise's life ever since the two of them met at a mutual friend's party in Copenhagen in the early nineties. They'd hit it off from the start and were like sisters to one another. Taking the ferry from Malmö, Louise would seek out Trine's company each time she required advice and felt lonely. Both women relocated to London on a modelling assignment and loved it so much that they decided to stay. When Trine met Jasper, a champion rugby player and fellow Dane, Louise instantly warmed to his easy-going nature and gained another friend. However, after Trine and Jasper married in a register office in Kensington, Louise felt like an outsider, wishing she too could meet and fall in love with someone as nice and reliable as Jasper.

She continued modelling for another agency and signed a contract with a magazine that required her to travel all over Europe for a period of time. Upon returning to London and the cosy flat she and Trine had rented when they first moved to London, Louise was invited to a party in Belsize Park. It wasn't until she was standing by herself in a corner of the large, brightly-lit room that she noticed a tall, muscular man with mousy blond hair, wearing a black suit, white T-shirt and a gold chain around his neck. As he approached her, a big grin lighting up his deep-set dark blue eyes, Louise heard him say: "I feel as if I know you. Have we met before?"

Twiddling with her bracelet, Louise blushed and shook her head. "I doubt it. What makes you think we did?" She'd never encountered anyone as straightforward as Mike Kershaw.

"Call it intuition, if you like. It feels as if I've known you all my life."

Well, that was twenty-three years ago and the start of something special.

As he wined and dined her in the most prestigious restaurants and nightclubs in London, she fell deeply in love and it wasn't long before she moved into his small yet elegant pad in Bermondsey. The apartment was located only a few blocks from where he was born and had lived with his parents, until his father died and Mike inherited the family car lot. They married a year after they first met and Trine was Louise's maid of honour at the small church in Bethnal Green.

Why am I taking a trip down memory lane? Louise wondered. It wasn't like her to dwell on the past. She'd left all of it behind when she'd moved away from Malmö, where her parents lived their whole lives. Louise kept her maiden name, Berg, after she married Mike; it was common for Swedish women to not abandon their surname and a tribute to Louise's heritage.

When Louise and Trine first retired, both women attempted to find work yet neither warmed to the idea of being employees. Passing an empty shop on Fulham Road, they knew instantly fate had steered them there. By then both of them led interesting lives with husbands who worked hard: Mike at the car lot he'd turned into a limousine service with his oldest friend, Steve; and Jasper had retired from his playing career, launching a rugby coaching programme for players all over Europe. In his spare time Jasper bought derelict buildings that he converted and put up for sale.

The two couples spent almost every weekend together and when Trine and Jasper had their first child, Zack, the family moved to Putney and into a large four-storey building where they soon had another child, Emilia, then two years later, Christian.

Around the time of Christian's birth, Louise persuaded Mike to move from Belsize Park to Barnes in southwest London, close to Hammersmith. Their new house was situated just off the high street, with lots of Swedes living in the area and a Swedish school nearby. After much deliberation, Mike relented to Louise's wish and commuted each day between Barnes and the business in Bermondsey. There were times when Louise felt guilty for forcing him into moving away from his beloved north London to Barnes, where he'd never envisaged they'd move into a house that Louise bought with funds from her modelling career. Indeed, the idea that he may resent her for it stayed with her for some time, yet as the years passed by, Louise stopped blaming herself and felt certain that Mike enjoyed living there as much as she did.

By then she and Trine had turned their clothes shop into a roaring success. Focusing on Scandinavian fashion designers, they regularly placed orders with Filippa K, House of Dagmar, Back's Designs and many more exclusive and trendy labels that were all the rage.

The Studio was their baby and their dream come true. They'd used their own money to refurbish the premises in shades of white, grey and silver. It wasn't long before The Studio became *the* place to shop for designer clothes. When *Vogue* described it as, "the most exciting boutique to shop in", women came rushing in to see it and spread the word. Louise and Trine's interior design investment soon turned into a goldmine, with clients queuing up outside the door, everyone eager to purchase the latest trends by designers they'd barely heard of until The Studio became an institution among the models and celebrities in Fulham and the neighbouring areas.

No matter how hard they worked to maintain their standards, Louise and Trine never fell out with each other. As tall and slim as her friend, Trine had long brown hair, freckles on her nose and was prone to wear tight-fitting jeans in whatever colourful shades fashion dictated at the time. With big brown eyes and a broad mouth, Trine always saw the best in people and rarely commented on their personal lives. Both women met up regularly for coffee or *fika*, the Swedish word for having a snack outside of work.

Where is he? Surely, Mike's not forgotten today is our twentieth wedding anniversary? Walking upstairs to the master bedroom, Louise contemplated how lucky she was to be married to a man who took pride in his appearance and worked hard. *He'll make it up to me. Mike and Steve must be caught up in some meeting*, she told herself, changing into a pair of black leather slacks and a lacy top.

However many times Mike insisted she wear a skirt or dress, showing off her long legs and figure, Louise preferred trousers and casual wear.

Putting on flat black shoes, she made the effort to apply makeup just the way he liked it, with smoky eyes and bronzer on her cheekbones, then brushed her hair until it shone.

Twenty years. Time sure flies. Louise wondered if he'd got caught up with a client. It was almost 6.00 pm and still no sign of him and his car.

She'd rushed home in her new BMW convertible, a gift she'd bestowed on herself when she turned forty-five. Returning downstairs to the kitchen, Louise looked outside the window, expecting to see his car in the driveway.

Recently, Mike had splashed out on a silver Jaguar, claiming it was appropriate when he met up with prestigious clients. The black limousine Mike's father had bought for him when Mike gained his driver's licence was too old and battered to drive for the Managing Director of a high-end car service.

As she climbed the stairs once more, Louise felt butterflies in the pit of her stomach. She reached for the eau de toilette on the glass shelf in her en suite bathroom and spritzed it on her neck, behind the ears and wrists. *This isn't like him . . . I know we've not spent much time together lately. What if he's upset with me? Maybe it's the reason he hasn't called?*

That morning, Mike had left before she got up. She'd caught a glimpse of him the previous night, just before he told her he'd been so late back due to a meeting. As he finished a mug of black coffee, he'd mumbled, "We'll talk in the morning," his eyes not meeting hers.

"Is something wrong?" she'd replied, searching for a sign that he wasn't upset with her. "It's our anniversary tomorrow. Let's do something special to celebrate it. Just you and me." She was aware that lately The Studio had taken up much of her attention with her and Trine working overtime most nights.

"Sure, I'll give you a call." Mike had taken his coffee mug to the kitchen before Louise could respond.

Now that she thought of it, Louise felt certain Mike was hiding something from her.

It was at times like this she wished her parents were alive. They'd died on their way to a friend's wedding in Vienna when their car collided with a van. The teenager driving it was found guilty of having too much alcohol in his system. In less than a few minutes, Louise lost her parents and everything they'd shared.

She'd just turned twenty and almost lost her will to live.

Everything she looked forward to when they were alive suddenly ceased to exist. After she'd received the terrible news of the fatal accident, Louise made up her mind there and then to leave Malmö for good. All her precious memories no longer mattered after she lost the two people who meant everything to her.

Except for her father's sister, Louise had no family left to care for her. Aunt Gabriella often called yet it was years since the two of them last met and spent time together. If it had not been for her closest friends and modelling career, Louise wouldn't have coped.

Seated on the edge of the large double bed, she let out a big sigh. *I miss Mamma and Pappa so much,* she thought. *No matter how long they've been gone, I'll never get over losing them.*

Elin and Simon Berg never had the opportunity to experience their only child's career and success. They'd not met Mike and never would. Louise hoped that they would have approved of him. She'd never seen anyone as much in love as they were.

Her parents were the perfect match. They'd doted on their daughter and wanted the best for her. Just as fair and slim as their child, Elin and Simon were eternal optimists and romantics.

Trine's always reminding me I ought to visit Gabriella. Malmö's so different nowadays, I'll probably not recognise it . . . It's almost seven o'clock. I'd better call him at work. Louise dialled Mike's number on her mobile.

Steve picked up on the third ring. "Kershaw & Matthews Limousine Service."

"It's me, Louise. Is Mike still at work?" Deep inside, Louise knew something was wrong. Mike had never let her down on their wedding anniversary until now. But Steve's response made her gasp.

"Mike's not come in to work since last week." There was an edge to his voice.

"I don't understand . . . Mike told me you've a lot of clients to look after. You're seriously telling me he's not been around for a week?" Louise's heart was beating frantically inside her chest.

"I assumed he'd told you," Steve replied in his usual direct manner.

"I don't get it . . . I'm sorry I called and disrupted you."

"That's okay. Mike's probably got something up his sleeve! Happy anniversary, darling."

Switching off her mobile, Louise let out another sigh. *Mike knows today's a special day. I'll give him more time to return home.* Recalling all the times he'd surprised her over the years in the most spectacular ways, she was on her way downstairs when her mobile rang. Mike's name was displayed on the screen.

Louise held her breath for a moment, a sense of foreboding overwhelming her as she picked up. "Mike! Where are you? I'm imagining all kinds of things! How long before you return home?"

"We need to talk. There's something I have to tell you." Mike sounded distant, as if they were strangers, not husband and wife. Not at all what she'd expected of him, today of all days.

"Can't it wait until you're home? Where are you? I talked to Steve. He told me you've not showed up at work since last week." Louise's mouth turned dry with fear.

"It's over. I'm not returning to you. Don't bother to try and change my mind. I'll pick up my belongings later." Mike's voice was deathly cold.

It was as if they'd never known each other, much less shared a life.

Feeling faint, Louise whispered, "You're kidding, right?"

"I've never been more serious than I am now," Mike replied. "We're through, Louise. Consider yourself dumped!"

The line went dead.

As the room started to spin, Louise couldn't fathom what had happened. Tears streamed down her face and neck. *Mike's left me! What did I do to make him treat me like this? On our anniversary of all days!* Reeling from shock, she swallowed hard, the room suddenly closing in on her. Her stomach ached so much she thought she'd be sick. Forcing herself to get a grip, she staggered upstairs and threw herself on the bed, not bothering to take off her shoes. Curled up in a ball of nerves and clutching a pillow, all she could think of was how cold he'd been when he told her they were finished. "This can't be happening to me! It just can't!" she cried aloud.

It was almost dark outside by the time Louise reached for the mobile on the bedside table and dialled Trine's number. Perhaps her old friend was still at The Studio, finishing off some last minute alterations before next week's fashion shoot?

The phone rang for what seemed like an eternity before she heard the familiar voice at the other end.

"Mike's left me!" Louise blurted out. "I can't cope on my own . . . please . . ."

As her friend's voice dissolved into sobs, Trine knew something awful had taken place. "You're at home?" she said. "I'll be with you shortly, just sit tight!" A knot the size of a football formed inside Trine's chest. Mike was a complete bastard to spring this on Louise on their anniversary. The man her best friend married was a worthless shit! "It won't take long, an hour maximum. Hang in there, I'm on my way!" Trine decided immediately that Louise would stay with her. All she had to do was to ensure nothing untoward took place between now and arriving at the house in Barnes. "We'll pack a suitcase and get you out of there. You're staying with us for the foreseeable future, until we know what's going on."

★

The following weeks passed by in a haze. Trine and Jasper took turns to watch over Louise. They'd persuaded her it was best that she stayed with them and Jasper convinced her he ought to pick up some of her belongings at the house. Neither Trine nor Louise had remembered to pack anything but a few pieces of clothing, a toothbrush and a pair of shoes. But ever since she arrived, Louise had confined herself to the guestroom and refused to get out of bed, except to shower.

Trine and Jasper had never seen her so distraught. Mike was a callous coward to end their marriage without warning over the phone! As much as they'd attempted to tempt her with food she normally liked, Louise barely touched it, causing her to lose at least a stone.

Watching her husband walk out the front door of their big and bustling home, Trine thought, *I hope Mike's not taken Louise's belongings, I'd not put it past him to stoop even lower than he already did!* If she ever saw him again, Trine would only be too pleased to wring his neck for all the pain and distress he'd subjected on her friend.

Her sentiment was confirmed when Jasper returned later that day, an angry expression in his normally kind blue eyes.

"You were right all along. Mike's picked up his things and helped himself to Louise's old paintings and furniture – the ones she inherited after her parents died! How will we tell her? It'll destroy her when she finds out."

Holding hands, the couple steered themselves to confront Louise with the news that Mike had already picked up his belongings. She looked so frail and upset, as if on the verge of a nervous breakdown.

Trine spoke first. She'd finished talking when to their surprise, Louise simply bowed her head, as if she'd already figured it out for herself.

"I wish he was dead!" she cried. "At least then I'd be able to bury him and put what happened behind me." Inwardly Louise wanted to cut him out of her life in the same way as he did with her. If only she knew the reason behind it! She'd spent a big part of her life with a man she loved and trusted. Yet all of it turned out to be a complete lie. Mike abandoned her without so much as an explanation, leaving her crushed to the core of her soul. All she could think of was how he sounded when he called that day. She repeated their conversation to herself so many times that all she wanted was to cry and sleep, wishing she could slip into oblivion and not wake up.

Later that week, Trine and Jasper's teenage son, Zack, went upstairs to check if she was alright, having already tried in vain to persuade her to join them downstairs in the kitchen for dinner. By then she'd lost so much weight they feared for her health. At fifteen, Zack was very mature for his age and viewed Louise as part of the family. Hearing him shout, "I can't wake her up!" Trine and Jasper ran upstairs and found Louise lying in bed, seemingly fast asleep. On the bedside table lay an empty bottle of sleeping pills neither of them recalled seeing before.

"Shit!" cried Trine. "She must have found it in the bathroom cabinet. I sometimes find it hard to sleep prior to a fashion show at The Studio . . . oh, why didn't I hide it?" The bottle contained at least twenty tablets, all of which were gone.

Attempting to console Zack, Trine quickly put a robe over Louise's cold body and prayed she wouldn't die. Jasper called an ambulance and arranged for a neighbour to babysit the younger children.

As the ambulance men carried Louise out on a stretcher, one of them asked if something had happened to cause her to take an overdose of sleeping tablets.

"Her husband dumped her on their twentieth anniversary," Trine replied, a desolate tear coursing down her cheek.

Nodding, the man said, "I see. Let's get her to the A&E as quickly as we can." It wasn't the first time he'd had a similar response, and wouldn't be the last. In his opinion the poor woman who lay unconscious in the ambulance was fortunate to be rid of someone as cruel as that. Looking at the three people who hovered over her, eyes glued to her face, he said, "She's lucky to have you. Is there anyone you can think of who should be informed? Those tablets are lethal, although I believe she'll survive."

Jasper shook his head. "She has an aunt who lives abroad. But Louise was adamant she was not to be disturbed when she first came to stay. We're here for her. We're her family now." He and Trine had tears in their eyes. If Zack hadn't found her lying in bed, comatose, Louise would not have survived. Instead she was vomiting up tablets after the ambulance men had inserted a drip to make her sick.

An hour later they were standing in the corridor outside the room in hospital, when a young nurse walked up to them and asked a few routine questions. "Your friend will recover but there's reason to believe she may do this again," she told them. "You must keep sleeping pills and other medication out of her reach."

"Please tell me the overdose didn't cause serious harm?" Trine asked in a low voice, so as to not wake Louise up. Sleeping soundly in the hospital bed, her friend looked so peaceful, yet Trine knew they had a long road ahead of them before she was truly on the mend.

"Your friend's fortunate in that your son found her when he did. She's over the worst hurdle. It's what happens next that matters more. I'm referring her to a therapist who specialises in trauma."

Almost a week passed before Louise willingly responded to questions. Her primary concern was the young boy who'd found her in the nick of time. Looking pale and exhausted, she leaned forward and touched Zack's arm.

"Are you alright? I'm desperately sorry you had to see me like that . . . there's a reason I did what I did, it won't happen again," she whispered, tears streaming down her face and onto the pillow.

"That's good to hear," Zack replied, squeezing her thin hand. "I'm glad you feel better." It seemed to him she'd lost even more weight after being on a drip since her admission to hospital.

The therapist, a middle-aged, bespectacled man, told them Louise was severely depressed yet not beyond repair. "Take one day at a time," he said. "Her entire world's been turned upside down. It will take a lot of patience and determination to get her back to how she used to be. Her entire emotional landscape has changed. You must make allowances for her as much as you can and permit her to vent her anger and grief on you. The time will come when you'll see that your friend's returned to you, albeit somewhat different." He prescribed antidepressants until Louise was capable of getting through the daily routine of getting up in the morning and caring for herself. "Some people take a long time to learn to cope," he explained. "Your friend may require counselling, although I suspect she's a lot stronger than she looks. Call me if you've cause for concern." Shaking their hands, he left the room.

Standing by the bed, Trine felt Louise's hand on hers.

"Please forgive me!" she cried, her eyes searching Trine's.

"There's nothing to forgive! Zack's fine. You must focus on getting better. It's the only thing that matters to us." Trine couldn't shake off the feeling of how hollow her words sounded. They'd been to hell and back in less than a few weeks, yet Louise had survived against all the odds.

A couple of days later, Louise was discharged and returned to live with the Larsen family. Lying in the same bed where Zack discovered her, she thought, *It's of no use to repeat what happened between me and Mike. If only I knew why he left me! I need answers, only then will I be able to get closure. He had no right to do what he did without so much as an explanation. I'm owed that at least.* She felt certain Mike had planned everything long before it actually took place. They had known each other far too long for her to let him walk away as if nothing happened.

The only sound coming from the living room was her friends' muffled voices, tinged with concern.

Deep down Louise knew without a doubt that the man she fell in love with wasn't the kind of person he'd led her and everyone else to believe. *The time will come when everything will be revealed*, she told herself, closing her mind to it for now.

CHAPTER TWO

ONE WEEK LATER, Louise insisted she felt more like herself and was ready to return to work. Privately she craved the distraction of the bustle of The Studio, knowing that would stop her dwelling on recent events. She and Trine were busy with the preparation of the autumn and winter stocktake, when out of the blue Trine commented, "You know, Jasper and I are very proud of you and how well you've coped in the last week. We think you ought to sell the house. We'll help you find a nice place to live; somewhere within walking distance of The Studio. What do you think?"

"I guess you're right," Louise replied after a moment's hesitation. "There's no reason for me to stay in the house anymore. I feel as if Mike's been gone a long time." That very afternoon she contacted a solicitor and filed for divorce.

"All I ask of him is that he gives up his share of the house. I want nothing of him," she reported back to Trine. Clearly, Mike never gave a damn about her so why should she care about him?

"Not even compensation for all the times you bailed him out at work?" Trine's tone was muted. No matter how successful The

Studio was, Louise deserved something after everything she'd been through.

Shaking her head, tears brimming in her eyes, Louise mumbled, "Not even after that." She turned her back on Trine and buried her head in a recent copy of *Vogue*, where The Studio was featured regularly as one of the most popular places to purchase Scandinavian designers' latest collections.

But Trine was much too angry to keep her thoughts to herself. "I understand you're too upset to think straight. Listen to me, please! That creep abandoned you. If I were in your shoes, I'd take him for everything he's got."

Turning to look at her, Louise grimaced. "I guess Mike's lucky I'm not like you. He and I had some good times. It wasn't all bad, at least not during the early part of our marriage . . ." Her voice faltered as she reached for the mug of steaming black coffee on the desk.

"Is that all you have to say? You've just admitted your relationship wasn't what it seemed. How come you never confided in me?"

"Because if I did, I'd have had to face up to the fact that we had our problems, same as everyone else." Louise raised herself from the stool and paced the room. "The truth is, I'm not sure why I felt that way. We had our ups and downs, who doesn't? In the last few years we started to drift apart. I wasn't keen on discussing it."

"Meaning what exactly?" Trine persisted, unable to drop the subject.

"I don't know! We were so much in love, travelling to Paris and Rome at a moment's notice, before we decided to settle in London. Those days were the happiest time for us both. I've no idea what changed between us. Mike was over the moon when he and Steve extended their business. I was convinced Mike and I would last forever. Looks like I was kidding myself all along."

Louise took a deep breath and sat down next to her friend.

"When did you suspect something was wrong?" Trine asked, searching Louise's eyes.

"I can't specify a moment in time, maybe around the time we moved to Barnes. Mike kept complaining about the distance to work and how exasperated he was with the commuting to and fro."

"Did . . . did either of you stray?" Trine dared to ask.

"Of course not!" Louise snapped. "The idea never entered my mind. I'd never do something like that to him." She felt insulted by Trine's suggestion she would.

"Perhaps Mike wasn't as loyal to you? You can be as angry as you like with me. The bottom line is this: Mike left you and doesn't give a damn about the consequences."

Trying her hardest to calm down, Louise nodded. "You've got a point. When I think about it, Mike came up with one excuse after another to avoid spending time together. But none of it matters now! It's too late to ask questions, I'll never know why he ended our marriage." She was shaking with rage, yet Trine persisted.

"Do you recall what I thought of him when we first met?"

"Not really, no. But I'm sure you're going to let me know!"

"Don't give me that, of course you do. Jasper and I told you Mike was envious of you. He resented your achievements. Even to the extent of how close you and I are! Mike wanted you all to himself. Surely, you must have had your doubts?"

"Maybe I did . . . The fact remains, Mike's gone. We're through. I don't wish to dwell in the past." Louise buried her head in her hands, desperate for the conversation to end.

"I get that. But don't you want to know the reason he left you? What Mike put you through was unacceptable."

"Sometimes people do things for no reason. I should have been able to read between the lines." Louise felt completely drained. Trine was only highlighting what she had struggled to deal with over the years.

"I've only got one more question for you. If you were as unfulfilled as you say, what prevented you from having a fling or putting an end to the marriage? You've got too much to give to settle for less than you deserve."

"I already told you the idea didn't occur to me!" Louise shouted. "I loved him and wanted our marriage to last."

"I see . . . I'm sorry, Louise, I don't mean to upset you. Was it maybe . . . did you feel he wasn't the kind of person you wanted to have a family with?" Trine's eagerness to get to the core of what may have been a consistent concern and cause for frustration between Louise and Mike was in danger of pushing her friend too far.

Louise sighed and closed her eyes for a moment. When she opened them, her voice was calmer. "We talked about having a child in the beginning of our marriage. Mike accepted I'm not the maternal type. At least that was what he told me back then. He agreed we were fine just the way we were. Perhaps that was a lie and the real reason he deserted me."

Pouring each of them more coffee, Trine knew Louise wasn't keen to answer more questions, much less discuss the reason Mike resented her so much he'd decided to leave her.

"Trine, I feel like you're blaming me for what happened," Louise said quietly. "Mike told me that he'd let me know if he changed his mind and wanted a child."

"I'm sorry I upset you." Trine covered Louise's hand with her own. "It's his fault if he didn't come clean about it. Mike's a bastard and a coward for treating you like that."

They stayed well away from the topic for the rest of the day, agreeing that it wasn't conducive to Louise's state of mind.

That evening Trine and Jasper once again offered to help Louise find a flat, ensuring she didn't have to live in a house full of memories. They sat together on the light brown suede sofa in their cosy yet untidy living room.

"You're bound to get a fair price for it," Jasper told her, the warmth in his blue eyes making Louise feel as if she belonged there with them. "Just be sure it's what you want. You're welcome to stay with us for as long as you wish. There's no rush."

"No, the time has come to move away from the area," she replied. "I will find somewhere else to live. Unless I do it now, I will never be able to move on. Barnes is a great area to live in but it's not for me anymore. I've googled flats to rent in Fulham and Chelsea, and quite a few seem to fit the bill. Besides, they're just a few blocks away from The Studio."

Jasper jumped up from the sofa and walked towards the small conservatory overlooking the back garden, then turned and asked, "You're quite certain it's what you want? So much has happened in a relatively short period of time. Perhaps you should stay put a while longer?" He had a worried expression in his eyes.

"I'm certain it'll be best for me. Mike's not coming back. The sooner I move on, the better." Louise's eyes were dark with pain.

Mike was always on her mind, but he was no longer the man she trusted and with whom she'd spent more than half of her life.

A week later, Louise moved into a two-bedroom flat just on the corner of The Studio and side street to Fulham Road. By then nearly a month had passed. Had someone told her that her life would be turned upside down so quickly, she'd never have believed it.

Close to local shops, cafés, bars and restaurants, Louise's new flat consisted of a large bedroom and en suite bathroom with a shower cabin and Jacuzzi, where she relaxed after work. The living room resembled a boudoir with a large walk-in closet in the hall and another small bedroom adjacent. She furnished the flat with a mixture of soft pastel-coloured furniture and what was left of her parent's belongings. Mike had taken her treasured antique chairs and tables, only leaving behind a fraction of the items that Louise had cherished.

It wasn't until she put the house up for sale and said goodbye to her neighbours that Louise felt close to tears. *Why did you leave me, Mike? What did I do to make you hate me so much?* she asked herself.

When Jasper first told her what he'd found when he'd been to the house during her hospital admission, Louise hadn't believed that Mike had taken her belongings. Looking back on it now, she felt nauseated at the thought of Mike stooping that low. It was as if everything they'd ever meant to one another was a complete lie.

As she turned for one last look around the picturesque house she'd lived in for so long, ideally situated in a quiet cul-de-sac and with rose bushes on either side of the front door, Louise's eyes fixed on a framed photo of the two of them on their wedding day, both smiling at the camera and looking as if they didn't have a care in the world. She'd decided to leave it behind in case Mike came back to ensure she'd not left something valuable. Staring at the familiar photo, Louise's mind reeled with anger. Marching up to the mantelpiece, she reached for it, bent down and placed it on the oak floor, then smashed it to pieces with her shoes.

It felt great to destroy evidence of a time they'd been happy. A time when she believed they'd last forever.

Overcome with emptiness, Louise slowly walked out the door, the sense of betrayal overwhelming her so much she could hardly breathe. It wasn't until she'd returned to the flat that she realised the pain she carried inside was still as sharp as the day he'd called to tell her they were finished.

Moving away from home wasn't going to be as simple a solution as she had been led to believe.

Weekdays passed by quickly with The Studio taking up most of Louise's time. The weekends were the hardest and each time she noticed couples walking by, holding hands, Louise felt the loneliest she'd ever been. In a bid to keep herself busy, she sold the jewellery Mike had given her on birthdays and anniversaries. He'd splashed out on exquisite pieces yet none of it appealed to her anymore. She now preferred understated yet elegant pieces as opposed to his big and ostentatious style.

One night towards the end of autumn, Louise and Trine were working late, when the former asked: "How come you and Jasper are as much in love as you were when you first met? What's your secret?" Louise sipped her coffee and waited for a reply.

"We're each other's best friend and soul mate. We've had our ups and downs, who doesn't? Jasper's obsession with refurbishing derelict houses sometimes gets on my nerves! I guess it keeps him occupied and gives him an alternative outlet to rugby."

"You're very fortunate to be married to someone as decent and reliable. I wish my marriage could have lasted."

"It's how life works out. Jasper and I happen to be right for each other. You'll find your perfect man, eventually."

"Are the two of you as passionate as you used to be?" Louise asked, embarrassed to enquire about something so personal.

"Most of the time. Listen to me, Louise, you've got to give

yourself time to heal. When you encounter the right person, you'll know it in here." Trine gestured at her heart.

"Nah, I don't think I ever will." She sighed. "Trine, why do you suppose Mike left me? Please be honest with me."

"Mike isn't the man you thought he was. He always put his own needs first. It was evident how much he resented your modelling career and this place. But he certainly never objected to the perks, money and material possessions. All of it enabled him to get what he wanted: a comfortable lifestyle. I'm sorry if what I say upsets you. You wanted the truth and I gave it to you."

"Then you should have confronted me with it earlier!" Louise felt awful. Her closest friend hadn't confided in her until it was too late.

"Would you have taken any notice? What goes on between a husband and wife is private. Plus I was worried we would fall out."

"I wish you had! It may have opened up my eyes to what was wrong with our marriage. You seem to think Mike resented me for not wanting to have a family."

"Stop blaming yourself for what happened! Mike chose to leave you and everything you shared. What took place is entirely down to him. Maybe he did resent you for a long time, but who cares? You did nothing wrong."

"We never said goodbye." Louise blinked back tears. "I've had an offer on the house. The estate agent informed me it's a family. I told them to go ahead and close the deal."

It was almost six months since she and Mike split up and the divorce had been finalised that week. Trine put an arm around her friend's shoulders. As far as she and Jasper were concerned, Mike deserved to rot in hell.

★

"I don't get it, why did you leave Louise for Abby?" Steve Matthews shook his head. "They're miles apart!"

Steve and Mike were having a drink in their local pub after work. They had known each other since nursery school and had grown up together. Their parents had socialised and it was only natural that their kids would be friends as well. When Mike's father died after decades of alcohol consumption and Steve's parents split up, they relied on each other for everything. With Mike leaving school and Steve out of a job at the local petrol station, they decided to enter into a partnership and revive the car lot that Timothy Kershaw had worked into the ground.

Mike loved to mingle with the pillars of the community, the richer the better. Bumping into Louise at an event in central London turned out to be the icing on the cake. He'd not been able to take his eyes off her. Lust at first sight, later turning into something more meaningful and marriage.

Forever obsessed with appearance, Mike fell for Louise's height, her blonde hair and her legs that went on forever. Yet there was something vulnerable about her beneath that breathtaking exterior. It wasn't until he managed to talk her into having dinner with him that Louise told him about her parents' untimely passing. From then on the two of them were inseparable and Mike knew he wanted her for himself.

Louise needed him; he made her feel safe and protected.

Yet Steve knew only too well that Mike wasn't the sort of man who wasted time on having regrets. *He's got the whole package: looks, business and money in the bank,* Steve thought inwardly. *I'll never get my head around the reason he left Louise. She did everything for him.*

Contrary to his well-groomed friend, Steve couldn't care less about his appearance. He had intense blue eyes, spiky short dark hair and a wrinkly face. Wearing a polo neck jumper and faded blue jeans with holes in the knees, he looked like a fading rock star and resembled Ronnie Wood. But as long as he had money to spend on beer and sexy young girls, everything was as it should be.

Pushing aside his glass of wine on the bar, Mike snapped: "You're actually comparing Abby with Louise? Can't we have a drink without you commenting on it every chance you get?" He took a swig of his wine, wishing he'd spent the evening on his own.

"Surely you must be fed up with Abby by now?" Steve asked.

"Listen to yourself – you'll be comparing Abby's and my place to Louise's house in Barnes next! I just found out she sold it to some family. It's typical that whatever Louise decides to do, I am the last to find out about it."

The people sitting close by averted their eyes. It was hard to believe the two men were acquainted; they looked as if they came from different planets. One so immaculate; the other like something the cat dragged in.

Changing the subject, Steve asked: "Will you exchange your Jaguar for the Porsche you talked about the other day?"

"Hardly. It needs too much work on it. Maybe I'll find a better one somewhere soon." Mike fiddled with the sleeves of his new leather jacket.

"Your old man would have had a fit if he could hear you talking like that! He wanted you to follow in his footsteps, not cater to the snobs of the neighbourhood." Steve thought it amusing how Mike bent over backwards to please the clients who had money and expensive taste, just like he did.

"It's got nothing to do with you! Dad left everything to me. He'd never have approved of our partnership, anyway."

"You're talking out of your posterior! Had it not been for my investment, there'd be no business at all. Your old man was indebted to his eyeballs. Louise knew it as well."

"Stay the hell away from my personal affairs," Mike hissed, gulping down his third glass of wine.

"You'd better stop right there. Louise is a class act compared with the likes of Abby." Steve's eyes narrowed. He and Mike never used to argue like they did now.

"Well, what about you and that slut, Camilla? She's not a patch on Paige. Why that gorgeous woman puts up with you, I'll never understand. She must be mad to think you'll change. Sex and booze are all you care about."

Both men glared at one another.

"Abby and I had a fling ages ago," Steve said eventually. "She's the sort of woman who takes a guy for everything he's got. You'd do well to bear it in mind."

"Yeah, well let me tell you something, mate. Abby and I are in love! There's nothing you can say that will stop me from being with her. Look at yourself: Paige is filing for divorce at long last! Don't look so surprised. You must have known she wouldn't stand by you forever? Your own wife can't stand you." Mike took great pleasure in seeing Steve cringe.

"Suit yourself. You and Abby are well suited. Both of you don't give a damn about anyone but yourselves; a match made in heaven!"

Grabbing his old denim jacket from behind the bar, Steve stormed out. The days when the two of them were close were long gone. Mike had changed for the worse some time ago and Steve had yet to discover the reason behind it.

Later, seated behind the steering wheel of his Jaguar, Mike admitted to himself that Steve had a point. He'd almost finished a packet of cigarettes due to all the tension he felt since the argument. *He's right,* he thought. *I acted on impulse where Abby's concerned. If only I'd taken some time to think it through. Why the hell couldn't Louise figure out how miserable I was? Abby will never replace her. Louise left me no option but to leave.*

Mike turned the car round and drove off.

CHAPTER THREE

December 2014

TRINE AND LOUISE were busy at work, planning the up-and-coming designers' show they'd held on an annual basis ever since The Studio became *the* place to shop for Scandinavian fashion. Turning to look at her friend, Trine asked if Louise missed Malmö.

"Don't tell me you don't miss the winters and Christmas? I miss Denmark this time of year."

Louise's eyes lit up at the mention of it. "I sure do. I'd give almost anything to be part of it: snow, Christmas trees and atmosphere. Mamma and Pappa loved this time of year, and they always had a houseful of people who shared the festive season with us."

"I'll always miss my roots. Not just over Christmas but Easter and Midsummer's Eve too." Trine had a wistful expression in her eyes.

Both women were orphaned with no siblings, thus stayed away from their birthplaces for fear of the absence of the people they loved. Trine lost her parents a few years after Louise's died. Unlike the Bergs' tragic but preventable accident, Trine's parents became ill one after the other and passed away with only months between them. The friends' respective losses brought them together and made them closer than ever.

"I guess I'm fortunate Gabriella is still alive. As far as I'm aware, she still lives in the same flat in central Malmö. We've not been in touch for a while. I miss her."

Up until the break-up, Louise had been in regular contact with her aunt. Yet since the divorce Louise had stopped calling, concerned that she'd have to confide in her aunt about it. Gabriella didn't approve of Mike who, in her opinion, wasn't right for her niece. Louise therefore told her nothing, knowing it was for the best, since Gabriella stuck to her guns and refused to change her mind. According to Gabriella, Mike was a selfish charmer who'd wormed his way into Louise's heart after Elin and Simon's untimely deaths and when Louise was at her most vulnerable.

Lost in thought, Louise was interrupted by an unexpected suggestion from Trine.

"Let's travel to Malmö in the spring! We'll take the train to Copenhagen while we're there. The Öresund Bridge is so beautiful and the scenery as you travel over the water is breathtaking. How about it? Please say yes, it'll do you good to leave London for a while."

"Perhaps you're right. I've not seen Gabriella for a long time. We'll look into it after Easter and treat ourselves to a nice hotel."

"Wouldn't you prefer to stay at your aunt's flat?"

"Please don't misinterpret what I'm about to say . . . Gabriella's very dear to me but I've not visited Malmö for a long time and a lot's happened since then. I genuinely don't think I'm ready to see her yet."

"You'd go there without letting her know? What if we bump into her or someone who knows her and us in the street? Malmö's a small town."

"I'll take the risk. Gabriella means the world to me yet I can't tell her that Mike and I are over. She detested him; I need more time to get over what happened first."

"You don't need to justify yourself to me. We'll travel to Malmö and if by chance you bump into your aunt, we'll tell a white lie and say we're over on a business trip to meet prospective new designers."

The next few months passed in a blur as Louise adapted to her new life as a single woman, living just off the Fulham Road. April arrived all too soon and after they'd placed orders with the leading Scandinavian fashion houses, Louise and Trine booked a flight and a boutique hotel in Little Square in the city centre.

The moment they arrived at Malmö Airport, both took a deep breath and inhaled the fresh air, so different to the pollution of London. The weather was sunny with a cool breeze. Taking a cab outside the airport, they were grateful they'd opted to wear jeans, T-shirts and jackets. They asked the cab driver to drop them close to the pedestrian walk, then stood, gazing around at the crowds of people talking and laughing. Many spoke a different language. Malmö, like London and so many parts of Europe, was inhabited with people from other cultures.

"Let's *fika* at Café Hollandia! I'm gasping for proper coffee and a cinnamon bun."

Minutes later, seated in a plush velvet chair at a table by the counter and drooling over the assortment of scrumptious delights before them, Louise and Trine decided to share a prawn and egg sandwich, followed by chocolate mousse gateaux.

"This is simply delicious," Trine declared, taking a bite of the cake and savouring it in her mouth. No matter how tasty the snacks were in her favourite Fulham café, nothing compared to Swedish confectionary in her view.

"Mamma used to take me here when she and I went shopping together. We'd cycle from our home in Limhamn and spend hours together talking and relaxing. Pappa and I visited art galleries every Saturday. I'll never forget all the special times we shared." Louise's voice faltered. Every time she returned to Malmö, the overwhelming sense of loss crushed her. This time wasn't any different. She'd never get over losing her parents.

"Life's much too precious to waste. Could you live here again?" Trine asked between mouthfuls of cake. She and Jasper had discussed it before the trip. Both agreed it would be the start of a new life for Louise and they'd look after the flat and The Studio if Louise wanted to return to Malmö. "You've been through so much in a short period of time. Jasper and I know you're not happy. However much you try to hide it, we can see straight through you. We love you too much to turn a blind eye to it. Face up to it, Louise. You've not been happy for a very long time. Not even when you and Mike were together. You know it just as much as we do."

"You seriously propose I relocate to Malmö? Is that the reason you persuaded me to come with you?" Louise wasn't sure if her friend was right. She'd lived in London for many years. Malmö hadn't changed that much yet Louise knew nothing was quite the way she remembered it. The political and cultural landscape had changed beyond recognition, both for better and worse. Furthermore, she'd lost touch with her aunt and close friends. What if she didn't fit in? "Malmö's not how it used to be. I can feel it in here." Louise pointed to her stomach.

"If that's how you feel, all I can tell you is that it takes time and perseverance to adjust. I know you're apprehensive of starting over but you needn't be! After decades in London, it won't take long to feel at home."

"But what about all the stories we've read in the press? Apparently, Malmö's a hostile place to live where ethnic minorities are concerned. Our Jewish and Muslim friends are attacked because of their faith and culture. London's not much better, yet these issues aren't as widely recognised as in a small city where the situation is highlighted in daily events."

"I know what you mean. But are you prepared to sacrifice your own happiness because a small group of people treat others despicably? Malmö is your birth city. You can't allow these things to dictate where and how you live. Besides, if everyone reasoned like that, the offenders would win."

"If I didn't know better, I'd imagine you want rid of me! Is that the real reason we're in Malmö? Trine, I'm forty-five years old, with a business and a home in London. I'm too old and set in my ways to start over. Don't you want us to work together anymore? I can't imagine a life without you, Jasper and the kids."

"You'll never get rid of us! I'm not a selfish person, Louise. If I were, I wouldn't tell you to move back to Malmö. I love our friendship and partnership but you're just going through the motions of everyday life. Seeing you so unhappy is killing me! I know you say you've come to terms with what happened with Mike and I wish that was true. You've not dealt with it sufficiently, Louise. Malmö is your chance for a new life. If you don't like it, all you have to do is book a flight back to London. We'll always be there for you."

"I can't fault your reasoning. Is Zack still upset about the night I took the overdose? You must tell him I was out of my mind after what Mike did. I'll never do something like that again. Please say you believe me."

"We know that. Zack's fine. Kids are a lot more resilient than you think." Trine omitted telling Louise her son had suffered with nightmares for a long time after he'd discovered her in a coma.

"Okay, I'll not lie and tell you the thought of moving back didn't cross my mind. And I'll admit I'm still miserable, but not like I was when everything blew up in my life. I appreciate your concern, but if I decide to move back it's got to be my decision, not someone else's. I'll think about it when we get back to London. Now, if you've finished eating, I suggest we take a trip down memory lane and visit the old familiar places we loved when we were young."

The days passed quickly as they walked through the city and along the coastline to Ribersborg and the sandy beaches where people sunbathed on the benches, stopping outside the restaurant Louise and her parents had frequented for dinner. Later in the evenings, the two friends visited Limhamn's Harbour, watching the boats on the Öresund strait and birds flying high in the sky. Louise took in the surroundings and wished they could have stayed a while longer. She'd made up her mind not to contact Gabriella. This was her opportunity to get away from Mike, their divorce and the unhappiness she'd carried inside her for so long.

As they walked back through the streets to the quaint hotel in Little Square, Louise realised she wasn't unhappy. Unlike the hectic life she lived in London, Malmö made her feel more at ease. It was as if something kept nagging at her to let go of the past.

They had dinner at a trendy brasserie not far from the central station, feasting on delicacies of the sea. Everything tasted fresh and the wine relaxed them sufficiently to laugh and joke until it was time to return to their hotel and pack. They spent the following morning in Copenhagen and took a cab across the bridge to Malmö and the airport.

During the flight, Trine looked at her friend and smiled. "I can tell you're feeling better. Don't worry about The Studio and me. We'll sort something out. The only thing that matters is you. Take all the time you require; everything will be alright."

Poor cow, Mike thought as he sat in his car, staring out at the home he and Louise had shared. *Louise must be devastated I dumped her. I can't believe the solicitor persuaded me to give up on my share of the house. At least I managed to get hold of some of the paintings and antiques Louise's parents left her.*

It still preyed on his mind how distraught she'd been when he called to tell her they were finished. Instead of celebrating their twentieth wedding anniversary, he'd broken her heart. Well, it served her right! If only she could have understood and read between the lines how miserable she'd made him. All she'd cared about was that bloody studio she and Trine worked at day and night. Mike knew full well Trine and Jasper had always detested him.

Thinking back to a deal he'd made with a client at the time he and Steve had invested in a business extension, he decided it was too late for regrets. *Louise got me out of a situation. Had she not repaid my debts Steve and I would have had to declare ourselves bankrupt. God alone knows where I'd have been now.* After that incident, Mike contacted a dealer he'd done business with in the past. Selling off a range of limousines behind Steve's back, Mike bought a number of vehicles he later sold for a huge profit via the dealer. Between them they'd made a small fortune and instead of putting his share back into the business – or indeed into his marriage – Mike opened up a separate account in his name and paid the profit into that. The dealer had sworn Mike to silence, saying he'd name him if he ever breathed a word about their arrangement. By the time

Mike realised the cars he'd received in exchange for the limousines originated from drugs and money laundering, the dealer had him firmly in his pocket. And what was worse, he'd mislaid the laptop containing all his account details in his haste to pack up and leave his marital home.

I've got to find that bloody laptop! If Louise knows about it . . . How could I have been so stupid to forget it? Mike knew if the file got into the wrong hands he'd at best incur Steve's wrath and at worst, serve a prison sentence. Neither option was in his best interest. *I wouldn't put it past Louise to hand the laptop over to her friends or the police,* he thought. *It leaves me no option but to contact the Larsens.*

Furious with himself for overlooking the significance of that laptop, Mike started his engine and drove as fast as he could towards his and Abby's flat.

CHAPTER FOUR

Natasha Sturgess stood in the recently decorated kitchen of the old Victorian house in which she'd lived with her husband, Robert, for at least two decades. They'd instantly fallen in love with the Chiswick property and paid their deposit soon after getting engaged.

Natasha and Robert had two sons aged sixteen and nineteen. Unable to conceive naturally, they'd spent a fortune on IVF until Natasha at long last became pregnant with their oldest son. After a few years passed, they were delighted to conceive their youngest without intervention. Contrary to Robert's stocky build, light brown eyes and ruddy complexion, Natasha was tiny; very slim and dark haired with green eyes. Ten years her forty-nine-year-old husband's junior, she wore a conservative style of clothing and appeared older than her years. Both she and Robert, who was young at heart, loved spending time together with their sons and circle of friends, including the Larsen, Kershaw and Matthews families.

After a brief stint as a stand-up comedian, Robert tried his luck as an actor and eventually became one of the most sought after names on the London stage. Meanwhile, Natasha started her own chocolatier's business on Chiswick High Street and had recently expanded her business with branches in Wimbledon and Ealing. Customers queued up outside her shops to purchase the most exquisite homemade chocolates and those that were especially ordered from Switzerland, Belgium and France. Recently Natasha had taken Louise and Trine's advice and invested in Swedish and Danish confectionery. Everything sold out so quickly that Natasha repeatedly placed orders with the wholesalers and spent nearly every weekend making her own delicious concoctions.

With an additional menagerie of stray cats and dogs to look after, the Sturgesses had their work cut out for them. They had the ideal marriage and were just as much in love as the day they'd met at a fundraising event in north London. Indeed, Natasha and Robert became the people to turn to in a crisis as they always lent a caring ear to anyone who required advice and support.

Yet today Natasha was close to tears. Trine had visited that morning to deliver some samples of Scandinavian designers. While having a gossip and snack, she'd confided in Natasha that the Kershaws were divorced. Seated at the round rustic table in the kitchen, dogs and cats scattered around their feet, Trine told Natasha that Mike had ended the marriage on their twentieth anniversary. She omitted to mention that Louise almost died after taking an overdose of sleeping tablets.

"Oh my God! You should have told me a lot sooner. I used to think they were so happy together. The perfect couple." Natasha pushed away her plate.

"Please keep it to yourself. Louise mustn't find out I've confided in you."

"Of course, I won't tell a soul. Just you wait until I see that man! Mike's *persona non grata* from now on. I'll have to tell Robert but it won't go further than that."

Sipping her mug of hot chocolate, Natasha asked, "Is there

someone else involved in this? Louise is stunning; Mike will never meet anyone like her."

"I've no idea. Louise is thinking of moving back to Malmö. Jasper and I want her to be happy. London's full of memories of her and Mike." Trine knew Louise wouldn't mind that she'd informed Natasha of the situation. Natasha was the kindest person they knew.

"Will she do it? What will happen to The Studio? Will you be able to run it by yourself?"

"I don't know, but I'll try my hardest. Jasper will give me a hand. Louise isn't happy, Tash. She blames herself for what happened. A change of scenery may benefit her."

The two women talked a while longer, then after Trine left, Natasha debated if she ought to call Louise or wait. They'd known each other for too long to ignore the situation. Dialling Louise's mobile number, Natasha sensed something was wrong when Louise answered in a subdued voice.

"Is there something I can do for you? Trine told me what happened. I'm so very sorry for you." Irrelevant of how successful she had been as model and also running a business, Louise had lost her parents at a young age and had no siblings. Natasha's heart bled for her friend.

"Not a lot but I'm grateful for the offer. We must get together soon; I've a lot on my mind at present." Louise wasn't in the mood to talk. She felt a lot better in herself yet had no intention of digging up the past. The wounds were still too raw.

Ending the conversation, Natasha thanked her lucky stars that she and Robert were blissfully happy.

"Did you manage to find us a bigger place to live?" Abby asked. "This flat's a dump!"

They'd just finished making love, but as Mike watched her get up and walk naked towards the small bathroom, with her long blonde extensions, big breasts and pouty lips, he felt a new stirring in his loins.

"That's not how you address someone who's just given you the best sex you've ever had!" He followed her into the bathroom, grabbed her arm and bent to kiss her mouth.

"Stop it," she snapped. "I've no desire to continue where we left off. Find us a nice place to live or you can kiss goodbye to sessions like the one we just indulged in." Abruptly she stepped into the tiny shower cabin and shut the glass door in his face.

Ignoring her wish that he kept his distance, Mike opened the door and squeezed in next to her. "Let's not argue about it. I'll see what I can do. We'll discuss it tonight after I've finished work." Sensing how enraged she was with him, he started to massage soap onto her body, suds of water and bubbles causing her to squeal in delight.

"You're a cocky bastard, aren't you? What makes you think I'm in the mood to have sex after the way you act? I'm serious, Mike. Unless you find us a decent place to live, I'm out of here, is that understood?" She'd bumped into the sleazy landlord on her way back from the grocery store. After the way he eyed her up and down, eyes glued to her breasts, she couldn't wait to move out of the shabby one-bedroom flat by Richmond station.

Feeling Mike pushing deep inside of her, Abby's long nails scraped down his back. Soon they started to climax. Lips brushing his, she threw her head back and laughed. "Did I mention Camilla and Steve are back together?" she said, the idea of her best friend and Steve sleeping together making her happy that she and Steve were no longer an item. Camilla was welcome to him. Steve wasn't much of a catch. For a start he was still in love with his wife and he never had money to waste on her. Mike, on the other hand, was her future. The only thing that came between them was his inability to find them a nice place to live.

Indeed, Abby wanted a big house in the heart of Richmond but Mike refused to comply. He'd already lost what he construed to be his share of the house he and Louise shared. The last thing he wanted was to splash out money on a property that would milk him dry in heating bills. Abby was fun to be with for now, but Mike had no idea if they'd last and wasn't willing to commit just yet.

Brushing past him in the bedroom, Abby pouted her lips and caressed his private parts. Moaning with pleasure despite already having been spent twice that morning, he caught her off guard and managed to position himself between her legs. Aching for him to thrust deeper inside of her, Abby dug her nails into Mike's neck and chest. Screaming in pain, Mike roughly pushed her aside and swore out loud.

"Shit, Abby! Look what you've done! How the hell will I be able to turn up at work? You've scratched me all over except the face!" Then, seeing how indifferent she was about it, Mike added, "You're vicious when you put your mind to it. How come you're such a bitch? I've gone out of my way to accommodate you." He pushed past her into the bathroom to spray disinfectant on his wounds, eyes tearing up when it started to work on his skin.

Standing behind him, Abby laughed. "You're great in bed! I can't imagine how you and Louise stuck it out for as long as you did." Her smile faded at the mention of that woman's name.

Mike glanced up at her reflection in the bathroom mirror. "It lasted for as long as it did because I was led to believe we were heading in the same direction."

"I'm surprised you didn't stray until we met," Abby retaliated, flicking back a strand of hair that had fallen in her eyes. "She must have meant a lot to you." She stressed the past tense.

"I stayed because I loved her and wanted us to have a family. Unfortunately for me, Louise wasn't the maternal type and had her own agenda. I wasn't part of it."

"You're not the sort of man who'd settle down with a family, surely? I obviously mistook you for wanting the same as Steve — sex and no strings attached."

"You did. I'm nothing like him! During our relationship I never so much as looked at another woman. Don't you dare compare me with that womaniser!" Mike's eyes were dark with anger.

"Lay off! I get it. You and your ex-wife wanted different things? Big deal. Sounds as if you're not over her yet. But let me tell you something: I'm no one's consolation prize. As for kids, you can forget about it. At least that's one thing I've in common with your ex-wife." Abby's shoulders began to shake. She'd had a hellish upbringing, with parents who were constantly at one another's throats.

Sensing how upset he'd made her, Mike turned to face her. "Hey, you and I don't know each other well enough to start thinking about that. I'm sorry I shouted at you. I'll buy a nice bottle of wine on my way back from work. We'll order a takeaway from the Thai restaurant in Kew." Seeing her expression soften, he pulled her into his arms.

"I meant what I just told you," Abby mumbled, her face buried in his neck. "I want us to move out of here."

Anger building up inside of him once more, Mike withdrew from her arms. "Now don't you call the shots with me! You wouldn't want to end up like Louise, would you?"

As she watched him get dressed and leave for work, Abby thought, *It's you who need to watch your back where I'm concerned,*

Mike. My dad lived to regret what he did to me. Pulling on her underwear, Abby smiled to herself. Steve had catered to her whims just like every man she was involved with. It was only a matter of time before Mike would as well.

"Stop what you're doing!" Steve protested as Camilla pulled him closer on the bed, his face buried in her ample cleavage.

"Abby's loss is my gain!" she moaned, legs straddled on either side of his back. "We're great together, aren't we?" she teased, kidding herself he had feelings for her. The only thing he wanted from her was sex.

Paige was the woman he loved yet Steve's insatiable sex drive had long caused her immeasurable pain and she'd refused to sleep with him ever since she'd found out he cheated on her years ago. The two first met at college when they were too young to commit to each other, but even then Steve knew she was the girl he wanted to marry. When she became pregnant their parents were incensed and didn't think the marriage would last. Paige was seventeen at the time and ecstatic to be a young mother with a baby and a husband. She'd always been a homemaker who took pleasure in doing housework and cooking since she was very young.

After Josh was born, Paige became pregnant again and gave birth to their second son, Alec, who like his brother meant everything to her. Unfortunately, by then Paige had realised that she and Steve weren't as happy as she'd first imagined. The cracks in the marriage were getting more obvious and when Steve admitted to having an affair with some temp at work, she kept her distance. If it weren't for their sons, she wouldn't have stayed for as long as she did.

Camilla had a feeling that Paige wasn't prepared to put up with her unfaithful husband much longer. Secretly, Camilla hoped that

Steve would want her to become a permanent fixture in his life. They were compatible in that both of them used the other. Camilla expected her bills to be paid in exchange for sex and Steve wanted a mistress to satisfy him.

But increasingly, Camilla was finding she wanted more than just a few hours now and then. She was tired of casual flings and craved the security of a home with a man who would look after her. Unless Steve got his priorities straight and sorted out his marriage to Paige, Camilla would start looking for a man who was capable of putting her first.

Steve doesn't give a damn about me. To him all I am is a free ride, literally. I'm fortunate we're both highly sexed. At least I get something out of it. And so Camilla pretended she didn't notice the grubby bedsit, dirty carpet and stained table by the window overlooking Kew Green.

She'd worked as a PA for Mike and Steve over the years. Abby, who did their accounts, had put her name forward and Camilla soon became the person they'd call in an emergency when they required assistance with client reports. Since they'd installed computers, Camilla's hours had decreased and she found it difficult to make ends meet. Meeting up for sex several times a week, in return for Steve paying her bills, was a mutually-satisfying arrangement.

At least I've not been subjected to what Abby endured, she thought, feeling Steve's mouth and hands on her breasts.

Camilla and Abby first met when they worked for a company that sold gadgets to large offices and corporations. Abby immediately befriended Camilla and taught her how to operate a computer. "You'll thank me one day," she'd told her. "Technology is developing beyond imagination. Soon everyone will be expected to either be part of it or risk losing out on jobs and social interaction."

She was right. A decade later, cyberspace was taking over people's lives.

"You're miles away!" Steve said, patting Camilla's behind and getting out of bed. "I'd best be off. Paige will wonder what happened to me if I'm late."

Watching him pulling on his boxer shorts, jeans and T-shirt, Camilla thought he looked old and haggard. There was stubble on his chin and his eyes had sunken into his square face. Steve wasn't as sexy as he'd been when he and Camilla first dated each other, during which time she saw other men and Steve slept with Abby. The latter fling ended when Abby set her sights on Mike, who'd by then ended his marriage to Louise.

Although Abby and Camilla were friends in the loose sense of the word, Abby never missed an opportunity to tell Camilla that Steve wouldn't have given a damn about her if he and Abby were still together. "You're relying on a man to provide for you, instead of supporting yourself," she would say in her usual direct way.

"You're no different! Mike's only with you because of the sex. Louise may not be his wife anymore, but you'll never measure up to her where Mike's concerned." Camilla was fed up with Abby constantly putting her down. Abby was only interested in money and material possessions. But unlike Steve, Mike never strayed when he and Louise were an item.

Returning to the present, Camilla sighed. Looking around her at the unmade bed and shabby furniture, she suddenly thought of her mother. She always relied on some man to pay her way. When she died at the age of sixty, looking at least twenty years older due to her alcohol and drug addiction, Camilla became scared that she would suffer the same fate.

They were a typical example of social heritage, in that both of them relied on men to finance their lives.

dress that clung to her body and accentuated the soft contour of her bosom and shapely legs, Steve had to physically restrain himself from taking her into his arms and carrying her to the bedroom. Yet as soon as she saw the way he looked at her, Paige kept her distance.

He'd fancied her rotten ever since he first laid eyes on her. No matter how many times he'd betrayed her, Steve knew he'd never be able to replace her.

"Please don't say that. You're just upset. I'm sorry I let you down in the past. I'll try my hardest not to do it again; all I ask is that you give me another chance." Steve took a step closer and reached for her hand.

"Get your grubby hands off me! I want you out of my life for good," Paige shouted, repulsed by his presence.

Taken aback by the sheer hatred in her eyes, Steve pleaded with her to not leave him. "I'm nothing without you, honey . . . please say you'll give me another chance!"

"I'm beyond caring. You are free to sleep around as much as you want." Paige paused for a moment, thinking. "Did you and Abby stop seeing each other when Mike arrived on the scene? Perhaps the three of you are a threesome?" It was the only query she had when he'd entered the house.

"Of course not! Abby was a mistake, just like everyone else. Whatever's going on between her and Mike is nothing to do with me."

"Once a cheat, always a cheat." Paige turned on her heel and left him standing there, his face white as a sheet. She wanted nothing more to do with him and he only had himself to blame.

Steve took a seat at the table where they'd shared so many happy moments together as a family, and absentmindedly picked at the surface that was beginning to fade and cause the wood to chip. Half an hour later, nursing a glass of wine and a stale biscuit, he heard her footsteps in the hall.

"Please don't leave. We need to talk," he said, thinking it odd she'd put on makeup on a week night.

"Your words fall on deaf ears. My solicitor said I've a right to claim half of everything. I'll make you pay for what you did to me! Whoever it is you're screwing will be revealed." Paige's voice shook with anger.

She'd given him the best years of her life. At forty-seven, Paige was ready to move on and had recently managed to find a job assisting elderly people with computer training. She'd bought a laptop years ago, thinking it would come in handy for all kinds of things.

She had met Liam after signing up to a cookery class in Richmond. Paige had been a housewife for many years with a deep desire to reconnect with the outside world and was slowly coming out of her self-inflicted prison. Liam was a former chef who'd moved to London from his native Dublin and started a catering business. They'd connected instantly and when he asked her out for a drink, Paige knew they were heading for more than a casual fling. His friendship meant a lot to her yet it didn't take long before they became lovers, meeting up in his flat in Kingston twice a week. Paige was adamant her sons mustn't find out about them until she and Steve were divorced. It was too risky to extend their nights together in case someone saw them and reported it to Josh and Alec.

"I don't depend on you, Steve. This house belongs to me; my father gave it to me after my mother passed away. They'd saved up for years! Your name may be on the deeds but my solicitor assured me my father's wishes will be taken into account." Ownership of the house had been playing on Paige's mind ever since she decided she wanted a divorce. After Alec was born, she'd gone against her father's wishes and signed over half of the house in Steve's name. Back then she was deeply in love with her husband and thought she was doing the right thing. Paige had bitterly regretted it ever since.

If Steve discovered she was in a relationship with someone else, he'd use it to his own advantage. Paige didn't believe anything he told her.

"Don't forget to lock up when you leave. I want you to pack your things and return your keys." She strode out to her car in the driveway. Suddenly, everything ceased to matter. All she cared about was the welfare of her sons and the man who awaited her in the flat in Kingston.

CHAPTER FIVE

"ARE YOU SURE you want to share your life with me?" Liam asked, holding her close in the big four-poster bed in his bedroom.

"One hundred per cent," Paige replied, snuggling up to him. They'd been drawn to each other like magnets the moment they first met. Both attempted to stay friends yet after Liam invited her to his flat for dinner, they wanted more than a casual relationship and never looked back.

Paige was attracted to Liam's warm personality, easy-going attitude and big smile. Tall, with hazel eyes and red hair, Liam was extremely fit and regularly worked out in the gym, cycled and went for a run every morning. At forty he was younger than Paige, with bags of energy and an aura of stability. Liam was the opposite of Steve in every way.

Paige's new love had relocated to London after he divorced. He'd been with his ex-wife for ten years and didn't have a family, yet every time Paige tried to discover the reason they'd split, Liam changed the subject. The only detail he told her was that he'd been depressed and had suffered a breakdown which led to the two of them breaking up.

Paige couldn't get her head around why any woman would want to divorce such a kind and loyal man. Much less that Liam stayed in a relationship that caused him to become depressed. She couldn't imagine him being anything other than what he was – calm, intuitive and utterly charming.

Kissing his cheek, Paige got out of bed and padded over to the window looking down on the street outside. Liam had furnished the flat entirely with furniture he bought at IKEA, all of it in muted colours. There were subtle spotlights in the ceiling.

"Steve's up to his old tricks," she said. "I won't let him fool me again. He came round unexpectedly last night. I can't wait for us to be divorced! My solicitor claims I'm entitled to half of everything. We'll have to keep a low profile a while longer or Steve will use it as an excuse to not declare his income." She wasn't willing to end up with nothing. Steve owed her big time! "I'm sorry you're caught up in our mess," she continued. "You're the only man for me. Steve's a lost cause; I can't figure out what women see in him. He looks awful."

Joining her by the window, Liam kissed her mouth. "Both of us have had our share of unhappiness. You're too good for him."

"Yeah, I suppose I am. Anyone who'd been through what I have wouldn't care what happens to him. I fell out of love with him years ago, yet he's still my sons' father. That won't change; I've just got to find a way to accept it. Are you alright? I hope my situation isn't bringing back memories of what took place between you and your wife."

It took Paige many weeks of gentle encouragement to persuade Liam to open up and tell her the truth. When he finally did, Paige didn't believe him. Liam wasn't a liar yet it seemed too grotesque. Liam O'Connor a victim of domestic violence? It was absurd to even think it.

It wasn't until he started to confide in her that Paige got the full picture. He'd married his childhood sweetheart, Molly, when they were in their early twenties. Working in a hardware store, Liam was promoted to manager of the entire chain all over Dublin. They'd been married for almost three years when the abuse started. At first it was a few snide remarks, camouflaged as jokes. When it escalated to arguments about everything and nothing, Liam suggested they seek out a counsellor. All hell broke loose and Molly started to drink heavily. She became aggressive. So much so that Liam stayed out of her way and avoided her altogether.

He slept on the couch at a work colleague's flat and only went home late at night when he knew she'd be asleep. One weekend as he was busy mowing the front lawn, Molly attacked him with a knife, stabbing him in the back. The wound wasn't too deep yet the incident was the start of a series of assaults that resulted in Liam fearing for his life and eventually filing for divorce. No matter how hard he tried to reason with her, Molly was beyond help.

Although he came through it externally, Liam felt like a complete failure for allowing her to vent her anger and frustration on him. Internally he was a mess and had it not been for the therapist who literally took him under his wing, Liam wouldn't have coped.

Over time the wounds turned into invisible scars that he carried inside of him every day. Meeting and falling in love with Paige was a miracle and shone a light on his life. Yet the knowledge that he had willingly subjected himself to his ex-wife's unstable and violent mental state and been a victim of abuse, stayed with him indefinitely. The stigma attached to being a man who couldn't defend himself made him feel inadequate and guilty for putting up with the ordeal.

Liam was a good man who'd fallen victim to a deeply disturbed woman he had loved and trusted. Falling in love with Paige was his biggest joy yet also his greatest sorrow. Not a day went by when he didn't worry that she would return to her estranged husband. Paige and Steve had a history together; a long marriage and sons. Liam wasn't convinced he stood a chance in comparison to what they shared. Seeing Paige so hell-bent on getting what she believed was owed to her, Liam wished he could whisk her away from all of it and take her to a remote island where no one could find them.

Kissing the nape of her neck, he whispered, "Please don't take this the wrong way. Until you can find it within yourself to let the past go, you and I will not have the life we dream of. It took me a very long time to fight my demons. I'm almost there but not quite. It's only natural to feel resentful of people who treat you badly. Yet you can't let it rule your life."

Turning to face him, Paige smiled. "Steve robbed me of the best years of my life and I will never forgive him for that. At least I've something to show for my so-called marriage: Josh and Alec are a credit to me. You mustn't waste energy on worrying about me. We must hold out a while longer. As soon as Steve and I are divorced, we will start to plan our future. Yours and mine." It infuriated her that after Steve's betrayal of trust and countless affairs, it was she who had to keep a low profile or risk losing everything, including part of the house her father gave her.

"What if you've still got feelings for him? You're blinded by anger now, but that will fade with time. Are you sure you want him out of your life?" Liam looked so upset that Paige might leave him and return to Steve, he was almost in tears.

Looking deep into his eyes, Paige replied, "That will never happen. I'm in love with *you*. You're all I've ever wanted in a man.

I know how hard it is for you to put your trust in me after what you went through, but you've got to believe that what I tell you is true. Just imagine how wonderful our life will be when all of this is behind us."

"I know what you say makes sense. I will be here for you when you need me. As long as you understand that I'll not hang around indefinitely. The days when I let someone rule my life are well and truly over. You have to proceed with the divorce irrespective of how things turn out financially! You and Steve need closure or we can kiss goodbye to our future life." Breathing in the scent of her eau de toilette and seeing her looking so beautiful made Liam insanely jealous that Paige's husband still was part of her life, so much so that he turned up at the house whenever he felt like it.

"I don't expect you to understand how much I detest him," she replied. "It's got nothing to do with revenge. All I want is my fair share of everything. I didn't waste all those years to end up with nothing!"

"But you've got me now," Liam persisted. "I'll look after you; you'll not go without anything. My income from the cookery classes and books and this flat . . . it will more than provide for us. We'll have everything we need."

"Let's go back to bed. I've no commitments that can't wait. Oh, Liam, I can't wait to introduce you to my boys! They'll be so happy to meet you!"

Brushing aside his nagging insecurity, Liam took her hand as they returned to the bed. Hours later, watching her put her clothes on and apply fresh makeup, Liam could not take his eyes off her. It never ceased to amaze him that she wanted him as much as he wanted her. She was everything to him and a part of him died inside each time she left.

★

Louise finally plucked up the courage to call Gabriella a couple of weeks after she returned to London.

"I'm surprised you remember my number!" her aunt snapped, entirely unaware her niece had been in Malmö.

"Please forgive me. I've had a lot on my mind." Louise felt terrible that she'd avoided her when she visited her native city.

"It's okay. How's that husband of yours?" Gabriella's voice had a sharp edge to it.

"Mike's busy as usual." She wasn't willing to reveal what happened over the phone. Louise tended to carry her emotions close to her chest and hadn't even visited her parents' graves. If she had, she'd have collapsed with grief. Losing Mike was bad enough, yet nothing compared to losing her parents.

"You sound upset. Did something happen I should know about?" Gabriella had an uncanny way of seeing through her, even if they couldn't see each other. They'd always been close, even more so when Louise's parents died.

After a moment debating whether or not to tell the truth, Louise relented. "I've had a hard time lately. Mike and I are divorced. He ended our marriage over the phone on our twentieth wedding anniversary. Trine and Jasper take very good care of me. Their son, Zack, found me unconscious in their guest room after I took an overdose of sleeping tablets. I'm okay now and recently moved into a flat close to The Studio. I sold the house in Barnes to a young family." Without thinking it through, Louise told her aunt everything.

The line went dead at the other end. After what seemed like an eternity, Louise heard her aunt cry, "I can't believe you kept it from me! Just you wait and see what I will do to that bastard!" At the other end of the line, Gabriella clutched her chest, tears blurring her vision. "I want you here with me so I can hold you close to me! Your parents would have been beside themselves. I always knew Mike was a manipulative shit who duped you into believing he cared for you."

"You really thought as much back then? But you never knew him!"

"There was no need. I'd heard enough. Oh, Louise, to think that I could have lost you! You're all I have left. I want us to spend more time together, before . . . before it's too late."

"I know you do, I do as well. Trine and Jasper think I ought to move back to Malmö." Louise neglected to mention she'd been there not so long ago. What Gabriella didn't know wouldn't hurt her.

"They're right. Promise me you'll come for a visit and tell the Larsens that I'm forever indebted to them for being there for you when you needed them the most."

"I will. We'll talk in a while. I'll call you very soon."

Later, Louise had gone to bed and was about to fall asleep, when the phone in the hall rang. Jumping out of bed to answer it, Louise was touched to hear her aunt's voice.

"I want you to move back so I can keep an eye on you. It'll be good for us both. London's too stressful. I'll even go so far as to make your favourite dessert, rhubarb pie with lemon sorbet. Malmö's turned into a cultural hub, but you'll get the peace and quiet you need here after what you've been through. Take all the time you need to settle your affairs in London, but don't take too long! I'm not as young as I used to be."

Imagining the two of them reunited after all the years they'd lived apart brought tears to Louise's eyes. "Have you stayed in touch with Kajsa and Martin?" she asked. "They're my oldest friends, yet I've not heard from them for a long time."

"Of course! Martin calls at least every week and Kajsa came round for a meal not so long ago. They always ask about you."

"And what about you? Have you met someone special?" Louise asked, wondering why her aunt stayed single all those years.

"Don't be so silly! Who'd have me? At my age work and good friends are all I need." A highly respected neurologist in Malmö's main hospital, Gabriella was still working full time at the age of seventy, having joined initially as a consultant and eventually being promoted to clinical director. She planned to retire from duty the following summer and already dreaded that she'd be surplus to requirements and get bored with sitting at home, waiting for friends to call her.

Louise's initial thought when she woke up the next morning was how much she was warming to the idea of returning to Malmö. She hadn't lived there since her parents died, yet in her heart she knew that her aunt and friends were right. There was no reason for her to remain in London except Trine and her family, and The Studio. Having breakfast in the small living room, Louise felt more alone than when Mike first left her. *I'll discuss it with Trine*, she decided, recalling the Larsens' promise to look after her flat and her share of the business in case she decided to return. *I'm lonely. Mamma loved dogs. Perhaps I ought to get a rescue dog to keep me company? I'll call Natasha tomorrow. She's bound to know of someone who's got puppies.*

She was browsing through an old photo album when Trine called to ask if she'd like to join them for lunch. "Jasper's been busy in the kitchen since dawn. The aroma is out of this world! We've got Sunday roast with hasselback potatoes and chocolate cake on the menu. Please say you'll come."

Salivating at the thought of all the food, Louise realised she was famished. "Alright! But I'll not stay for long. Tell Jasper I want him to prepare a large G&T. I'll catch a cab." Louise refused to use the local transport that never arrived on time and had sold her BMW convertible after she moved into her flat, only a few minutes' walk from The Studio.

Contrary to what she'd told them, Trine, Jasper and the kids persuaded her to stay much longer. Just as she was about to accept a lift home from Jasper, Trine took her aside.

"Do you recall that guy you used to date when your parents were alive? I can't for the life of me remember his name. He was so sweet."

"Why are you bringing him up now? Nicklas and I were kids."

"That's the one! Nicklas. You were deeply in love with each other. I wonder what happened to him."

"He's probably married with five kids. Honestly, I can't figure you out, sometimes! Do you recall every guy you've dated? I sure don't."

"Nicklas wasn't just a fling. The two of you were inseparable. Don't you ever look back and wonder what might have happened had you not met Mike and moved to London?"

"Not really. What's the point? Life's transient. Nothing stays the same."

Later, seated in Jasper's van on the way back to Fulham, Louise couldn't shake off Trine's comments. *I hope Nicklas has found someone who loves and understands him,* she thought, then pushed his image to the back of her mind.

"Why are you in such a bad mood?" Mike asked when he and Abby finished making love on the living room couch.

"Have a guess! You still haven't found us a nice place to live." She got up from the couch and wandered off into the bathroom.

"Has it not dawned on you we are in a relationship? You and Louise are in the past!"

Mike felt rage bubbling up inside of him. Lately it was becoming an increasingly familiar feeling. "I forbid you to mention her name! Louise is nothing to do with you. She and I didn't work out, period!" he shouted, so angry froth was building up in the corners of his mouth.

"If that's the case, then maybe the two of you should try again," Abby said, returning to the living room, a spiteful expression on her face. "Camilla said Steve told her Louise is single. You dumped her, Mike! I'm the only woman who gets you. Anyway, I don't want us to argue anymore. I've got something to tell you." The tone of her voice alerted him to the fact she'd been keeping something from him. Walking up to him, Abby softened her face and whispered, "Don't you know how much you mean to me? I can't be without you. I know you feel the same way about me."

As she stood there in front of him, her naked body glowing from the sun streaming through the window, Mike's rage subsided. He was torn between pushing her away and listening to what she wanted to say to him. "Don't imagine I'm putty in your hands," he grunted. "Just come out with it – I'm already late for a meeting." He brushed past her and picked up his tie from the floor.

"Suit yourself. You'll find out sooner or later."

"What are you talking about?" Mike's face dropped when he heard her reply.

"I'm pregnant. Isn't it great? It's what you always wanted." She took his hand and placed it on her abdomen.

"But . . . but we've always taken precautions . . . How can this be?"

"You don't know at your age?" she teased.

Truthfully, Abby hadn't suspected she was pregnant for a long time. Her periods had always been irregular and she never focused on parts of her body below the navel due to her father's assaults. Having resorted to plastic enhancement of her breasts, she ignored any symptoms of swelling and tenderness. So it came as a total shock when, after many weeks, she suddenly realised that she'd not had any cramps in her abdomen, usually a sign of an impending period. Her mind reeling with the implications, Abby bought a pregnancy testing kit and discovered the truth.

Taking a few moments to register what she told him, Mike's face softened, a smile playing on his lips. "You're absolutely sure you're pregnant? I'm going to be a father?"

"I stopped taking the pill some time ago as I thought it's what you wanted," Abby said meekly, worried she had misread him. "But, yes, you're right! It's all I ever wanted. I can't get my head around it: we're having a baby! Let's celebrate tonight. I'll open up a bottle of champagne for you; pregnant women are not supposed to drink . . ."

Suddenly everything fell into place and all the doubts he'd had over leaving his wife vanished. Abby wasn't as beautiful or sophisticated as Louise, yet she gave him what Louise denied – the prospect of becoming a father. He would always be grateful to her for that.

". . . No, I'm sure a couple of glasses won't harm the baby. Just promise me one thing: please don't mention your ex-wife's name. She was wrong to deny you the opportunity to have a child." Privately, Abby hoped Mike would ask her to marry him. Everything had gone according to plan. Abby always got what she wanted in the end. Ever since she and Steve broke up, she'd set her sights on Mike. "Surely now you know we've got to find a bigger place to live?" she added sweetly.

★

59

Half an hour later, Mike climbed out of his Jaguar, eager to get the meeting out of the way. *I'm going to be a father! I can't believe it. I gave up on this such a long time ago.* He was so excited and couldn't wait to tell Steve when he turned up at the office twenty minutes later.

"Abby's pregnant? You're kidding, right? How far gone is she? I never viewed her as the maternal type . . ."

Mike's face turned flustered and angry. "I can tell you're not pleased for me. Well, I don't give a damn! I've never felt as happy as I am now."

Pacing the crammed office, Steve glared at him. "For what it's worth, I think you're making a big mistake."

"You think so, do you? Well, you're wrong. Louise deprived me of what I wanted the most. The only thing she cared about was herself and that damn Studio! I was her husband but my needs never mattered to her."

"Alright, I'm sorry I upset you. Paige and I have problems of our own. She always puts our sons before me and I never stood a chance to be the husband she wanted me to be. If only she'd let me come near her . . ."

"You've only got yourself to blame. Paige deserves a medal for putting up with you for as long as she did. You ought to be ashamed of yourself!"

"Is that so? What about you and the way you treated your wife? Abby may be more fun in bed, yet that's as far as it goes. I should know since I slept with her! Ending our affair was the best decision I ever made. To Abby you're just a ticket to an easy life." Steve spat the words in Mike's face.

"You're insinuating she's been cheating on me? I was under the impression the two of you were through when she and I started dating?" Mike's voice was a mere whisper.

"Calm down! I'd never betray you. Abby and I were over long before you were on the scene. She meant nothing to me; Paige is the only woman I love." Steve was petrified that Mike would find out he and Abby got together so soon after they'd split up. "I'd never leave Paige of my own free will," he added, feeling dreadful they were heading for divorce.

"Answer my question! Were the two of you still sleeping together when Abby and I started seeing each other?" Mike's eyes flared.

"Of course not! How far gone is she?" Steve asked, holding his breath.

"She didn't tell me. I'll find out tonight. Why do you want to know? Are you implying my girlfriend is lying to me?"

"Can't I enquire when my best friend will become a father? Hell, I'll even volunteer to be the child's Godparent!"

Satisfied with Steve's response, Mike shook his head. "We'll see about that. You're not exactly a role model for your own kids!"

Gazing at each other, the two men suddenly burst into laughter.

"Can you get it into your head I'll soon be a father?" Mike asked.

"You'd better believe it, mate," Steve replied, thinking how awful it would be if the baby wasn't Mike's. The thought preyed on Steve's mind throughout the remainder of the day.

CHAPTER SIX

June 2015

ABBY MADE AN appointment with her gynaecologist a few days later to confirm the pregnancy. She managed to persuade Mike she would be alright on her own. At first he insisted she let him come with her but when she told him it'd be awkward to have him present during the examination, Mike relented, saying he understood.

"Okay, I'll come with you when you have a scan instead," he said. "It's not as if I haven't seen you naked before."

"Sorry, Mike, I'm finding it really difficult to cope with all the hormones!" Abby offered by way of explanation. "Please be patient with me."

To her delight, Mike had already found them a big house in Chiswick, which he decided to rent prior to making an offer. They filled it with furniture from a local store, except for the bed and cot, which Mike insisted they buy from a retailer who was one of his clients. Louise's late parents' pieces, which Mike had taken from the house in Barnes, fitted perfectly in the living room.

"How far gone am I?" Abby asked the young female gynaecologist.

"Four months. The baby is due to be born shortly before Christmas."

"That's great news, my partner will be thrilled . . ." But inwardly Abby cringed.

"You don't seem happy about it," the gynaecologist remarked, concerned. "Is there something you wish to discuss?"

"Only that I'm not sure who the father is," Abby admitted. "Please say you won't tell my partner!" She was petrified about the implications.

"What we talk about here is confidential. It's up to you whether you want to confide in your partner or not. Are you worried about going through labour? Most women are the first time."

"No, no, I'm not. Thank you for confirming my suspicion that I'm further along than I initially believed. It's alright. My partner's the father."

Abby left the clinic in a haste and decided to have a drink in the wine bar across the street. *One glass of wine won't harm the baby. It's giving birth to it that scares the living daylights out of me! Well, it's too late for regrets now. I'm having that baby even if it kills me. It's my only opportunity to ensure I'll get the life I always dreamed of.*

"Have you decided about Malmö yet?" Trine enquired when they locked up and left The Studio late one evening. They'd sold out on every designer's latest collection and didn't get the time to have a single break throughout the day.

"Let's have a *fika* in Bluebird's café; we'll discuss it there," Louise said, as they were standing outside on the pavement in the blustery rain.

"Okay, but we'll have to run or get completely soaked!" Trine laughed. They'd forgotten to bring an umbrella with them. In

London that was as bad as carrying valuables and expecting not to get robbed.

"So, what's it going to be? Will you take some time out and relocate to Malmö or stay in London?" Trine repeated her question as soon as they'd ordered coffee and croissants. The café was packed with locals and tourists.

"I don't think it would work out; London's been my home for too long. What will I do in Malmö? I've got The Studio to consider and you."

"I told you: Jasper and I will take care of it. If you don't like living there, you can always return. Of course I'd prefer you to stay, but your happiness comes first." Trine was convinced Louise needed a change of scenery even if only for a short period of time. She'd moved on physically but had a long way to go until she healed emotionally. Trine wanted her to distance herself from everything that had happened with Mike.

"I know you mean well. But what if I don't like Malmö as much as I used to? The problem with living abroad for a long time is you think everything stays the same, exactly as it used to be. But it doesn't. London's my home town now; it's the only city I feel at home in."

"I feel the same about Copenhagen. Although if I didn't have kids I wouldn't think twice about moving back. The nature, standard of living and life in general are better. Jasper feels the same as I do yet we've created a life here and it's our children's home."

"But I've also made a life for myself here! What have I got in Malmö apart from Gabriella? As much as I love and miss her, I can't live my life around her. I'd go mad if I didn't have a job." She decided to change the subject. "Natasha's throwing her annual chocolatier party tomorrow night. The invitation arrived in the mail yesterday. Let's forget about work and Malmö and enjoy ourselves."

"Okay, I received mine as well. Natasha and Robert are such a good antidote to this persistent rain! But, Louise . . . Just remember that however much Malmö's changed, there are moments in life when it's good to return to one's roots. You've been through so much recently, you've not found the time to digest everything."

Trine's advice made sense but it was too soon to make a decision. Louise still wasn't convinced moving back to her birthplace would improve her life.

The following evening, Louise and Trine arrived at the Sturgess' house. Busy entertaining the guests with jokes and scrumptious chocolate treats, Robert and Natasha were in their element. Everyone was talking and laughing and tasting Natasha's latest concoctions.

Natasha made up her own recipes and had everything wrapped up in cute boxes featuring her business logo and delivered to customers all over the UK. A friend who helped out from time to time had decorated her shop and Natasha recruited several members of staff. Natasha's chocolatiers had made a huge profit in the first year and maintained its top position among the competition ever since.

Nowadays, Natasha only helped out in the shop a couple of days a week, her main focus being to develop as many new recipes as possible, without losing the quality of her brand. Combined with Robert's increasing success as a stage actor, both were at the top of their trade yet always found the time to socialise and be there for their friends.

Wearing a cashmere jacket and skirt, her dark hair in a ponytail and no makeup, Natasha greeted Louise and Trine with open arms.

"I'm so pleased you're here! You must taste my new recipe of chocolate mousse with brandy and liquorice. I swear by it."

Grimacing at the ingredients, Trine shook her head. "I'll stick to hot chocolate with rum," she laughed, embracing her hostess then walking into the adjacent room where Robert held court with some of the guests.

"How are you feeling?" Natasha asked Louise, a sympathetic expression in her eyes.

"I'm okay. Since moving into a flat and getting back to work I've returned to the land of the living." Louise wished she didn't have to talk about how she felt all the time. People meant well but all she wanted was to move on.

"Have you considered getting a pet? I have a friend who runs a kennel. She's got a couple of Labrador puppies that need to be rehomed. They make lovely companions! I can give her a call if you're interested?"

Taken aback by Natasha's proposition, Louise slowly shook her head. "It's funny you should mention this – I was thinking about it just the other day. Yes, I know the breed very well. My mother had quite a few rescue dogs. Regrettably, I'm at work all day thus am unable to have a pet. It wouldn't be fair to leave it alone for so long. I'm grateful you thought of me."

"What a pity. Most people aren't willing to have a dog that's been rescued. They assume it will incur complications but that's not true. Robert and I have more pets than we can handle, yet I wouldn't be without them as they give us immeasurable joy and the kids love them. Whenever I feel down about something, they're always there for me, in a way that humans aren't. At least say you'll come with me to my friend's kennel, the puppies are adorable."

Listening to her, Louise realised how much she'd missed being surrounded by dogs. The last time she had one was when she still lived at home with her parents. "Alright! Just give me a call when you plan to visit your friend and I'll come with you."

"I can do better than that. My friend is a breeder, but she also rehomes rescue dogs. She's just received a beautiful chocolate-coloured Labrador puppy. You've got to see him! Apparently, he's been abandoned by the owner whose boyfriend made her give him up."

"That's awful!" Louise didn't add she knew what it felt like to be abandoned by someone she trusted.

"I'll call my friend and tell her we'll come over tomorrow. It's Sunday so you won't have to take time off work. What do you think?"

After a moment's thought, Louise nodded her approval.

"Great! I'll pick you up at ten o'clock. Tell you what, I'll ask my friend to reserve the puppy, just in case you change your mind and decide to buy him. Will your landlord disapprove?"

"No, the previous tenant kept a dog and cat . . ." Louise replied in a tense voice. Everything was happening too quickly. First the divorce, then Trine and Jasper's suggestion she move back to Malmö, now Natasha persuading her to get a dog.

"Don't look so worried. You know what they say: animals choose us, not the other way round. You may not even be to his liking!"

But when Louise and Natasha arrived at the kennel in Thames Ditton the next day, it was evident how much the puppies approved of her. Louise was looking around her at the dogs playing and barking when a small puppy with chocolate brown fur and big brown eyes jumped up on her lap, making itself comfortable.

"That's Rufus, the puppy I told you about!" the breeder exclaimed. "He's had a bad start in life, yet is the most affectionate little creature I've ever come across. He's gorgeous."

"You've already named him?" Louise asked, stroking his soft fur. As if he'd always known her, Rufus snuggled up to her and promptly fell asleep.

"Yes, don't you think it suits him?"

"Oh, look, he's taken to you instantly!" Natasha said happily. "What do you think? Will you have him or not?" It was time to decide if the small creature snoring softly on her lap was coming home with her.

"He's beautiful. Yes. You've twisted my arm – I'll have him if I may?" Louise felt quite shaken. Only yesterday she'd been weighing the pros and cons of returning to Malmö and now here she was, with a dog on her lap – a dog she'd just decided to buy and care for.

"Of course!" The breeder smiled, looking first at Louise and then Natasha. "I was hoping someone as kind and genuine as yourself would want to buy him. He'll be a wonderful companion."

Looking down at the little dog, Louise felt happier than she'd been in a long time. Rufus instantly made her feel more alive and now that she had him, she didn't feel lonely. "When can I collect him?"

"Why don't you go out and buy a dog bed and some food first? I'll have his vaccination card and bowls ready for you when you pick him up, say Tuesday?"

"That's wonderful! I'll come over on Tuesday afternoon after work."

Paying over the asking price as a token of gratitude, Louise couldn't wait to return and collect Rufus. The puppy seemed to sense he belonged to her, wagging his tail as she bent to kiss his head before she and Natasha left.

Seated in Natasha's old station wagon, Louise kissed her friend's cheek. "I don't know how to thank you for persuading me to come with you to the kennel! Rufus is the best thing that's happened to me in a long time. I can't wait to bring him home with me."

Paige wandered through the rooms in the house she and Steve had shared for many years. Picking up a framed photograph of them and the boys, she let out a big sigh. *We look so happy. Steve and I were in love but all of it was a lie I held onto for the sake of our marriage and sons. Steve never ceased to let me down, not even when I was pregnant. I constantly turned a blind eye to his affairs.*

Every time he walked in the door, Steve had taken a shower and pretended everything was as it should be. Back then, Paige never rejected him. Thinking about how naïve she had been, Paige started to cry.

He made a fool of me and everything we shared! Oh, why didn't I take my father's advice? Dad paid for this house and put it in my name. What possessed me to include Steve's name on the deed? He repaid me by having sex with any woman who was willing to sleep with him! Well, this time he will part with half of what he owns. I'll not be tricked out of what belongs to me.

She had yet to discover the identity of his latest girlfriend, knowing in that way she'd stand a better chance of getting what she was entitled to. Yet she couldn't stop wondering. A neighbour who lived across the street, had told Paige how she'd often noticed Steve walking hand-in-hand with a dark-haired woman in Kew. *Louise told me that Mike and Steve employed someone to do the admin for them. Abby dated Steve for a while, then after they finished Steve got involved with her friend Camilla who fits the description of a woman with long dark hair. Louise was of the opinion that Camilla sets her heart on married men. What if Steve's having a fling with her?*

Steve was attracted to women who wore short skirts and revealing tops. Camilla certainly fitted the bill.

Paige vaguely recalled that Natasha heard someone say that Camilla's mother also relied on men to pay the bills in exchange for sex. Camilla must have inherited her mother's dependency on men to deliver what she was incapable of.

The neighbour offered to keep her eyes open and report back to Paige. It felt horrible that her neighbour knew about her husband's extramarital affair, even worse that Steve still lied to her and pretended he'd changed.

I'll do whatever it takes to reclaim what's mine, she vowed, willing herself to stop taking a trip down memory lane and focus on her and Liam's future. After all, he and the boys were all that mattered now. She and Steve were through . . . or did Liam have a point when he asked if she still had feelings for her estranged husband?

Only Paige held the answer and there and then she was too confused to own up to her own true feelings.

CHAPTER SEVEN

October 2015

Rufus settled in with Louise in no time at all. He was the sweetest dog, so affectionate, and followed Louise everywhere she went in the flat.

The Larsen children took turns to visit and take Rufus out for a walk, pleading with their parents to have him over the odd weekend when Louise and Trine were busy stocktaking in The Studio.

In October Louise at long last made up her mind to visit Gabriella and her potential new home before winter and the snow would prevent her bringing Rufus to Copenhagen and driving over the Öresund Bridge to Malmö. She'd had him vaccinated and microchipped; all that remained was to apply for his passport and abide Scandinavian legislation.

"I told Gabriella I would stay for a short time and see how I got on. She's over the moon and insists we stay in her flat," Louise said when Trine came round after work late one Friday night.

"Have you thought about what you'll do when you live there?"

"It's too soon. I always fancied the idea of opening my own boutique in Malmö one day. Maybe it's something I can look into. Are you sure you'll cope with The Studio while I'm away? I know Jasper will be on hand, but it's a lot to take on board on your own.

Between us we have our hands full." Louise debated if it'd be best to employ someone to handle her duties.

"Don't worry about me! If needs be Jasper will assist with stocktakes and spreadsheets and all the things you're so good at. I'll keep you updated on what's going on. We're still partners. If you decide to remain in Malmö, Jasper and I will buy you out at a fair price. Who knows? You may need the funds to start a new boutique."

"As long as you're sure you're okay with me and Rufus spending the foreseeable future in Malmö, I don't see any reason it can't work out."

Rufus sat on the settee between them. Trine reached down to stroke his soft fur. "You've got yourself a true friend in this little fellow. Will Gabriella mind having him in the flat? As I recall, she's very particular about everything – what if there's an accident and her best china is damaged?"

"We'll only stay for a short time. I intend to find a nice flat for us to live in. Gabriella is lovely but I don't wish to live with her indefinitely."

"Might the landlord permit you to sublet this place? That way you'll be able to store your belongings in the small bedroom. If not, I'll get Jasper to pick them up and put everything in our spare room."

"You're very kind. I think I'd prefer that to having some stranger rummage through my things. If I decide to stay in Malmö, they can be shipped over to me later."

Louise had spent the last few months planning everything in her head, and now it was wonderful to know that if things didn't work out, she'd still have the flat in London and her old job and business.

"You must be so excited! When are you planning on leaving?"

Trine asked, helping herself to some more wine and a generous slice of custard pie. They'd eaten homemade salmon fishcakes with mashed potatoes, salad and a baguette that Louise had baked herself. She'd developed quite an appetite recently, with which she credited Rufus. Having the small dog gave her a reason to get up in the morning and she got plenty of exercise taking him out for a walk three times a day. The rest of the time Rufus entertained them and the customers at The Studio, where he'd follow everyone around and make funny noises each time someone entered. "Perhaps you'll meet a nice, handsome Swede and fall in love?" Trine dared to suggest. She and Jasper couldn't persuade Louise to allow them to set her up on a date with one of Jasper's friends.

"Don't be so silly! It wasn't so long ago I got divorced. I'm relocating to Malmö to start afresh, not get involved with some man."

"How do you think you'd feel if you bumped into Nicklas?"

"There's always a possibility I might. Yet I don't think it will happen, somehow. Either way, Nicklas will most likely be in a relationship."

"Perhaps, but that's not the point. How would you feel after all those years?"

"How would I know? Nicklas was part of my life when we were young and thought we had the rest of our lives to look forward to. What does anyone know at that age? My parents died and his . . . well, I've no idea what became of them, only that Nicklas went through a rough time and had his own problems."

"Meaning what exactly?" Trine was all ears. She'd met him briefly one Midsummer's Eve and remembered how kind he was to her and how very much in love he was with Louise. After that day Trine and Louise lost touch for a short while and when Louise's parents died it wasn't something Trine kept in mind. By then they'd signed their contracts with the modelling agency and eventually moved to London.

"Oh, nothing in particular. You must recall what it was like for him and the others back then? Nicklas felt like an outsider. I was too wrapped up with myself after Mamma and Pappa died . . . I'd behave differently if it happened now. That's the benefit of hindsight talking."

"I know what you mean. I had no idea how he felt. As for Sweden and people's attitudes, even less. Let's hope he's found what he was looking for after the two of you parted."

Both women became momentarily lost in thought, contemplating how life may have turned out had they not moved away.

In early November Abby was rushed to hospital and after a mammoth forty-hour labour she gave birth to a boy. She and Mike named him Timmy, short for Timothy, after Mike's dad.

Premature by one month, Timmy was slightly underweight at 2kg and placed in an incubator for three weeks. To her relief, Mike didn't ask awkward questions and happily accepted that the baby had been born earlier than his due date. Thanks to her, Mike got his biggest wish and she intended to ensure he didn't forget it. With a bit of luck Mike wouldn't suspect the baby might not be his.

Abby had never wanted a child of her own after what her parents put her through. Her mother turned a blind eye each time her father forced himself on her. It started when Abby was five years old and continued until she was sixteen. Every time she went to bed he'd knock on her door and enter.

It didn't matter however much she pleaded with him to leave her alone, he kept hurting her and told her if she talked about it at school or with her friends, no one would believe her and her mother would put her into care.

She was lucky he didn't get her pregnant before she managed to get the school nurse to give her a prescription for the pill on the pretext that she'd started her periods and was involved with some boy. The older Abby became, the more her father demanded of her until she couldn't take it anymore and ran away from home, finding shelter at women's refuges and sleeping rough on the streets of London. Anything was better than returning to the hellish life she'd had at home. Eventually Abby found a job as waitress in a lap dancing club, which was where she and Camilla first met. They'd kept in touch ever since.

Despite their different backgrounds, they had a lot in common. Just like her mother, Camilla relied on men to pay her way. Unlike Abby, she didn't aspire to much, only that she had a roof over her head and enough money to survive.

Since Abby was very young, all she wanted was to be in control of her life. No man was allowed to get close to her. As soon as he did, Abby ended things between them and cut him off for good. That was, until she met Steve while working at his office. Abby wrongly assumed she'd struck gold. Unknown to her, Steve was addicted to sex and all she was to him was a fling, since he had no intention of leaving his wife for her or anyone else. Despite the fact he had a good income and was Mike's business partner, Steve rarely had money to spend. Most of his earnings went towards the upkeep of his wife and children, and what was left soon vanished on cheap motels and bedsits where he'd arrange to have sex. Yet for all his faults, Steve could be the sweetest of men she'd come across. He made her feel loved and protected despite her inability to respond.

Abby's father's betrayal of her went deeper than the physical abuse to which he'd subjected her. She didn't delude herself that one day she'd meet someone and fall in love. In her mind men only wanted one thing: sex. She decided that the only way forward was to manipulate any man that took an interest in her.

Ensuring that she was the only woman in their life, Abby duped them into thinking they could confide their deepest secrets to her, especially business deals and bank details. It made them feel powerful and in control.

Little did they know she'd use it against them and to her own advantage.

Apart from Steve, who never had money to spare, Abby wormed her way into men's lives and bank accounts. She learned how to hack into accounts online and managed to withdraw large sums of money. As soon as she got what she wanted, she moved on to the next unsuspecting victim, before her initial target became suspicious and checked his statements.

Abby had Mike in her sights for a long time and when Steve had a one-night stand with some office temp behind her back, Abby called it quits between them. Since Mike was married to Louise, Abby decided to stay patient a while longer.

She couldn't believe her luck when Mike asked her out for a drink, and confided in her that he and Louise were finished and that it was only a matter of time until they divorced. Wary as to whether he was telling the truth or spinning a yarn to get her into bed, Abby kept him at arms' length and succumbed once again to Steve when he told her he'd made a mistake getting involved with someone else behind her back.

"Me and you, we're perfect for one another in and out of bed!" Steve turned on the charm. "When I'm with you I don't feel inadequate like I do with Paige. She constantly puts me down. I can't help I'm highly sexed . . . unlike her. She won't let me come near her!" Steve's complaints were unable to silence the small voice inside, telling him he was a liar and cheat. In his own weird way, Steve loved his wife yet was incapable of staying faithful to her.

Abby and Steve continued to meet behind Mike's back for a short while. Abby was well aware Mike would cut her out of his life if he found out about their affair and that she'd betrayed him in more ways than one. For the time being she had no option but to keep a low profile and put her plan on hold a while longer. Either that or she'd risk losing everything she had.

As soon as I get him to marry me, half of what he owns will be mine, she told herself, paying no attention to the tiny sleeping infant in the crib next to her in the sterile hospital room.

The labour had been nothing compared with the pain she'd endured during her father's repeated rapes. She'd never said anything to anyone, except Camilla. Yet even her friend didn't know the full story. Steve was the only person who knew what happened the last time Abby's father attempted to molest her. When Steve confided in Abby that Paige wouldn't let him come near her, Abby opened up about what her father did to her. It was a secret that she'd long since put to the back of her mind as it was much too painful to confront herself with. But there was something about Steve that allowed her to let her guard down.

Abby told him how she'd kept in touch with her parents' next door neighbour who informed her they'd split up, filed for divorce and that her mother lived by herself in the house. Fed up with sleeping rough, Abby decided to return home for a few nights and clear her head. She was desperate for a shower and change of clothes.

The house looked exactly as it did when she left. Same tacky old furniture, the shabby interior in urgent need of refurbishment, dirty carpets and curtains. She'd searched everywhere for her mother to no avail, assuming she'd turn up later.

After she made herself a sandwich and had a glass of water, Abby instinctively brought the kitchen knife with her upstairs to her old bedroom. It was a ritual she'd adopted when she'd slept rough on the streets of London and it had saved her life numerous times. Falling into a restless sleep, she was woken by the sound of someone entering the room.

Suddenly Abby felt a hand over her mouth and heard a voice say, "You're back home where you belong." To her horror, the voice belonged to her father, who'd returned to pick up his belongings. "Keep your mouth shut and do what I say, there's a good girl."

Feeling his sour breath on her face and hands ripping her T-shirt and underwear, Abby managed to pull out the knife from under the pillow. With one deft swipe, she stuck it into his right hand just as he was about to spread her legs.

"You little whore! I'll kill you for what you did!" he screamed, dragging himself half naked out of bed, leaving a trail of blood on the bed linen, pillow and floor as he crawled towards the door. Immobilised with fear, Abby watched as he cried out in pain and staggered down the stairs. Minutes later she heard the front door slam behind him.

Half an hour later, Abby forced herself to leave the room and check whether he'd truly left or was still somewhere in the house. Satisfied he wasn't there, she cleaned up the bloodstains in the bedroom, on the doors and staircase. She put the bed linen together with her soiled T-shirt and underwear in a black bin bag and ensured there were no traces of what happened. She went into the kitchen, where she proceeded to clear up after the remainder of the meal she'd prepared earlier, rinsed the knife and

WE NEVER SAID GOODBYE

returned it to a drawer next to the sink.

It wasn't until she locked the front door behind her on her way to catch the early morning bus, bin bag in hand, that Abby realised the old bastard wouldn't get the opportunity to hurt her again. She would never return to that house, and she would take all necessary steps to ensure she couldn't be found.

Seated at the back of the empty bus, she started to shake so much she thought she would have a nervous breakdown. Abby thanked her lucky stars she had the sense to bring a knife with her upstairs to her old bedroom.

Arriving in London, she disposed of the bin bag after getting off the bus and vowed to never rely on anyone but herself. From that day onwards men became objects to control and dump as she pleased. Steve could have been different, but after his indiscretion with the office temp, he and Abby parted ways. Mike wasn't aware of it yet but he would be as soon as he checked his bank statement. The baby was just insurance that everything she wanted would come true. The pain she endured giving birth to it was a small price to pay for what she would get in return.

"Please look after my baby while I sleep," she said to the middle-aged nurse who entered the room to check on them.

"Of course I will, love. You'll need your strength to look after him," she replied, thinking it was odd the mother showed no interest in her own child. Perhaps she resented him for all the pain he'd caused her during labour? The kind nurse turned off the light, leaving the door slightly open and left.

Unknown to her, Abby was already busy making plans that didn't include Mike or the baby.

Mike was in a lousy mood. Although he was thrilled he at long last had a son, it hadn't escaped his notice that Timmy had been born premature. *It's only a month*, he told himself. *I'm allowing my suspicion to overshadow what ought to be the happiest time of my life.*

What disturbed him most was how indifferent Abby seemed towards her own child and that she didn't display emotion, not even during labour when she must have been in excruciating pain. He made a mental note to ask Steve if there was something he should know about Abby's past.

In the pub after work he brought up the subject tentatively. Steve mentioned he knew she hadn't had a happy childhood but nothing else. Mike wondered if he'd been sworn to secrecy about Abby's past.

As the days and weeks passed without Abby displaying a maternal interest, Mike became more concerned. *Steve's right*, he thought, *she's not exactly 'mother of the year'. She's great in bed, sure, but that's as far as it goes. I've never even heard her say she loves our son.*

Timmy was the perfect baby, sleeping through the night and content to be bottle-fed rather than breastfed. The last thing Abby wanted was to have him too close to her; the idea of him being physically attached to her repulsed her. Yet when Mike suggested they took turns to feed him, Abby exploded with anger.

"Don't tell me how to behave with my own son!" she shouted at Mike and slammed the nursery door in his face. Her abusive father had instilled a deep-rooted defence mechanism that kicked in whenever someone attempted to get too close. Love was always the furthest thing from her mind, and she was awash with conflicting feelings for her baby.

Now whatever Mike asked of her, Abby ignored. It was as if she'd turned into a stranger who couldn't care less about him or their son. He'd get back from work to find her in bed fast asleep or in the bathroom, applying makeup.

Having regained her slim figure, Abby started to wear the

skimpy outfits and tight fitting jeans she loved. Mike had been attracted to how she looked before she became pregnant yet part of him wished she would wear clothes that befitted a mother instead of a single woman who went out clubbing.

Arriving early at the car lot one morning close to Christmas, Mike entered his and Steve's offices in another foul mood.

"Have you prepared for the meeting with our new client this afternoon?" Steve enquired, busy printing out a Word document.

"Sure. How about you? Did you investigate his background? It sounds too good to be true to me. He's invested in other services and now he wants to do the same where we are concerned. It's too much of a coincidence in my opinion."

"What for? I believe him. He's worked his way up from nothing, just like we did. Stop worrying so much."

"That's easy for you to say. You've never risked anything in your entire life except your marriage and that's never bothered you! I, not you, built this company from nothing. All you ever did was to invest in it."

"Is that all you can say? I worked my arse off for you! The money you're referring to was my life savings. Unlike you, I haven't inherited anything! Tell me, Mike, what's this really about? You're constantly picking fights with me. Is Abby not turning out to be the woman you thought she was? She's hardly in the same league as Louise, is she? Perhaps you've realised your mistake and want out?"

"Don't you dare talk about her like that! Abby's the mother of my son. I wouldn't have him if it weren't for her. Perhaps you're jealous it's me she wants? It can't be much fun shagging Camilla!" There was a vicious expression in Mike's eyes.

"What's Camilla got to do with anything?" Steve shouted. "You've got what you wanted, Mike. Stop trying to convince me that Abby makes you happy. Be grateful for what you have and leave me alone!"

Realising he'd gone too far, Mike put up his hands. "Okay, okay. I'm sorry I gave you a hard time. Hell, on one hand I'm over the moon to be a father. On the other hand, I just don't know where I stand with Abby. One minute she's all over me like a rash, the next she won't speak to me. I'm worried she doesn't care about Timmy. Please, Steve, you must tell me as much as you can about her past. Don't say she's turned out the way she has because of her background. Everyone's got a past, but they don't turn their backs on love and affection."

"Sorry, mate, but that's not my forte. Whatever she told me stays between her and me. I may be many things, but I'm not a gossip. You want to know more, go ask her yourself."

Beside himself with rage, Mike strode up to Steve and looked him in the eyes. "Are the two of you carrying on behind my back? Tell me now or I swear I'll beat you until you confess!" Suddenly, everything he'd told himself with regard to Timmy's premature birth didn't add up.

"I'll not dignify that with an answer. Don't you ever accuse me of that again!"

"Why not? Sleeping around never bothered you before. Why are you getting so upset when I want to know if you and Abby still see each other?"

"What you're really asking is if I think she's capable of two-timing you. I told you, ask her yourself! If what you believe is true, it sure as hell has nothing to do with me. I'll tell you something, shall I? You may think of me as you wish. The bottom line is that I've got no one who cares about me. Oh, I know it's my own fault it's all over with Paige. Why would any woman, especially someone as genuine and lovely as her, want to be with a guy who's incapable of keeping his trousers up?" There were tears in Steve's eyes, but Mike didn't care.

"If you're lying to me . . . If I find out you and her are still at it . . . you're dead!" Mike knew that if his suspicions were confirmed, then he'd left Louise for no good reason other than to prove to himself he was better off without her. That wouldn't count for much in the long run.

"Don't lie to yourself," Steve said, furiously wiping at his eyes with his sleeves. "Abby's not the reason you dumped Louise. You two were over a long time ago. Both of you just went through the motions of everyday life. Neither of your hearts was in it anymore. Had you not left her when you did, Louise would have come to her senses sooner or later." Seeing Mike's look of utter fury, Steve changed tack.

"As far as Paige is concerned . . . well, you've been right all along. I failed her, Mike. You're my best and oldest friend. We can rip each other's hair out and still remain close, yet both of us lost the women we love."

"Listen to how pathetic you sound. You're old enough to be a grandfather but all you can think of is chasing after women half your age! You're like a dog on heat. Unlike you, all I care about is my son. I'm going to ask Abby to marry me."

Steve slumped down on a chair by the desk and covered his face with his hands. "You can't be serious . . . please say you're kidding? It's too grotesque to contemplate. For a start, you're not in love with her. All you have to do is stay together until Timmy's older. Abby's only looking out for herself."

"You're mistaken about her. Maybe that's how it was between you and her. Abby made a huge sacrifice, having my baby."

"Bullshit, Mike! She got pregnant on purpose. Abby's relying on you to give her everything she wants. What will you do if it turns out that I'm right?" Steve almost pitied Mike, thinking him a gullible idiot for believing Abby cared about him.

"We're fine! I won't abandon her the way you've abandoned your marriage and sons. You and I are miles apart. It's your own fault no one gives a damn about you."

Steve's eyes turned dark with anger. "I'd stop now if I were you," he replied, acutely conscious of the fact he'd let down his wife and sons. Mike's cruel words made sense and it was too late to have regrets. "Louise always used to worry you'd lose everything you've achieved. Looks like she may be right! I'd go so far as to say that she must be counting her blessings you're no longer a part of her life."

"You're wrong," Mike whispered, all colour drained from his face. "Louise knew how much this place means to me. She'd never have wanted us to get divorced." His eyes narrowed. "Rumour has it Paige's involved with someone else. Apparently, someone saw them holding hands in the street the other day." It felt great to see Steve's face crumble.

"You're lying! Paige would never see someone behind my back. You're just jealous that despite everything she and I went through, we're still on speaking terms. You chose to leave Louise and shack up with Abby; you've made your bed – now go lie in it!"

They attended the meeting and managed to stay civil with one another throughout the day, yet soon after Steve helped wrap up a series of limousine deals that injected some much-needed cash into the business, he left the premises without so much as a good-bye, thinking, *Why is Mike taking such great pleasure in hurting me? If that baby turns out to be mine, Paige will never let me get away with it and will get her hands on everything!*

CHAPTER EIGHT

ABBY WAS BESIDE herself with worry that Mike suspected the baby wasn't his. He'd stopped asking awkward questions about her inability to bond with her son. Instead he'd begun to talk about how their child would one day succeed him at Kershaw & Matthews Limousine Service.

Meanwhile Steve was on the brink of a nervous breakdown after Paige filed for divorce, Mike told Abby one evening when they sat down for dinner in the large kitchen, the baby in his crib upstairs in the nursery.

"I intend to buy him out at a reasonable prize, although it won't be anything like he expects. Soon I'll set up a trust fund in Timmy's name. It'll be available to him when he turns twenty-one." Mike's chest swelled with pride at the prospect of one day entering into partnership with his son.

Her heart racing in her chest, Abby's face turned crimson. "I'd have preferred that you discussed that with me first. After all, I am his mother."

Lately, she'd spent more time with Timmy, and was tentatively beginning to bond with him. Sometimes when she held him in her arms, he'd look at her and cause her heart to melt. Despite her insistence that he meant nothing to her, Abby couldn't help but admit to herself how defenceless he was and completely dependent on her. It was the first time she felt a sense of belonging towards another human being.

But bonding was proving to be a struggle for Abby. She knew it was partly due to the long and difficult labour, and her inability to process and express emotions. She was in two minds whether to have him adopted or take him with her when she left.

Ever since her father started to abuse her sexually, Abby had distanced herself from everything that required emotional input. Sex was at the best of times a chore she put up with to further her own interests and at worst something that had to be endured much the same way as she did with her father. Irrelevant of which, Abby didn't permit herself to give a damn.

At school no one had suspected what went on at home. It wasn't until she befriended Camilla, that Abby opened up about what her father did to her.

Shocked that her friend kept everything to herself, Camilla felt tears sting her eyes. "You never told anyone? Not even the school nurse?"

"You seriously think they would have believed me? Mum never cared about me, why would anyone else?" Abby's eyes were hard and unforgiving. "A teacher or nurse would have reported it to social services."

It was obvious to Camilla that Abby would have resented any interference, as what happened with her father was too horrific to address.

"I'd have been accused of making it up. No one stands by some kid! My own mother paved the way for my father to do as he liked with me."

Returning to the here and now, Abby reprimanded herself. *I can't afford to get emotionally attached. All I want is a place that belongs to me, not to Mike and Timmy. Somewhere I'll be safe and where no one will hurt me. Mike's got what he always wanted: a son and heir to his business. I'll have to find a way to gain access to Timmy's trust fund!*

As the years went by, Abby never saw or heard from her parents again. Eventually her old neighbour informed her they'd died and left nothing of value except the derelict house, which Abby promptly put up for sale. She'd only received a small sum for it since her father owed money on a loan he'd never bothered to settle.

The money Abby had accumulated from hacking into other people's accounts would suffice for the remainder of her life. Yet due to everything life had thrown at her, Abby wasn't prepared to leave Mike and the baby she'd given him until she'd profited further.

No, Abby would no longer be easy prey to anyone. Her father's depraved assault served as a warning to never put her trust in anyone. She had to do whatever it took to ensure she would never have to depend on anyone ever again.

With that in mind, Abby had hacked into Mike's account several times, stealing large sums of money and covering her tracks by opening up new accounts in false identities, then closing them one after another.

The fool that he is, Steve's never had much money of his own, Abby thought. *Mike, on the other hand, got Louise to pay off his and Steve's debts. Mike's kept everyone in the dark about it. But he will never track the missing money I stole from his secret account. I'll set my plan to clear out Timmy's account in action soon.*

Abby excused herself from the table and went upstairs to check on Timmy, pulling the blanket over his small body. She tiptoed into the bedroom, where she took off her clothes and got into bed, her mind preoccupied with all the money she'd steal from Timmy's account.

"I can't live like this any longer!"

Liam and Paige were on their way home from an art gallery in Mortlake. They'd managed to get a rare entire day to themselves, after he persuaded her the chance of bumping into someone they knew was slim.

"What do you mean? We've had a wonderful time so far." Paige had never seen Liam as distracted as he was now. They'd met up at his flat and made love, then ventured into Kingston and after that Barnes and Mortlake. Lunch was a hot dog with relish in the bistro Paige had often taken her kids to when they were young. The place looked exactly as it used to, and was badly in need of updating.

"Which is the reason I want to spend every day with you, not contend with a few stolen moments now and then! What's taking so long? You and Steve should be divorced soon. Have you had second thoughts?" Liam's eyes were full of despair. He loved her so much that he constantly worried he'd lose her along with his self-respect.

Standing on the pavement outside the quaint old gallery, Paige kissed his lips. "Don't you know how much you mean to me? Hearing you talk like that makes me sad. How many more times do I have to tell you Steve and I are over for good? All I want is half of what he's got! It's the reason the divorce is dragging on." Seeing the unhappiness in Liam's eyes made her hate Steve more than ever.

"What I can't understand is why we can't come out in the open. Why are you so determined we keep our relationship secret from everyone we know? We're in love! It makes me feel as if I did something wrong."

"You know the reason. I can't give up on what belongs to me! Not after everything Steve put me through. I'll not succumb to him any longer." Paige pulled out a silk handkerchief she kept in her bag and blew her nose. If it weren't for her and her father's inheritance, they wouldn't have a roof over their heads. Steve wasn't capable of supporting his own family, much less buy a house and pay the boys' school fees. Paige had sacrificed everything to give them a good start in life.

"How long? Are we talking weeks, months or even years before we can properly commit to each other? Steve's a shit. I love you so much I positively ache when we're apart! I don't understand how you can stand to live in the same house as that man." Liam had left everything he owned behind him when he moved to London. That was years ago now and he'd managed to start afresh. "Perhaps it's best we see less of each other until your divorce is finalised. Call me when you've got a timescale."

Paige dabbed at her eyes and nodded. "You're right as usual. I've no right to put you through all of this. We can't go on the way we are now. We deserve to be happy together and that will not happen unless Steve and I sort everything out between us. But Liam, I owe it to my sons and myself not to walk away empty-handed. I took on so many jobs just to make ends meet! Steve's not pulling the wool over my eyes any more than he already did." She started to cry, thinking she would die if Liam ended their relationship.

"All I ask is that you don't walk away from me," Liam replied, reaching out to stroke her arm. "We've endured so much together. Promise me you won't let Steve talk you into staying married to him. You must get closure. Let him go, I beg of you!"

"I already did. This isn't personal, Liam, all I want is what's owed to me. I'm so sorry my personal affairs cause you so much stress. But the bottom line is that I can't and won't let Steve take away any more of my self-respect and pride. Not even for you. If I do, I'll never forgive myself. Please try to understand."

Registering everything she told him, Liam bowed his head. "I hear you. We'll talk soon. It'll give us time to put things into perspective." He was desperate to be with her and ask her to become his wife, but unless Paige found the strength to cut Steve out of her life, Liam was convinced they didn't have a future together.

Kissing him one final time, Paige looked deep into his eyes and told him she loved him. "I won't give up on us," she said, then hailed a black cab passing by, climbed into the back seat and buried her face in her hands.

"When will you get us a decent place to meet up?" Camilla asked the minute Steve walked in the door.

They'd split up then got back together numerous times. Neither of them missed the other yet they depended on one another; Camilla for the money to pay her bills and Steve for the sex. Now Paige had filed for divorce, Steve knew his needs wouldn't be met at home.

Fed up with Camilla's constant demands, Steve regarded the brash woman who had contributed to his demise. "I never heard you complain until now."

Seating herself on his lap, Camilla asked, "What's up?" Her hand lingered on his crotch.

"Don't! The day's gone from bad to worse. Mike's always on my case. I think he's losing it, big time." Steve pushed her aside.

"Really? I got the impression he and Abby are playing happy families."

"So did I. But Mike's got it into his head she's been carrying on behind his back. I never saw him acting so weird before, almost as if he's paranoid."

"What's that got to do with us? Are you and Abby still seeing each other?" Camilla's eyes narrowed. Despite their friendship, she was under no illusions where Abby was concerned. She always got whatever she set her sights on. If Abby and Mike split up, Camilla knew Abby would eventually worm her way back into Steve's affections. He'd always had a soft spot for her. "Talk about having your cake and eating it! You're certain you don't want her back?" she asked in a subdued voice.

Wearing a woolly jumper and stained jeans, Steve looked haggard and older than his years. "Look, baby, you and me . . . it's not working out. We're good together in bed, but it doesn't go any further than that. You always knew the score. I don't want to continue the way we are. We're through. You can stay here until the end of the month, seeing as I've paid the rent until then. After that you're on your own. I don't need more complications in my life. If Paige finds out about us I stand to lose everything!"

Camilla swallowed hard and turned her back on him. "You can't just leave me!" she cried. "I depend on you to pay my bills! You and Paige are over. Pay her what she's owed and get it over and done with. Set yourself free and start over with me! Unless you do, I won't be responsible for my actions . . . Imagine what your soon-to-be-ex-wife will do to you if she finds out we've been sleeping together right under her nose! I'll tell her you and Abby slept together around the same time as Mike dumped Louise and got involved with Abby!" She whirled around, looking him square in the eyes so he could see she wasn't joking.

As far as Camilla was concerned, Steve could rot in hell as long as she still had a roof over her head. She simply wasn't willing to scrape by on whatever job she managed to find anymore. Unless Steve came to his senses, she'd no option but to return to the sleazy nightclub and subject herself to the men who came to ogle the topless lap dancers. At forty it was demeaning to strip for money, and she knew that one thing would soon lead to another. Camilla's greatest fear was that she'd end up like her mother and meet up with clients in some cheap motel. The mere thought of it made her cringe inside.

"Are you ... *blackmailing* me?" Steve spluttered. "If the answer's yes, be warned! I'll tell Mike and everyone I know exactly what you're like. You won't stand a chance of getting a job, ever again! Between us, Mike and I will make sure you're persona non grata." He paused to wipe spittle from the side of his mouth. "Just look at yourself, mutton dressed as lamb. You're damaged goods!"

Tears threatening to blur her vision, Camilla whispered, "I never knew you could be so vicious ... I'll be out of here first thing in the morning. Just so you know, I wouldn't have anything more to do with you even if you were the only man on the planet! I'm not that desperate." She wanted to say he'd better watch his back. If Paige found out about their dalliance, she'd inform her solicitor, who in turn would state adultery as cause for the divorce. Paige desperately required proof of Steve's infidelity and Camilla was only too pleased to assist. "You and Mike are as rotten as each other," she said quietly. "What a pity the two of you aren't gay, you'd make the perfect couple."

"Look who's talking!" Steve replied. "You're nothing but a cheap whore who sleeps with men in exchange for getting her bills paid!" Brushing past her, he stormed out, not bothering to shut the door behind him.

Camilla reeled with anger. *The bastard! How dare Steve talk to me like that? He won't get away with it — I'll own up to Paige about every-thing.* Hastily she packed her belongings.

That day taught her a valid lesson. Until then she'd permitted men to exploit her in return for money.

Mum warned me to not end up like she did, worn out and with no one who gave a damn whether she lived or died, Camilla thought, telling herself that no matter how hard things turned out to be, she'd take responsibility for herself. From now on, no man would rule her. She'd never again let anyone belittle her the way Steve had. Her only concern was how she'd be able to cope on her own without someone willing to pay for services rendered.

"What are you doing on my doorstep?" Abby hissed, her face dark as thunder. "Mike's on his way home. Leave now or he'll draw the wrong conclusion!"

"You're talking rubbish. Mike knows we're not together any-more," Steve replied. "Just tell me one thing and I'll leave. Am I the baby's father? Camilla and I are finished. She threatened to tell Paige about us. You'd better tell me the truth! I've got nothing to lose."

Consumed with fear that Mike would return any minute, Abby stammered, "I-I've n-no idea what you're talking about."

"Liar! Is that baby mine?" Steve raised his voice so much that he gave her no option but to let him inside.

"You're out of your mind! Of course Mike's the father. As soon as we started to date, I stopped taking the pill."

"You're quite sure of that? Just don't get any ideas about involving Mike and Paige! You and Camilla spend your entire lives tricking men into looking after you. It won't be long before Mike realises he made a big mistake, getting involved with you. It's only a matter of time before he sees through you."

"Don't you dare take that tone with me. You can't touch us! As for Camilla, she's perfectly capable of taking care of herself. It's Paige I pity the most. Camilla and I saw her the other day in Mortlake, on our way to a friend's birthday party. She was with some guy; they were kissing! Apparently, someone told Natasha about it, saying a reliable source said Paige and that guy are deeply in love and that she can't wait to get divorced. You revolt me, Steve, thinking you've got the right to play with people's feelings and pretend you've got morals after the way you've behaved. Get the hell away from me and my baby or I'll make sure you'll regret it." Abby pushed him aside and slammed the door in his shocked face.

Returning to his car, Steve sat behind the steering wheel, devastated at the news that Paige had met someone else. *I'll tell her I found out about it,* he resolved. *What hypocrisy! All the time I've been racked with guilt, she's been carrying on with him behind my back!*

Steve simply couldn't get his head around it. He didn't understand why she was so angry with him. So both of them had made mistakes. He most of all, yet that was no excuse for her to treat him in that way.

Driving off in the old battered Volvo Louise had sold him twenty years ago, Steve vowed to return and persuade Abby to tell him the truth about whether or not he was the baby's biological father. "She didn't even offer to let me see him," he muttered, before his thoughts turned to Paige and some stranger making love to his estranged wife.

Paige was on her way out to do the weekly shop when she heard a noise coming from the front door. Running into the hall to see what it was, she noticed a medium-sized brown envelope on the doormat.

I wonder who it's from? There's a mailbox outside at the front of the house. Why didn't whoever it was put it inside the box?

Picking it up, Paige brought it with her into the kitchen and laid it on the table. Finishing her mug of coffee, she slit open the envelope with a knife and read the note inside. So as to convince herself she wasn't dreaming, Paige read the words out loud.

I know who your husband sleeps with behind your back, the note said. It was signed, *From someone who wishes you well.*

Too numb to react to what she'd just read, Paige returned the note inside the envelope and pocket of her jacket.

Who wants me to know about Steve and some woman having an affair? I knew it! Paige pulled out a bottle of white wine from the fridge and poured herself a glass. This was cause for celebration.

She finally had proof of her husband being unfaithful to her.

She'd barely finished drinking, when she heard Steve come inside and into the kitchen. "Hi, honey. What are you doing, nursing a glass of wine at this time of day?" She wanted to throw the letter at him and see the reaction on his face yet managed to refrain so she could find out who wrote it first.

"What do you want? I told you I want you to pack your stuff and move out!"

"Can't we talk about it like adults?" Steve asked, desperate to know if Abby's friend was right about Paige and some man.

"It's too late for that. You may pour yourself a glass of wine, after that I want you gone! I've a busy day tomorrow." She could tell he'd been trying to figure out how to get her to change her mind and cancel the divorce.

"How come, are you seeing someone else?" Steve enquired, eyes searching hers.

Paige frowned. "Only the usual people . . . is there anything else you wish to know?"

Fed up with walking on eggshells, Steve came out with it. "I hope whoever it is treats you well."

Paige's face drained of colour. "Stop talking in riddles! Why on earth are you insinuating I've met someone? I want you to leave this instant! Find yourself somewhere else to live, please." Ignoring him, she went up to the kitchen sink and started rinsing glasses and plates.

"Please! Can't you at least be honest with me? I wish I was able to undo what I did wrong. Just hear me out."

"It's of no concern to me. I've moved on and I want you to as well. We're getting divorced, Steve. I've nothing more to say to you." She'd wasted too long trying to turn him into someone he wasn't – decent, honest, eyes only for her. "Get it through your thick skull: we're over!"

He had the nerve to turn up unexpectedly, claiming he loved her when all along he was still betraying her. The letter confirmed her suspicions. She knew him too well to fall for his lies and charm.

Desperate to reach out to her, Steve mumbled, "I've changed, Paige. Please let me prove it to you, for old times' sake. You're the only woman I love and always will be." His eyes begged her to not give up on him and the marriage.

"Then prove how much you love me by giving me half of everything you've got," Paige snapped.

Steve stood there, mute.

"No? Then just leave! You're all mouth and no trousers. I gave you the best years of my life and you . . . you think you can talk me into taking you back by saying you love me. You don't know the meaning of the word!"

Anger building up inside, Steve hissed, "I'm not going anywhere. This place belongs to me as well. I worked my arse off to pay for the interior decorations and bills."

"That's nothing compared to what my father did for you! Why, he trusted you to be there for me, not screw girls no older than our sons! I know you're sleeping around despite your best efforts to persuade me you're not."

"Like you, you mean? At least have the guts to tell me!" Steve shouted.

"I owe you nothing! Get the hell away from me." She was getting more upset by the minute. What the hell gave him the right to interrogate her?

"This isn't over by a long shot; you're playing with our lives. Everything we've achieved is falling apart . . . I won't give up on us!"

"Are you insane? You single-handedly destroyed our marriage. I'll never forgive you for all the times you lied and cheated on me. All I feel for you is contempt and revulsion. What I do and who I see have nothing to do with you. I've every right to be happy." Paige calmed down sufficiently to finish the washing up.

Feeling drained, Steve slumped down on a chair at the table. "I'll pick up my things later in the week and be out of your hair as soon as I've found somewhere to live. You needn't worry about me, I'll not bother you again." Raising himself from the chair, Steve walked out of the kitchen, minutes later closing the front door behind him. They were over for good. Thirty years of her love had come to an end and he only had himself to blame for it.

CHAPTER NINE

WHAT IF I'M right and the baby isn't mine? Mike downed his third glass of wine in the pub. *Is Steve capable of lying to me too? Perhaps he just pretends to be my friend. A womaniser and adulterer, yes. But would he stoop so low as to father a child and let another man think it's his?* Steve insisted he and Abby had already stopped seeing each other by the time Mike appeared on the scene. Timmy was everything to him and the reason he left Louise was to start over and have a family. It didn't bear thinking about Abby's betrayal with his best friend. Leaving the pub an hour later, Mike got into his car and drove home unsteadily.

"Louise, it's me, Gabriella. I wish you'd decide a date when you and Rufus are coming over. It's getting cold. Malmö's always at its best in the spring and summer. Mind you, the long dark winter months are quite cosy. I get to catch up on reading all the books I've put aside for quiet nights at home."

Louise was acutely aware of how much her aunt looked forward to her niece and dog staying with her in the flat. Gabriella had long since redecorated the guest room and hall, making room for their belongings. She'd even called Louise's old friends, Kajsa and Martin, informing them of her niece's imminent arrival.

"I'm not as young as I used to be, at my time of life every day counts."

"When you put it like that, I feel guilty for postponing the move."

"Wait till you find out what I'm about to do," Gabriella said in a low voice.

"You must tell me now! Please don't say you've handed in your resignation at the hospital. Top neurologists like you are hard to find."

"That's just it. I've decided to work part time a while longer, then retire. Someone's got to make room for the next generation. It may as well be me." Gabriella didn't sound in the least upset she would soon retire from work at the hospital after nearly forty-five years.

When she's gone I'll have no family left. Gabriella's right. It's high time I started planning our departure, Louise thought, making a mental note of setting the wheels in motion and discussing the details with Trine and Jasper.

She'd left Malmö all those years ago and was on her way back.

Paige was carrying her shopping to the car park outside Sainsbury's when her eyes fell on a tall, dark-haired woman she recalled from somewhere. Packing the shopping into the boot of her Mercedes, Paige heard the woman call her name.

"Can we talk? My name's Camilla Jessup."

Taking a closer look at her, thinking she must have encountered her in the past, Paige replied cautiously, "Who are you and what do you want from me?"

"We have a mutual friend. Natasha Sturgess introduced us at her annual Christmas bash. I recognised you just now in the supermarket. Steve and I are acquainted," Camilla added, feeling awkward and painfully aware of the other woman's disapproval. Compared to her own skimpy outfit, Paige looked elegant in a demure dress; her soft, curly blonde hair scraped off her pretty face.

"I saw you and Steve years ago. I know you're divorcing him." Camilla fiddled with her long hair, wondering if she'd made a mistake in approaching Steve's estranged wife. After she'd left the dingy bedsit, Camilla moved into a friend's studio flat in Ham where she slept on the couch until she could find somewhere to rent.

"What's that got to do with you? If you have something to tell me you may as well spit it out. I've no time for chit-chat." Paige knew Camilla's type only too well. It was obvious the vulgar woman standing there had had an affair with Steve.

"I've got something to tell you. Something you may want to hear." Camilla watched Paige get into the front seat of the car and roll down the window.

"Have you now? Well, I don't give a damn! You're not the first woman Steve's had a fling with and sure as hell won't be the last!" Paige snapped, eager to get out of there.

"Don't I know it! All I ask is that you hear me out. I wish you no harm. You'll thank me for it one day."

"I doubt that will ever be the case. There's nothing you can say to me that I haven't heard before." It used to hurt Paige deeply every time she was confronted with one of Steve's extra marital affairs, but over the years she had gradually got used to it and eventually stopped caring. "Alright, we may as well get it out of the way. Get in." Paige saw the confused expression in Camilla's eyes as she opened the passenger door and got in, thinking to herself, *She's exactly how Steve likes them, cheap and easy to string along. What's wrong with me? Why am I prepared to talk to some woman my soon-to-be ex-husband had an affair with?* "Are you and Steve still together?" Paige's voice sounded oddly detached.

"Not anymore. Steve ended it a short while ago. Just so you know, I never intended to hurt you, it just happened. I'm on your side. What I'm about to say may come as a shock to you."

"Save your breath! It's not something I've not heard before. Steve slept around constantly throughout our so-called marriage. My biggest mistake was to marry him and stay for as long as I did. So, what have you got to tell me that I don't already know?" The other woman's presence and cheap scent were making her nauseous.

"That I'm willing to testify that I and Steve have been lovers on and off for a long time. It'll contribute to your claiming half of everything during the divorce." She calmly awaited Paige's response.

"Why are you going behind Steve's back?" Paige said, after a pause. "Did he screw you over like he did me? Is there someone else on the scene? You're surely not doing this without getting something in return."

"Steve lied to me: he told me the two of you were over! It was I who wrote that letter!" Camilla cried, overwhelmed by what she'd done.

"Why?" Paige asked in an incredulous voice. Perhaps that woman was the answer to her problem after all? Turning to look at her, she continued, "I don't understand how you can live with yourself and stoop so low as to have an affair with a married man. Surely you knew he has children? He must have mentioned them. How old are you, forty? Are you really so desperate to get a man, that you jump into bed with anyone who propositions you?" Paige felt nothing but contempt for her sort.

"But he said you were over and getting divorced!" Camilla felt hideous for what she'd put the other woman through. Men like Steve only thought of themselves and to hell with the consequences. "I'm so sorry I caused you and your kids so much pain! You're too good for him. I never knew you were so nice and pretty," she continued, incapable of comprehending why any man would want to stray when they had someone as beautiful as Paige in their life.

Registering her words, Paige muttered, "You're not so bad yourself, only foolish and naïve to allow men to treat you badly. Having an affair with a married man is beyond contempt."

"My mother was the same. She always slept with men in return for money. I read somewhere that it's referred to as social heritage. The apple doesn't fall far from the tree, as they say. Anyway, there's something else you ought to know." Camilla prayed her revelation wouldn't backfire in her face.

"I'm all ears."

"Steve's been involved with someone else on and off. It's the same woman who recently had a baby with Mike Kershaw. You probably know him. He and his ex-wife Louise got divorced last year."

Paige's face dropped. This was better than anything she could have hoped for. If what Camilla insinuated was true, Steve hadn't only betrayed his wife but also his oldest friend and business associate.

"I've no proof. But think about it. If what I've told you is true, you'll get everything you're entitled to. Abby is the woman's name; we've known each other for years. You can't tell her I told you about the baby! It may turn out I'm wrong and that Mike's the father, but I somehow doubt it. The dates don't add up. The baby was born premature. Please say you forgive me for what I did to you."

Too stunned to think straight, Paige put a hand to her mouth, stifling a sob. "Steve fathered a child with Abby, pulling it off as Mike's?" She was visibly shaken and it took her a few moments to compose herself sufficiently to reply, "I can see you regret what you did, Camilla. Yet if Steve hadn't dumped you, would you still confess to me about you and him? I think both of us know the answer . . ."

"You're right, I wouldn't, but I came to my senses and wrote that note. Surely, it counts for something? Deep down, I'm not a bad person."

"What makes you think that baby isn't Mike's? Lots of babies are premature."

"I know how my friend operates. Abby will do whatever it takes to further her own interests. She wants enough money to lead an independent life. As for me, all I've ever wanted is to meet a good, decent man who will love and take care of me. Steve's an idiot for treating you like he did!" Camilla sensed Paige was thawing towards her.

"Steve's actions don't affect me anymore. He's the father of our children, nothing more. Even that he manages to fail at. Fancy that, Steve and Mike getting it on with the same woman! Mike and Abby are doomed to fail. I've resigned myself to the fact Steve will never change. It's Louise I feel sorry for, after everything she did for Mike. He and Steve wouldn't still have the business if it weren't for her generosity. I'm grateful you wrote that letter, Camilla, even more so that you had the guts to approach me. But what about you? Are you sure you will be able to reject Steve if he wants to pick up from where you left off?"

Paige searched Camilla's eyes. They'd been talking in the car for nearly twenty minutes.

"I wouldn't take him back if he was the only man on the planet! Steve had plenty of opportunities to prove he cared. Men like him never do."

Camilla scribbled down her number on a piece of paper and handed it to Paige. "Call me if there's anything you need. Leave a message on my mobile and I'll get back to you." After waiting for Paige to write down her number in exchange, Camilla got out, waved and walked off.

Sitting by herself in the car a while longer, Paige abruptly shook her head and laughed out loud. "I got what I want! Thanks to Camilla's admissions, Liam and I are closer than ever to getting the life we deserve." She decided to call her solicitor as soon as she returned home and made a mental note to confide in Natasha about the unexpected conversation.

"Why do you look so shocked? You knew Mike and Abby had a baby," Trine said to Louise as they ate at a nearby restaurant in Fulham. They'd been working late at The Studio to ensure Trine was up to speed with everything Louise normally handled.

"Yes, of course I know that. What I wasn't aware of is that Mike may not be the baby's father. What makes you think he isn't?" Louise's head was full of everything she had to do before she and Rufus left for Sweden.

"It's something Natasha told me the other day. Apparently Paige encountered Steve's mistress, Camilla. We met her at one of Natasha and Robert's annual get-togethers, do you remember? Tall, dark hair, short skirt, does that ring a bell? Natasha and Abby have known each other for some time. Anyway, according to Camilla, Steve and Abby continued to see one another after Mike and Abby started dating. See what I mean?"

"Kind of . . . Well, I'm sure glad Rufus and I are moving to Malmö! Mike's welcome to her and Steve's betrayal of him. At least in Malmö I won't have to worry about bumping into someone who knows them and tells me all the latest gossip," Louise replied, a tiny voice inside her urging her to not get upset.

She'd coped so well recently and had no intention of fretting about Mike every time someone mentioned his name. Mike chose to leave her, not the other way round. Whatever happened to him was nothing to do with her anymore.

"I only told you about it because I didn't want you to hear it from someone else," Trine said hastily. "Don't even consider either of them! Mike made his bed and deserves everything he gets. As for Abby, all I can say is what goes around comes around. It's the baby I feel sorry for – with parents like that it will grow up in an environment devoid of love and stability." Trine's eyes clouded over.

Signalling for a waitress to bring the bill, the friends changed the topic of conversation and discussed Louise and Rufus' imminent departure to Malmö.

"I will call you every day to make sure you're okay. Jasper's promised he'll take care of all your duties. Everything will work out just fine!"

"I don't how I'd have coped this past year had it not been for the two of you," Louise said. "I'm so very blessed and grateful to have you in my life. Oh, and before I forget: Mike left his old laptop behind in the house in Barnes. I brought it with me to the flat. The thought of calling him and ask him to collect it doesn't appeal to me! Please say you'll take it and store it in the attic?"

"Of course we will. Mike forgot to take his laptop with him

when he stole the antique pieces you inherited from your parents? I wonder what's on it. Did you take a look?" Trine's eyes lit up at the prospect of that man hiding something that wasn't intended for anyone's eyes but his.

"No, I've no interest in anything that's associated with him," Louise replied, thinking it wouldn't harm her to at least dig it out of the box she'd put it in when she moved to the flat.

Just then the young waitress appeared with the bill and after they'd split it between them, Trine and Louise parted outside on the pavement.

"I can't get my head around the fact that you're moving to Malmö. You must be so excited. Jasper and I will look after the flat until you decide if you want to give notice in which case we'll store the furniture and everything else. Give Rufus a hug from me!"

It was exactly one month until they were traveling to Malmö. Rufus' inoculations were up-to-date and the vet had issued his passport. Gabriella had already arranged for a taxi to pick them up at Copenhagen Airport and take them over the bridge to Malmö. At Gabriella's request, Louise got in touch with her old friends, Kajsa and Martin. Both were delighted to hear from her and said they couldn't wait to see her after such a long time. Happy her friends still lived in Malmö, Louise felt assured that apart from her aunt, she and Rufus were off to a good start.

It wasn't until later that evening just as she was about to go to bed, that Louise remembered Mike's old laptop. After rummaging through some boxes in the closet in the spare room, she finally found it at the bottom of a drawer.

I ought to get rid of it. Mike's laptop is nothing to do with me, she told herself, recalling what Trine said about the baby and Natasha's suspicion Steve may be the father. *I'll just take a quick look at it, then hand it over to Trine and Jasper to store in the house,* she thought, bringing it with her to her bedroom.

Following behind her, Rufus curled up on the bed and fell asleep.

Half an hour later, still attempting to figure out Mike's password, Louise recalled his obsession with cars, particularly old American vehicles. She tapped in the word 'Edsel'. Bingo! She'd managed to gain access to his old files, among them a statement of a business bank account Mike opened in his own name years ago.

It didn't feel right to view his private documents yet Mike obviously didn't care or he'd have deleted the details. Louise's eyes fixed on a large deposit of £2 million. The date coincided directly with a time Mike begged her to lend him money to pay off a debt on which Kershaw & Matthews Limousine Service were incurring hefty interest. Staring at the screen, Louise felt sick.

Mike tricked me to pay off his and Steve's debts several times! The naïve fool I was, I trusted him. Not only did I get them out of a hole, but Mike also made a tidy profit from some client and paid it into his own account! I bet Steve didn't even know about it . . . at least I hope that's the case. Those two are thick as thieves.

Confused as to what to do with the damning evidence of Mike's criminal activity, Louise turned off the laptop and placed it on the table in the kitchen. Biting the bullet, she dialled Steve's mobile number, uncertain as to what to say to him yet adamant to get to the bottom of his eventual part in Mike's scam.

"Hi, it's me, Louise," she said in a shaky voice. "I'm sorry if I'm calling at an inconvenient time. There's something I need you to clarify."

"Louise? It's great to hear from you! I met up with Robert the other day. He mentioned you're thinking of returning to Malmö." Steve was surprised to hear from his colleague's ex-wife. After what Mike did to her, he'd concluded she want nothing more to do with either of them.

"Yeah . . . I've not made up my mind yet. Anyway, can you recall if Mike opened a business account in his own name, apart from your joint account? It suddenly dawned on me that Mike left behind some paperwork in the house in Barnes and I may have made a mistake in shredding them before I had a proper look . . ." Louise held her breath.

"You're too good to him! After the way he behaved, I'd expect you to cut off his genitals, not worry about some documents he left behind. Nah, Mike would have told me if he'd opened an account in his own name. He's had his own personal bank account since he finished college but nothing else that I'm aware of."

"I'm sorry I bothered you. Great! At least now I don't have to worry about it anymore. You're quite right; Mike's whereabouts aren't anything to do with me. Give my best wishes to Paige and the boys."

There was a moment of silence. "I take it you know we're getting divorced? I made such a mess of my life, Louise. Take good care of yourself." He switched off his mobile before she could reply.

I was right all along, Louise thought. *Mike betrayed both of us. I'd have heard it in his voice if Steve lied to me. A womaniser, sure, yet he'd not stoop so low as to steal from his friend! I'll confide in Trine and Jasper tomorrow; it's too late to do something now. Mike duped everyone around him.*

Louise willed herself to put the matter out of her mind until the next day when she would bring Mike's laptop with her to The Studio and reveal everything to her friend.

"How dare you go behind my back and sign a deal with a rival firm?" Mike was reeling with anger. Steve had just told him he'd taken the liberty of making a decision on their behalf, while Mike was away at a meeting.

"You know it's our only chance to ensure our competitors don't steal our clients by offering less expensive options. Together we'll maintain our position in the market instead of losing out to everyone." Steve was livid that Mike questioned his capability to decide what was best for them in the current market. They'd been close to declaring themselves bankrupt lately; Louise's gift didn't cover the consistent struggle to survive and draw a salary. Recently, Steve had even abstained from that, as he believed that everything they'd made was best placed in the business.

Clearly Mike didn't share his opinion. To him the company was his domain to rule as he wished. He'd inherited it from his father and gladly accepted Steve's investment in return for an equal share in the company.

"We're in a league of our own! No one comes close to what we offer," Mike snapped, adding, "You're an idiot. The minute I turn my back, you sign a deal with a minicab firm. What the hell were you thinking?"

"You really need to ask? For the benefit of the company, of course! You should try it." Steve resented Mike for coming and going as he pleased. He hadn't put in a full day's work for ages.

"You signed a deal that stipulates that we have to ensure that most vehicles are available to the minicab firm whenever they require it, in return for 50% of the profit. Meanwhile, our loyal, long-standing clients will have to wait until the same cars are available to them – clients who pay five times the amount it costs to book a cab! It's insane and will ruin us, Steve. I will ensure that you pay the difference out of your share of the business!"

"What bloody share? You're living on another planet. We don't even have sufficient funds to sell up and make a profit!" Steve never felt as angry as he did there and then. Unlike Mike, he didn't splash out on cars and fancy clothes, only cheap motels for his sordid sexual encounters.

Mike took a step closer to Steve and snarled at him. "Thanks to you we'll come across as desperate. Had it not been for my dad and me, you wouldn't have a job! You ought to be grateful to me and show some respect."

"Like you do towards me, right? You were only too pleased to take my money and for us to enter into partnership." Steve suddenly recalled Louise's strange late-night query about whether Mike had opened a business account in his own name. He decided to keep it to himself a while longer. "In the event I decided to sell my share, you wouldn't have the funds to buy me out," he commented instead.

"There you go again, claiming you're indispensable," Mike mocked him. "This is *my* business; you're just an employee answering to *me!*"

Exasperated with his behaviour, Steve saw red and punched him in the face. "That's for all the times you've put me down! If you continue in the same manner I'll pull the plug on you and your precious company." He started to walk away.

Incensed Steve had the nerve to attack him, Mike came after him and twisted his arm, then dragged him backwards and pinned him against the desk. "I'd love to finish what we've started but we've a meeting to attend!" Panting, he realised what he'd done and stepped back, releasing the other man. *What the hell is happening to us?* Mike thought then, scared he'd pushed Steve too far. *We used to be close . . . I must cut down on booze; it's making me aggressive and irrational.* He'd concluded Abby wasn't interested in him and the baby, only what was in it for her. If she'd pawned off another man's child on him, Mike had no option but to seek legal advice.

But irrelevant of whether or not Timmy was his, he'd prevent Abby from taking his son away from him. *I've got to set up a trust fund in his name*, Mike reminded himself, his face aching from Steve's punch.

Rubbing his sore arm, Steve led the way out of there in silence, Mike following closely behind.

Recalling he'd left his old laptop at the house in Barnes, Mike began to fret that Steve would somehow get hold of it and put two and two together.

If he discovers I opened a secret account and hid a large sum of money, Steve will kill me, he thought to himself. *How could I have been so negligent as to forget about that damn laptop?*

According to a neighbour, the house had been sold to a young family who renovated it and added an extension. They'd hired a skip to get rid of everything that was left behind. Mike had combed through the skip under the cover of darkness, but to no avail. Desperate to find the laptop, Mike felt certain Louise must have come across it and stored it at a friend's place when she moved out.

What if she or one of her friends figured out the password and discovered I've got a secret account? Mike was frantic to get hold of the laptop and file, knowing he had to ensure it didn't get into the wrong hands. *I'll start with Natasha and Robert. If Louise confided in them about the file, they'd not tell anyone except the Larsens.* Mike detested Trine and Jasper, who didn't think he was worthy of Louise.

Yes, the Sturgesses were his best bet to begin with. Mike prayed that they'd hold the key to his predicament.

Thinking it was the sound of her husband's car in the driveway, Natasha opened the front door, her welcoming expression darkening when she saw who was standing on the doorstep. "You! What brings you here?"

"I was passing and immediately thought of you and Robert," Mike replied, leaning forward to kiss her cheek. "I've something I wish to discuss with him." He looked rather wild-eyed, and there was a large bruise forming on his cheek.

Feeling nervous, Natasha prayed Robert was on his way home after his matinee performance at The Haymarket Theatre. "We're invited to meet friends for dinner. Robert just called to say he won't be long." She hoped her admission would cause Mike to leave. Seeing him after such a long time reminded her unpleasantly of what he'd put Louise through.

Wondering why Natasha didn't make the effort to dress up, instead of wearing an old cardigan, torn black trousers, flat shoes and no makeup, Mike had the feeling she was lying to him.

"What do you want from us, Mike? Tell the truth for once in your life!"

"Can't I say hello to my old friends? Surely, you want to know what became of me?" he teased.

"Not at all. We're disgusted with you for what you did to Louise. No one saw it coming."

Surrounded by shoes and jackets scattered on the floor in the entrance hall, Mike glared at her. "I should have known you'd take her side! There's two sides to everything."

"Is that so? Perhaps you can enlighten me." The anger Natasha felt when Trine told her Louise took an overdose of sleeping pills was close to spilling over. "You left her on your twentieth wedding anniversary! What did you expect us to think?" Her voice was shaking.

"Look, I've not come here to cause an argument. Tell Robert I'll wait for him outside in my car. I'm sorry I upset you." He was about to kiss her cheek a second time but Natasha recoiled.

Normally she'd have offered him something to drink but Mike didn't deserve her kindness after the way he'd treated her friend. As he climbed into his car, Natasha went inside and called her husband. "Mike's here! He's waiting for you outside in his car. Please hurry home. I told him we're invited to friends for dinner."

Hearing the distress in her voice, Robert told her to calm down. "You mustn't let him get to you, my darling. Mike probably came round to give us his side of the story. Don't worry, I'm on my way."

Minutes passed. She was on the verge of calling him again, when Robert's car rolled up outside. Standing at the kitchen window, Natasha watched her husband park up, step out of the car and walk towards Mike's vehicle.

"What are you doing here, Mike? Natasha told me you've something to ask me."

"Natasha got the wrong end of the stick. I had no choice but to end my marriage to Louise. It's a great pity my so-called friends don't give me the benefit of the doubt!" Mike said, his voice raised in anger.

"You abandoned your own wife without warning and explanation – on your twentieth wedding anniversary of all days! Louise was devastated, Mike. Yet here you are, bold as ever, without regrets and expecting us to act as if nothing happened." Robert spoke quietly but firmly.

"Louise isn't a victim! Her wishes and work always took priority over me!"

"So you decided to exact your revenge?" Robert shook his head. They'd never been close, yet they'd always been civil with one another.

"Think what you like! I don't give a damn. I came here to ask

113

a favour of you . . . for old times' sake," Mike muttered, watching Robert's face contort with anger.

"You're out of your mind to even ask!"

"Steady on, mate, you're not on stage now," Mike mocked him, an evil expression in his eyes.

"That's enough! Unless you leave immediately, I will call the police."

Sensing he'd better do as he was told, Mike put his hands up. "I didn't come here to cause a scene. I'm sorry Louise had such a hard time. These things happen."

Robert sighed. Such drama should be reserved for the stage. "You said you wanted me to do you a favour."

"It's not a big deal . . . Look, mate, I mislaid my old laptop. It was in my office at our old house . . . you wouldn't know what became of it? I've got some important files on it."

"You came all the way for that? Sorry, *mate,* I've no idea what you're talking about. Now don't trouble us again, is that understood? Neither of us knows the whereabouts of some damn laptop."

"Please, Robert, can't you ask Trine and Jasper about it for me?" Mike begged. "They want nothing to do with me."

"You've got a nerve, after the way you treated Louise! I know you stole her parent's old furniture and got her to bail you out." Relieved Natasha had left the front door open, Robert turned and walked up the driveway without so much as a backward glance at Mike.

"What did he want from you?" Natasha asked as soon as he entered.

"He asked me to help him locate an old laptop he left behind in the house in Barnes. I told him we don't want anything more to do with him." Robert's mouth was set in a thin line, a sign he'd reached the limit of what he was prepared to tolerate.

Natasha couldn't stop thinking about Mike's odd request, making a mental note to call Trine the following day and ask if she and Jasper ever came across Mike's old laptop. On his part, Robert couldn't shake off the feeling that Mike was keeping something from him. Was it possible that he'd stored some file on the laptop containing information he didn't want Louise to see? He continued mulling it over for the duration of the evening.

They'd returned home after dinner at their friends' house when Robert turned to his wife and said, "Mike's up to something. We've got to locate that laptop."

"How? Paige told me Louise is moving back to Malmö. I refuse to get her involved in Mike's affairs! She's suffered enough."

"You're right as usual. I'll talk to Jasper when I've calmed down. I'm starving! We hardly ate a thing at the Bensons' tonight. Vegetarian lasagne isn't our thing. Come on, I'll make us a cup of tea and a sandwich." Robert kissed her on the lips and went into the kitchen. It had been a long day. Hopefully Mike had got the message and would stay out of their lives for good.

Chapter Ten

November 2015

Furious that Robert had rejected his plea for help, Mike drove to the office and was relieved Steve saw fit to not show his face. Glancing at his reflection in the mirror above the sink, Mike saw his left cheek was bruised and noticed for the first time it was throbbing. He put ice on it from the freezer in the staff room.

I've got to find that laptop, he thought. *If the Sturgesses and Larsens tell Steve about this, he'll become suspicious. That damn file is on it! Brentwood LTD gave me a cheque for £2 million and told me to open a separate account. Fortunately for me, neither Louise nor Steve suspected anything. It was around that time I persuaded Louise to credit the joint account with nearly £250K to clear the company debt. She got us out of a sticky situation, claiming she only did it because we were married. It never occurred to her that due to her determination to not start a family, I was deprived of a child! Bailing us out was the least she could have done.*

Mike was just as upset now about Louise's refusal to have children as he ever had been, and truly believed the money he'd paid into his account was his to spend as he pleased. He had kept the £2 million he'd put in the secret account, enabling him to buy a series of sports cars that he stored in a warehouse not far from

Kingston. He kept the details in a drawer at the house, to which only he had the key.

If someone found out about the account, Mike knew he'd risk being sued for fraud and may lose the business as a direct consequence. The prospect of Louise finding out what had really happened to the money and Steve's reaction when he discovered his oldest friend and associate had betrayed him didn't bear thinking of.

I'd have no option but to go bankrupt as the money would go towards what I owe those two! Mike's stomach twisted. *As if that wouldn't be bad enough, Abby will leave me and take the baby with her. It'd be my own fault for leaving that damn laptop behind!* He'd not even dared to check his monthly statements online since early spring in the event Abby or Steve figured out the password. Deciding now was as good time as any to do it, Mike dialled his bank manager's direct line.

"Mr Stoppard speaking. May I take your name?"

"Kershaw. Mike Kershaw. I'm pushed for time so let's get on with it."

"Mr Kershaw, I've not heard from you for some time. What can I do for you?"

"Please be so good as to give me the balance of my account."

"Of course. It'll only take a couple of minutes," the branch manager replied stiffly, irritated that Mike didn't take the time to be civil.

After what seemed like a very long pause, Mike was initially relieved to hear the other man's voice. "There seems to be a problem, Mr Kershaw. Did you withdraw a large sum of money recently?"

"Of course not! If I did, I wouldn't be calling to check the balance. What's wrong?" Mike could feel a splitting headache coming on.

"I don't wish to upset you . . ."

"Don't talk in riddles! Tell me what's wrong." Mike's face was turning a furious red.

"Since 10th April someone has regularly withdrawn money from the account adding up to the total sum of £1.2 million. The last withdrawal was on 5th September this year."

Thinking this was the other man's idea of a joke, Mike swore out loud. "You idiot! I've no time to play silly buggers. I want to know the balance of my account."

"I can assure you I'd never joke about something as serious as this. The balance of your account is £800,000."

"What? You're seriously expecting me to believe that?"

"That appears to be the case, sir."

"Then someone must have hacked into my account! You've got to do something about it!" Mike was close to losing his temper altogether.

"There's nothing that can be done. Are you absolutely sure you've not withdrawn the amount yourself?"

"You're insinuating I stole from my own account? Clearly, this is a discrepancy on the bank's part. You must reinstate the money that's gone missing. If you refuse, you leave me no option but to sue you for negligence!" Mike was on the verge of a breakdown. *If only I hadn't mislaid that damn laptop*, he thought, wondering who had got hold of the details and hacked into his account.

A million thoughts rushed through his mind. Could Steve have found out about the account somehow? Or Louise? Perhaps she came across the laptop when she packed her belongings? Either way, Mike wasn't going to let them get away with it. Hearing the bank manager's distant voice at the other end of the line, saying "We've never encountered anything like it before. It's bound to be a scam. Nothing to do with the bank," Mike nearly had a fit.

"You insist I had something to do with it? I asked you to give me the balance and you respond like this! Unless you immediately investigate the matter and get back to me, I'll get my lawyer involved."

"I'm sorry you feel the need to incriminate the bank in your personal affairs. We'll certainly investigate the matter and report back to you. I bid you good day, Mr Kershaw."

Mike broke into a cold sweat when the line went dead. *The bastard! Except me, no one's got access to the account. Louise and Steve wouldn't go behind my back and steal from me . . . It's got to be someone else. When I find out who it is, their life will not be worth living!*

What's taking her so long? Paige glanced at her wristwatch in irritation. She'd ordered a mug of tea and a bun in the rundown café in Kew Green. Signalling at the waitress to bring her the bill, Paige saw the familiar figure rush inside, apologising for the delay.

"The traffic's awful this time of day!" Camilla exclaimed, throwing her jacket and bag on the floor between them.

"We arranged to meet at 2.00 pm; you're an hour late!" Paige snapped, surveying the woman she'd befriended not so long ago. "Did anyone recognise you when you walked in?"

"Not that I recall. I was about to leave my mother's old flat when one of her ex-boyfriends turned up, saying she'd left me pieces of costume jewellery. Just my luck if it turns out to be worthless!" Camilla sighed and browsed the small menu.

"Haven't you learned from your mistakes? You're still relying on others to pay your bills," Paige commented, frowning.

"I'm sorry I spoke!" Camilla retaliated. After all, it was hardly her fault Paige allowed Steve to walk all over her. "Look, I'm sorry I spoke out of turn, but you've got to stop blaming me and Steve for the breakup of your marriage. What we did was wrong, yet you've got to accept some of the responsibility. You chose to stay married to him despite everything he did."

Determined to not let the other woman get too familiar, Paige asked, "Have you found out any more about your friend's baby? Is Steve the father?" The tension between them was palpable.

"I've no idea! If I were you I'd confront him with it. If he refuses to cooperate, your solicitor must request a paternity test."

"How about you ask that friend of yours? If the two of you are as close as you say, she's bound to confide in you."

"I can't! Abby will get suspicious if I ask too many questions. We've had our ups and downs over the years; I don't want us to fall out again."

"Please level with me and tell me if you believe Steve is the baby's father. I was a fool to put up with Steve's affairs for as long as I did. You're no different for relying on him when everything else fails." A part of Paige pitied Camilla and Abby for offering themselves to men who used them.

"I told you I'll do whatever it takes to help you get what you're owed! But there's something I need to confess first . . ." Camilla swallowed. "Steve and I had a one-night stand. I know I should have rejected him but I've nowhere to live and the bills are mounting up."

"I knew you'd take him back, eventually. Why are you so keen to let him exploit you? I genuinely thought you'd learned your lesson." Paige watched Camilla's face crumple, tears brimming in her eyes.

"You think this is how I want to behave? I'm ashamed of who I am – someone who relies on married men to pay the bills! I'm not proud of what I did. At my age I should be able to support myself. The last thing I want is to end up like my mother:

lonely, destitute and beyond repair." She reached for Paige's hand. "Please say you believe me?"

"It's of no consequence what I or anyone else thinks of you! You're right; I was a fool putting up with Steve's affairs for as long as I did. You're an idiot as well for relying on him when everything else fails."

Letting go of her hand, Camilla replied, "I'll never forgive myself for what I did to you." She burst into fresh tears.

Paige felt awful for causing the other woman to feel inadequate. After all, it wasn't Camilla's fault she'd inherited her mother's dependency on men to put a roof over her head and pay the bills. Seeing her so upset, Paige didn't have the heart to further add to what she'd already accused her of.

"Oh, Camilla . . . I do believe you when you say you've turned a new leaf. I want you to come and stay with me in the house. I gave Steve his marching orders! Tell me something: it was he, not you, who ended things between you the second time as well? Please be honest with me."

"Y . . . ee . . . s. I'm sorry I didn't tell you. Steve finished things between us twice. Are you serious about wanting me to move in with you?" Camilla whispered.

"I've been in your shoes, putting my trust in a man who's incapable of changing his ways. Your friend has a point; we need to be in charge of our own lives! I meant what I said earlier. Deep down you're not a bad person, only hurting and confused." Paige suddenly viewed Camilla in a different light.

"Won't your boys object to my presence?" Camilla asked.

"I've brought them up to be decent and considerate."

"But I deceived you! Will you ever be able to forgive and trust me?" At that point, Camilla broke down and cried so much she couldn't speak properly. By then everyone in the café was staring at them.

"I honestly don't know. It remains to be seen. From now on you must promise me you'll stop meeting up with Steve or working at his and Mike's office. We'll think of something eventually."

Paige was grateful that Camilla had admitted her one-night stand with Steve.

Unknown to him, Steve's estranged wife and mistress were about to cohabit in the house he and Paige had shared for most of their marriage.

"Did you discover who hacked into my account?" Mike asked, seated opposite the bank manager. They were in the offices of the main building, close to Marble Arch.

"Sadly, no," Mr Stoppard replied, his rigid manner belying his dislike of this most demanding customer. "Our fraud department confirms someone's helped themselves to your money on and off since 10th April."

"What the hell am I supposed to do now?" Mike hissed, wanting to wring the older man's neck.

"Whatever you deem necessary. The matter is out of our hands. Please excuse me but I've got to leave. My colleagues are waiting for me." Mr Stoppard raised himself from the chair and started to walk towards the door, further indicating the meeting had come to an end.

"You'll pay for this!" Mike spat at him.

"Is that a threat, sir? If the answer's yes, I'm left no alternative but to alert our security department." Mr Stoppard had witnessed too many people attempting to pull the wool over his eyes, when in fact it was they who'd initiated the entire scam. From experience the bank manager felt certain Mike Kershaw belonged in the same category.

Opening the door to him, he made it abundantly clear he wasn't willing to discuss the matter further.

Paige entered the house in time to answer the phone.

"Mrs Matthews? I'm pleased I managed to get hold of you." The voice belonged to Justin Pollock, her appointed solicitor.

"What can I do for you?" Paige asked, wondering if Steve's solicitor had been in touch with him.

"Are you and Mr Matthews still living together? If the answer's yes, I strongly advise that you ask him to leave. You need to keep a distance from one another. We don't want him to find out you're claiming half of everything including his business. Do I make myself understood?"

"Steve already knows that. What's it got to do with me if he questions it? I've done nothing wrong! Steve's to blame for everything."

"Of course. My only concern is that he doesn't find a reason to pin something on you since you're divorcing him on grounds of adultery." The solicitor's tone became more serious. "Mrs Matthews, your estranged husband mustn't be alerted to your personal affairs. If you're involved with someone, I firmly suggest you keep a low profile until the divorce is finalised. Forgive me for asking, but are you seeing someone?"

"As a matter of fact, I am. We're in love and want to get married as soon as I'm divorced," Paige retaliated sharply, her heart racing inside her chest. Steve had ruined so much for her, the idea that he'd be able to turn the tables on her made her nauseous.

"I'm sorry if I upset you," Mr Pollock said, after a brief pause.

"No . . . It's I who ought to apologise for being defensive," Paige told him, mortified that she'd lashed out at him.

"Please see it from my point of view. If you and your . . . *friend* are seen in public, it could be construed that you've been having an affair behind your husband's back for some time. Mr Matthews may even point the finger at you. The law will not consider the grounds for divorce versus settlement. However, I will do my utmost to prove how badly your husband's infidelity throughout the marriage has affected you emotionally. In my experience, each case is treated individually and I've had much success in the past."

"You're asking me to keep a low profile until it's over? To pretend I'm not involved with someone? How will I be able to keep up this charade?" Paige felt sick. It was bad enough that Liam told her it was best they kept their distance until she and Steve sorted things between them. Yet now her solicitor advised her to not have anything to do with him whatsoever, not even a phone call. Paige wasn't sure if she would be able to survive without his reassurance and support.

"I strongly advise that you and your . . . *friend* use the utmost discretion until a short period of time has passed after the divorce is finalised."

"But we love each other! I may lose him if we have to be apart!"

"Then so be it, Mrs Matthews. Life's not fair at the best of times."

"I can't be expected to put my life on hold! Steve's the one who's had affairs for years, not I!"

"Then you must prove it. Give me the proof I need to fight your corner and I'll do my best for you."

"I've not got it . . . yet. All I have is his latest mistress' admission and offer to testify to the fact. It's slightly complicated, as we've become friendly with each other. I've offered her to come and stay with me until she can find somewhere to live. Steve ended the affair a while ago." Paige realised that socialising with her estranged husband's former mistress made her look stupid and naïve.

"Well, as decent as that may seem, I'm confident it will harm your case. You must ask her to sign a written statement. Let me have her details and I'll ensure it'll be dealt with immediately. My PA will get in touch soon. Remember what I told you and everything will be alright."

Paige sat by the phone for almost an hour, attempting to digest his advice.

It was just as well she and Liam had already decided it was best to keep a distance until she and Steve were divorced. But what hurt the most was that it was she who now had to display a squeaky clean façade when Steve was the one who was unfaithful throughout the marriage. "Mr Pollock's right, life's not fair at the best of times," Paige said out loud, wishing Liam were there with her.

Calling him later that night, Paige told him what the solicitor had advised. "It's for the best," she said, tears brimming in her eyes. Hearing his voice yet not being able to see and touch him hurt more than she'd imagined.

"It won't be for long," Liam replied. "We'll soon be together. I love you, Paige. The thought of you is what keeps me going. We've been through so much, it will not kill us to be apart a while longer." Abruptly he turned off his mobile.

His last words echoed in her ears, reminding her of Burt Bacharach's 'A House Is Not A Home'. Without Liam in her life to love and share things with, Paige felt the house she'd lived in for so long became a prison of which she couldn't wait to rid herself. It was just an empty place to live in until they were reunited.

CHAPTER ELEVEN

ON THE EVE of Louise and Rufus' departure to Malmö, Trine and Jasper helped to pack up the furniture and store it in the flat's spare room. Louise had the landlord's permission to sublet the flat until she knew if they'd stay put in Malmö or return to London. Until then, Trine and Jasper would be looking after it.

"I'll miss you so much!" Trine sighed. "We'll call and email each other often and I'll come over to visit you as soon as I can."

Trine and Jasper were adamant about taking them to the airport early the next morning, before returning to The Studio in time for deliveries and stocktake. Jasper had appointed someone to assist him with his property business, enabling him to be available whenever Trine required.

"I can't imagine my life without you, who will I turn to when I need advice? You're always there for me." Louise almost started to cry at the thought of leaving her best friend behind.

"You'll be fine! Gabriella will be there for you and you've got friends in Malmö."

"I've not seen Kajsa and Martin since I moved to London. We kept in touch over the years, the odd phone call and letter. You're the only person who knows me inside out."

"Just give yourself the opportunity to settle in and get to know them again. View it as a new chapter in your life. Malmö's changed since you left; it'll take a while to adapt to a small city." Trine suddenly thought of something. "By the way, Natasha called last night. She told me Mike came round to ask Robert about a laptop he'd left behind in Barnes. Robert was so upset with him over the way he treated you, he asked him to leave and not return. You mentioned this the other day – did you find the laptop in the end?"

Taken aback that Mike saw fit to bother the Sturgesses, Louise shook her head. "It's just like him to upset people! Yes, I did. I found it in the bottom of a drawer. It contains a file with details of Mike's bank account. He opened it in his own name behind Steve's back." She wanted to confide in Trine further, but decided it wasn't in either of their interests. Mike was no longer part of their lives.

"Wow! Are you telling me Mike stashed away money that doesn't belong to him?"

Trine's eyes widened. "I'm not sure. All I could figure out when I browsed the file was that Mike deposited a large amount of money into the account, £2 million to be exact, around the time he pleaded with me to settle his and Steve's debt."

"Are you sure? If that's true then Mike committed fraud! Not only did he get you to bail him and Steve out, he also got someone to pay him a large sum of money for services rendered that presumably Steve didn't know about! No wonder Mike's frantic to trace that laptop. He'll stop at nothing to get it back! His life's not worth living if he doesn't." Trine briefed Jasper on it as soon as he walked in the door with a stack of boxes to store the rest of Louise's belongings.

"That son of a bitch! Mike's such a hypocrite. First he gets

Louise to bail him out, then he screws Steve over. If Steve finds out about it, all hell will break loose." Jasper couldn't believe how dumb Mike was to risk everything he and Steve had achieved for some shady deal. "Two million pounds is a huge amount and should have been split equally between them."

Louise decided then to confide what else she knew. "According to the recent statement, Mike – or someone else – made regular withdrawals that add up to the sum of £1.2 million . . ."

"You're kidding!" Trine exclaimed. "Mike obviously forgot he set up the account online where anyone can gain access to the details if they've got the password. No one in their right mind does what he did. He stole from you, Louise! If someone's done the same to him I hope they get away with it. It serves him right."

"It appears the withdrawals occurred six months ago. Anyway, it's nothing to do with me. I'm just relieved he's no longer part of my life," Louise replied.

"But he took you for almost everything you've got! That laptop proves what a dubious person Mike is. If I were you, I'd report it to the police." Trine was incensed that Louise would let him get away with treating her like that.

"No, I don't want the police involved. We're divorced. I don't wish to dwell on the past. It's the reason I decided to relocate to Malmö. The future's what matters now." Louise was determined to not be dragged back into Mike's shady affairs.

"I agree with you. Mike will get his comeuppance one way or another. It's only a matter of time. If Mike wasn't the one withdrawing all that money, who can it be?" Jasper wondered, attempting to come up with a plausible answer.

"If someone fleeced him out of £1.2 million I sure as hell wouldn't want to be in their shoes. Mike won't let them get away with it. He'll make them pay!" Louise's mind worked overtime to figure out if it could be anyone she knew, but she was unable to think of anyone who was capable of doing something like that. She asked her friends what she should do with the incriminating evidence, and Jasper offered to store the laptop at their house, just in case things should turn even nastier than they already were.

Over dinner that night in Bluebird restaurant on King's Road, they focused on the present and Louise's imminent departure to Malmö.

Raising her glass, Trine toasted her friend and wished her a great life.

She and Jasper were on their way home, when the latter said, "I'm pleased Louise is getting on with her life in a city where Mike can't find her."

Deep in thought, Mike didn't hear Abby ask, "Did I mention Camilla and I met up for lunch yesterday? She and Steve called it quits. Camilla thinks he's involved with someone else." Sensing he had other things on his mind, she added, "Why don't you pour yourself another glass of red wine while I get dinner ready? Caesar's salad with baguette okay with you?"

When he didn't reply, Abby went up to him. "Is everything okay? I've been thinking about what you said last night."

"What do you mean?" Mike couldn't for the life of him recall what they'd talked about.

"Your wish that we formalise our relationship, silly!" Abby purred in his ear. "I know you'd had a bit to drink, but can't you remember suggesting that we get married? Maybe it's not such a bad idea now we've got Timmy. It'll make us even closer and be good for our son's future . . ." They'd not argued as much lately and Mike had stopped complaining to her about everything that went on at work.

Turning to look at her from his position on a stool at the kitchen bar, Mike snapped, "You didn't seem keen, remember? Forget it. The moment's passed!"

Baffled he had addressed her in such a brusque manner, Abby replied, "Don't snap at me! What's up? I can tell something's bothering you." A part of her was hurt he'd discarded the idea of marriage. Yet a bigger part was relieved she didn't have to pretend it mattered.

Mike took a long swig of red wine. "Someone's stolen a large sum of my money from my account. I only found out about it when I checked the balance last week. I don't suppose you'd know anything about it?"

"What's that supposed to mean? I don't have access to your bank details! Are you accusing me of stealing from you?" Abby pretended to be offended so as to not arouse further suspicion.

"Someone hacked into my account! You and Camilla had access to Kershaw & Matthews' account details when you looked after the accounts and office administration. They were written down on a piece of paper we kept in a drawer." He omitted to mention he'd not recorded the details of his personal account, only the company's. Mike kept the other details in a locked drawer in his office, in the event he forgot about them. "The PIN number was in the same drawer," he added, referring again to Kershaw & Matthews' joint account. Without realising it, Mike raised his voice so much that Timmy woke upstairs and started to cry.

"Look what you've done! It took ages to get him to sleep. I haven't the faintest idea of what bank details you mean. Steve's the one you should ask. Give him a hard time instead!" Abby shouted, running upstairs to ensure the baby was alright. They'd bonded even more since Mike often worked late and didn't return home until after mealtimes and Timmy's evening baths.

Desperate for Mike to not see through her, Abby prayed she'd covered her tracks. She'd hacked into people's bank accounts so many times yet never got caught. Primarily, she didn't want to lose her child, having warmed to the idea of bringing him with her if she and Mike didn't work out. It seemed to her that time had arrived earlier than she'd anticipated.

Mike can't find out it was me who took that money! If he does, I'll end up in prison and Mike will get custody of Timmy. Abby had discovered his PIN number, password and account details before Mike installed a lock.

The men whose bank accounts she'd emptied in the past never suspected a thing until after she'd ended the relationship. Even if they had, Abby was careful to not leave any signs. She'd learned from the best hackers and advanced her skill over the years. She never contemplated hacking into Steve's account, since there wasn't any point as he rarely had money to spare. Abby had decided not to confide in Camilla as it may have compromised her and the baby if the other woman knew of it. Although they'd known each other for a long time, they'd never been that close.

Hearing his footsteps outside the nursery, Abby took a deep breath, gently pulling the sleeping baby closer to her until his head and face were buried in her neck.

"I'll locate that laptop if it kills me!" Mike hissed, entering the nursery and taking in the scene in front of him.

Scared he'd frighten the baby, Abby pretended she didn't hear him, asking, "Are you and Louise still in touch? Who else would be able to steal from you except her? You probably gave her the details of your account."

"No, Louise didn't know about it. Look, I'm sorry I shouted at you earlier. I'm just so damn angry someone hacked into my account," Mike said in a calmer voice.

"It's okay. I'd feel the same if roles were reversed. You've a lot on your mind."

Relieved he didn't suspect her anymore, Abby made a mental note to call Natasha and ask if she knew of the laptop's whereabouts.

"I've got to leave; I'm late as it is for a meeting. We'll talk later, honey." Mike walked up to them and kissed the baby's forehead, looked her in the eyes and left.

Phew! That was too close for comfort, Abby thought. *I'll call Natasha and Trine tomorrow.* The time had come when she needed to make plans for her and the baby.

The following morning Abby called Natasha on a pay-as-you-go mobile she'd bought in the event she needed to cover her tracks. Disguising her voice, she told her a former client had asked her to get information of Mike's account.

"My name's Lis. I used to temp at Kershaw & Matthews Limousine Service. Apparently the client suspects they committed fraud."

"I recognise your voice. Have we been introduced? Mike came over to ask about the laptop. Trine and Jasper Larsen are storing it in their house. I hope your client gets the answers he needs."

Ignoring Natasha's initial comment, Abby thanked her and switched off the mobile. She made a mental note to destroy the pay-as-you-go SIM card in case Natasha called using that number. So the laptop was at the Larsen house. With a bit of luck no one would gain access to it and discover Mike's account details. *Timmy and I are okay for the time being. There's no reason for me to get in touch with Trine, I'll keep a low profile where Louise's friends are concerned.*

Unbeknown to Abby, Natasha called Trine and told her about 'Lis'. "I thought I recognised her voice yet couldn't figure out who it was," she said. "You must help me to refresh my memory.

There can't be that many people who've been involved with Mike and Steve's business over the years."

"Perhaps you're right. Only two women spring to mind: Abby Logan and Camilla Jessup. They've been friends for a long time, and both worked for Mike and Steve, looking after the accounts and running the office . . . Do you suppose one of them pretended to be someone named Lis?"

"I'm not a hundred per cent sure, but the woman who called me could have been Abby. I've met her a few times when she and Camilla attended our Christmas parties . . . Abby's accent is very guttural. Lis didn't exactly have the same voice, but a similar accent . . ." Natasha was extremely pleased she'd called to ask for Trine's advice.

"It makes perfect sense that Abby's the one who hacked into Mike's account!" Trine said in a jubilant voice.

"Maybe. But how can we be certain Mike's not withdrawn the money himself?" Natasha asked.

"We weren't until now. Abby impersonated some woman who doesn't exist. The only reason she did it is because it was she who withdrew that money."

"But we don't have any proof!"

"That's okay. At least now we know what the two of them did. Mike paid a large sum of money into a secret account behind Louise and Steve's back. Abby hacked into the account and stole more than half of the money. I'd go so far as to say those two are perfectly suited." Trine thanked her lucky stars Louise was safely tucked away in Malmö. When Steve caught out Mike and Abby, they'd get what they deserved.

"You're forgetting there's a baby involved in this," Natasha reminded her.

Feeling sick at the idea of an innocent child falling victim to his parents' criminal activity, Trine murmured, "We must ensure that baby comes to no harm."

"We must involve Steve in this. Camilla and Paige suspect he's that child's father! If Abby and Mike end up in prison, someone's got to take responsibility for him," Trine added, vowing to make sure Mike's misdemeanours wouldn't remain a secret for much longer.

Too agitated to put the matter to the back of her mind, Abby wondered why Mike was delayed. He'd told her he'd be back so they could talk. Dialling Steve's mobile number, she let out a big sigh when he answered.

"It's me. Can you recall if Mike opened another bank account?" she asked, coming straight to the point.

"Why do you want to know?" It wasn't so long ago that Louise enquired about it as well. He was baffled that both women deemed it sufficiently interesting to get in touch and ask about it. "I've no idea if Mike's opened another account. Surely, that's nothing to do with me? Why are you calling? The last time we talked you made it perfectly clear you want nothing to do with me!"

"That's right. This isn't about us. Mike's upset someone hacked into his account. Apparently, someone stole a lot of money."

"But I don't know anything about some account Mike supposedly opened in his own name!"

"I believe you. Please keep our conversation confidential, Steve. Mike suspects everyone around him of stealing from him, me included."

She'd planted a seed in Steve's mind. If Mike continued to suspect her, at least Steve knew about the account and may decide to question Mike and discover his old friend had tricked him out of a lot of money. *I'll be home free!* Abby smiled. *The police will get the fraud team involved. I've not left any tracks. Mike will be the one who ends up in prison, not me!*

Unfortunately for Steve, it was Abby and Camilla who were responsible for accounts and bookkeeping, giving Abby the perfect opportunity to fiddle the account figures and gain access to Mike's bank details. Steve's trust in Mike meant he had no reason to check up on his old friend and business partner.

"Camilla informed me Paige filed for divorce," she said in a kind voice. "I'm sorry the two of you can't work things out." Out of all the men she was involved with, Steve was the only man who despite his addiction to sex treated her with a level of respect. In Abby's mind that counted for something.

"I never knew you two were still in touch. I got the impression you're not as close as you used to be."

"Whatever gave you that idea? We lead different lives, that's all."

"Mike's always fighting with me. Looks like the two of you are getting on. Can't say I'm surprised. He constantly berates me for screwing around and thinks I've only got myself to blame for the divorce." Steve sounded fed up.

"He's got a point! The way you've treated your own wife is simply disgraceful."

"Is it, really? How about the way you and Mike behave? You're both as bad as each other! Your relationship is a joke. Who's kidding themselves now?"

"I'm sorry you feel that way. Mike and I have our problems but both of us only want what's best for Timmy. That's more than you ever cared for your sons!" Abby ended the call before Steve had the opportunity to tell her he didn't believe Mike was the father.

★

Camilla had been living in Paige and Steve's house for nearly two weeks when Paige asked if she'd found a job. "You've got many skills," she said, "particularly the ability to communicate with people of all ages. I've seen it with my own eyes. That combined with hard work will eventually contribute to getting a job you like."

They were in the front garden, catching a few rays of sunshine. Steve had recently picked up his things and moved into a one-bedroom flat in Wimbledon. He'd at long last listened to Paige, who made it abundantly clear their divorce wasn't up for discussion. "I've wasted too many years catering to your needs. It's my turn now," she'd said, helping him pack. They'd agreed he could return to collect the rest of his belongings when they were divorced.

"I don't understand how you and Camilla can share a house. You're always giving me a hard time yet you found it in your heart to forgive her," he'd complained.

"That's because I know she's learned from her mistakes. Unlike you, Camilla's capable of changing."

"I'm not like you, Paige," Camilla said, breaking Paige's train of thought. "I try so hard to not rely on anyone but myself, yet no one gives me a break. I must have applied for at least ten jobs." She breathed in the chilly air, wishing she was able to contribute more towards food and household bills. Paige didn't expect her to, only that they took turns to cook, clean and shop. Wearing heavy layers of clothing and boots, both women had spent the morning in a local garden centre, stocking up on plants, soil and tools. They'd bought a Christmas tree and Paige had brought down the previous year's decorations from the attic.

"You're too hard on yourself! Look, I've got a proposition for you. It suddenly dawned on me we're both at a crossroads in life."

Paige hadn't told Camilla about Liam, concerned she wouldn't be able to keep it to herself. Justin Pollock repeatedly reminded Paige she must keep a low profile or risk losing her share of Steve's income and savings. The solicitor had managed to secure the house, claiming it had been her father's wish that his daughter inherited it in the event she and Steve were divorced. "The house is mine to do with as I please. I've decided to redecorate the bedrooms and turn two into offices. One for me; the other for you. You see, I have a proposition for you. It's high time someone offered a matchmaking service for mature people. We want to be different to other services who rely on members to go on one date after another. We're offering a personalised service to people who wish to meet that special someone to share their lives with. We'll match people's profiles, lifestyles and credentials. I want you to be my business partner."

Stunned that Paige suggested they work together on an equal basis, Camilla was at a loss for words. "You're the kindest person I know but I can't possibly accept. For a start I've not got the funds to invest and I don't feel that I can contribute as much as you can. I won't sponge off you, Paige!" She was close to tears. Ever since her mother died and Steve dumped her, Camilla had taken a long, hard look at herself.

When Paige suggested she moved in with her, it was as if she'd been given a second chance in life. But that was as far as it went. Camilla was too proud to accept a job she wasn't qualified to do and have an equal share in Paige's business.

"You're selling yourself short," Paige protested. "I just told you how good you are with people. It's the most important commodity for a matchmaker. I'm intuitive and technical. Between us we'll succeed. Most significantly, both of us have quite a lot of experience and we've certainly suffered heartache."

Listening to her, Camilla couldn't deny they'd make a good team. "I'll consider it on one condition. You must let me invest some money as well. At a recent auction an expert evaluated my mother's collection of costume jewellery. It's not worth a fortune and won't substitute for the real article, but I've decided to accept an offer of £10k."

Touched that Camilla wanted to invest in the business and was willing to sell her mother's jewellery to do so, Paige smiled. "You must put aside a few pieces to remember her by."

"Is that a yes, you'll permit me to invest in your scheme?"

"Absolutely. It shows how committed you are for us to succeed. We'll be equal partners. All I require of you is a yes or no."

"Yes! Oh, Paige, you're too good to me. I hope I can live up to it." Camilla followed her inside to the kitchen, feeling happier than she ever had been in her entire life.

"Let's celebrate in style!" Paige pulled out an expensive bottle of white wine from the fridge. They had a lot to discuss and plan yet both felt certain that the concept would benefit many potential clients who preferred not to take a chance on the numerous online dating sites that catered to younger people.

"We'll come up with an angle that specifically offers a service for mature people," Paige said, conscious of the fact both of them were about to enter a new phase in their lives. "You may eventually find the right person to share your life with." It wasn't just Camilla who'd benefitted from their newfound friendship; Paige dwelled less on her marriage to Steve since Camilla came to live with her and generally felt much better than she had in a long time.

"Like you, you mean? Josh told me he saw you with some man in the street. He and Alec want you to be happy."

"How did he find out I'm seeing someone?" Although her

heart fluttered at the fact that her secret was out, Paige loved that her boys instantly felt at ease with Camilla. Neither of them referred to her fling with their father – it was in the past and unnecessary to bring up the sordid details of their father's actions.

"Apparently, he and Alec saw you walking with your arms around each other. They were waiting for you to tell them. You deserve to be happy more than anyone I know, me included. Here's to us and our new venture!"

Pouring them a glass of wine each, while she considered the implications of her sons knowing about her lover, Paige changed the subject. "We've got to come up with a name."

Sipping her wine, Camilla had a wistful expression in her eyes. "How about 'Forever Yours'?" she asked.

"That's it! Well, we'd better get a good night's sleep. Tomorrow we'll start to develop a website that appeals to everyone who wants to meet someone special. It will take time to establish ourselves but it will be worth it in the end."

"Steve will be shocked when he finds out we're starting a business together," Camilla commented, thinking life wasn't so bad after all.

"Good, that serves him right!" Paige's head was spinning with everything that lay ahead of them and the amount of wine she'd consumed to celebrate her and Camilla's new venture.

"Can we talk?" Steve asked Mike as they came out of a meeting.

Recently both had kept a distance and managed to be civil with one another. Despite Mike's initial anger that Steve had signed a deal with a local minicab service, he had to admit it was in their favour as both companies benefitted from the new partnership.

"Sure. What's on your mind?" Mike asked, eyes glued on his partner.

Sitting down in the black leather chair that was his favourite piece of furniture in the office, Steve returned his gaze. "What's going on between you and Abby?"

"You want to talk about my personal life?"

"Yes. Abby called me the other day, saying someone hacked into your account. She sounded scared."

Swallowing hard, Mike broke out in a cold sweat. Everything depended on his response. "What do you mean? Abby's fine. I just got upset someone stole from me. We've sorted things out between us. I've got everything under control."

"Then you won't mind I ask you a couple of questions?"

"Go ahead."

"How come you didn't bother to tell me you opened a separate business account?"

"I wasn't aware I had to inform you of everything I do." Mike tried to keep calm.

"Not even that you kept it secret?"

"Don't patronise me! I don't know why you think I've got something to hide." He was getting angrier by the minute. "I don't answer to you! Now it's my turn to confront you. What the hell is going on between you and Abby? Answer me!" Mike felt certain they were carrying on behind his back. Why else would they talk on the phone?

"You need to talk to her, Mike," Steve said, just as Mike saw red and lunged for him.

"I warned you to not play games with me!" He shouted so loudly everyone outside the office could hear him and wrapped his hands around Steve's throat.

"And I warned you to not get involved with her! Abby's been through a lot in the past." Steve managed to cut loose from Mike's grip on his neck. "You're deluding yourself if you think the two of you will have a future. Abby's capable of more than you give her credit for! She always gets what she wants, eventually . . ."

Uncertain as to what Steve meant, Mike changed tack. "I know you only want what's best for me. Do me a favour; don't talk about Abby, okay? She and I understand each other." Mike put on his jacket, smiled strangely and walked out.

CHAPTER TWELVE

Louise had been living in Malmö for nearly two months when she got in touch with Kajsa Jansson and Martin Norell. As soon as they heard from her, they talked her into meeting them at Café Hollandia in the pedestrian walk. Malmö's oldest café, it was located only a five-minute walk from Gabriella's flat.

Louise and Rufus had settled in the minute they entered the spacious and elegant home Gabriella bought in the 1970s. Surrounded by Malmö's best restaurants and cafés, city life and close to nearby coastline and beaches, it was a stylishly decorated flat, with antique furniture and a roof terrace overlooking the Öresund strait and Denmark. Gabriella was in her element. Living on her own wasn't all it was cut out to be; she had missed her niece over the years and loved fussing over her and her cute dog.

Determined not to put her aunt out and to find a place of her own, Louise put down her name with several estate agents, listing her favourite areas, Fridhem and Limhamn, where she was born and had lived with her parents.

"How wonderful you've arranged to meet your friends at Café Hollandia. You must tell them I want them to come round for dinner on Saturday." Gabriella hadn't seen Kajsa and Martin for a little while and was just as keen to meet them as Louise. Having now semi-retired, the highly respected neurologist spent her days off on a golf course in the countryside not far from Malmö. "Malmö's expanded a lot in recent years," she continued. "You must visit Turning Torso in the West Harbour. It's the tallest building complex in all of Scandinavia, and is quite striking." Gabriella detested some of the new apartment blocks in the old part of the city; in her opinion they spoiled the atmosphere and didn't blend in with the old buildings and cobbled streets.

Louise loved Little Square and Big Square, where people met up to eat and drink in trendy restaurants and cafés. She and Rufus walked for hours in the numerous parks, their favourites being Palace Park and Malmö's largest park, Willow Park. She purchased a bike and it felt wonderful to ride along the designated cycle tracks all over Malmö. Buying continental food at Möllevång Square with its pop-up restaurants, wine bars and delicatessen reminded Louise of Soho in London. She hadn't exercised a fraction as much in Barnes and Fulham as she did in her native city, and here she went to bed at ten o'clock every night.

Each time Trine called, she heard just how happy her friend was, and was keen to reassure her everything was going smoothly back in London. "Jasper and I work really well together in The Studio," she said. "He's cut down on his rugby coaching to be available to me from time to time."

"Did Mike get in touch regarding his laptop?"

"Not yet. He's probably keeping a low profile for a while in case we're on to him."

It felt surreal to both that they were living in different cities. Trine missed Louise's presence in her life, in particular at The Studio where customers frequently asked after her.

"You must visit soon," Louise said, feeling homesick despite her newfound happiness as she imagined what went on in London in her absence.

It was cold outside and Christmas was fast approaching. The weather forecast predicted snow and sleet during the festive season, and everywhere she went, children and adults talked and laughed around her.

Meeting up with Kajsa and Martin two weeks before Christmas at Café Hollandia made Louise feel slightly tense and nostalgic. Her parents, Elin and Simon, often spent Sunday afternoons there, ordering hot chocolate with whipped cream, cinnamon buns and gingerbread. All of it seemed such a long time ago now yet was still fresh in Louise's mind.

She'd barely walked in the door to the old, quaint café with uniformed waitresses behind the large cake and sandwich counter, when Louise spotted her two friends sitting at a table by the window. As she passed the paintings on the walls, oriental rugs on the oak floor and cosy old furniture, she didn't think the café had changed much at all.

Kajsa stood to greet and hug Louise, a welcoming smile on her face. She had hardly aged. Wearing a black floaty skirt, fitted top and ankle boots, she looked very pretty with her long curly brown hair hanging loosely around her shoulders, big brown eyes and bright red lipstick. Martin was slightly taller than the two women, sporting a brown leather jacket, matching trousers and black jumper he'd recently purchased in Copenhagen.

"You look just as beautiful as you always did!" he exclaimed. "Welcome back to Malmö. Kajsa and I missed our little get-togethers when you left."

He and Kajsa had always been there for her and vice versa since the three of them first met at college. They'd lost touch when Louise moved to London, their friendship put on hold.

"Gabriella told us you're divorced," said Kajsa, seated between Louise and Martin at the small table. "You should have got in touch."

"I'm sorry . . . it wasn't the first thing that entered my mind," Louise admitted. "It's taken me until now to make sense of it and I'm not over it yet. I doubt I ever will be."

Martin reached for her hand. "We understand. As long as you know Kajsa and I are here for you. On a happier note, Nils and I just got engaged. Both of you are invited to our celebration party in Limhamn's Smoke House. We've rented the entire place next Friday night. The party kicks off at 6.00 pm. You'd better be there!"

Martin and his fiancé, Nils Fredriksson, were ex models who met when they were signed with the same agency in Stockholm. They'd lived together for many years and co-owned Sweden's largest and most famous male modelling agency. Both loved sports, music festivals and travelling to exotic places around the world. At six feet tall, Nils was of an athletic build with jet-black hair and blue eyes. Slightly heavier and broad shouldered, with brown eyes and fair hair, Martin was nearly as tall as Nils and more outgoing. Nils was slightly introverted yet as soon as he felt at ease with Martin's friends, he treated them as his own. Both were fiercely loyal and everyone who met them, either as models or as friends, were in awe of their relationship and success. They'd recently opened a branch in Copenhagen where they lived in a big town house not far from Tivoli Gardens.

Louise had met Nils a couple of times over the years and looked forward to seeing him at the engagement party the following week. "I'd not miss it for the world!" she said, squeezing Martin's hand. She'd forgotten how good it felt to be surrounded by her friends.

"Nils recently inherited a flat in the West Harbour. We're letting it to an Italian couple. Malmö's considered to be quite the cultural hub nowadays. People from all over the world live here at least part of the year. It must feel strange to return after so many years in London?" Martin asked her.

"Sometimes I feel like a fish out of water. Fortunately, I'm not alone. Gabriella and Rufus, that's my Labrador, keep me company and now I'm reunited with the two of you. But I miss my best friend, Trine, who's in charge of The Studio, our joint venture. You remember my Danish friend, don't you? She and I met in Copenhagen and signed with the same agency. We've been friends for a long time."

"I recall she used to wear her hair in a ponytail and had lots of freckles on her face! She seemed to be a lovely person. I'm pleased you had someone to turn to when things went awry." Kajsa would have loved to have been there for Louise.

"Trine still looks the same, except for the ponytail. I'm lucky we've stayed friends over the years. With the exception of my parents passing, my divorce was the hardest time of my life and Trine got me through it. I'll always be grateful to her and her family for that. Anyway, together we've opened The Studio – a boutique that stocks Scandinavian designer collections and is incredibly popular with the locals in Fulham and Chelsea. Apparently, the latest stock sold out before it even arrived in the shop!" She had a wistful expression in her eyes. However much she'd adapted to life in Malmö during the short time she'd been there, Louise wished she had something that belonged to her. Since she left London, The Studio ceased to be part of her life and she missed the daily routine.

"By the way your face lights up when you talk about it, I can tell how much you miss it," Kajsa commented. An A-grade student at school, she'd worked as an interpreter for various large corporations. Kajsa spoke several languages, among them Chinese, Italian and French. Recently, she'd left a good position and started work as a librarian in Malmö City Library, one of Malmö's oldest and most prestigious institutions and buildings. Louise recalled all the times they'd spent there as students, catching up on the latest gossip and titles worthy of reading.

"Don't you miss your well-paid job?" Martin asked her. Since she'd opted to leave her former workplace, Kajsa had taken a big pay cut. Living in a small two-bedroom flat with a balcony overlooking Möllevång Square, Kajsa had recently paid off the mortgage, and was ecstatic that her home at long last belonged to her, not the building society.

"It depends on how you view it. To me what matters the most is quality of life. I managed to save up to buy my flat, yet I never felt job satisfaction. At least now I'm able to do what I love – assisting with anything from recommending books to helping older people get acquainted with modern technology. Not a day goes by when I don't feel I've landed the job of my dreams!" She oozed contentment.

"I wish I could find something that makes me feel like you do." Louise sighed. "As things stand, all I do is go for long walks, cycle and spend time re-acquainting myself with my native city. It's great I'm able to spend time with Gabriella, and Rufus is adorable, but I need more to be fulfilled . . ." Her voice faltered. Louise didn't regret moving away from London; she only wished she had something that belonged to her. An idea about opening a ladies' boutique that stocked international designer collections for mature women was slowly taking shape in her mind yet she didn't know how to go about it. She kept it to herself for the time being.

"Is Gabriella alright?" Kajsa broke into Louise's thoughts. "I've not seen her for a while. You know, when I was young I used to think she was gay." Kajsa usually expressed opinions most people kept to themselves, yet back then she'd been too young and inexperienced to speak her mind.

"It never crossed my mind!" Louise was taken aback by the bold statement. "What made you think that?"

"I can't put my finger on it. Perhaps because I never saw her go out on a date with a man."

"That's hardly a reason to assume she's gay! Are you of the same opinion as Kajsa, Martin?" Louise noticed her friends exchange a glance.

"Gabriella's personal life is nothing to do with us," he replied, glaring at Kajsa for crossing a line.

"That's not what I asked. Kajsa expressed her opinion, I want yours as well."

Fiddling with his napkin, Martin pushed aside his plate and finished his coffee. They'd thoroughly enjoyed their open sandwiches with prawns, eggs and lettuce, and strawberry mousse cakes for dessert. The last thing he wanted now was to offend Louise by admitting what he believed was true and thereby ruin what up to now had been a lovely chat among old friends. "You really want to know what I think?"

"Definitely."

"Okay, I'd never have mentioned it if Kajsa hadn't said what she did and you didn't ask. In my opinion Gabriella may be gay but that's of no relevance. You must make up your own mind."

"How? She and I haven't seen each other for years! Surely, my parents must have known about it?" Louise regretted pursuing the matter. Now she'd entered unfamiliar territory.

"Gabriella may wish to tell you in her own time. We're only

148

speculating! Her generation keeps anything of a sexual nature close to their chests. The last thing you should do is embarrass her." Martin felt sorry for anyone who denied their sexuality yet was painfully aware of how much Gabriella detested interference in her life. Irrespective of which, she may belong to a category of people who preferred to stay single. "Don't concern yourself with it," he reassured her. "The two of you get along famously. You're the daughter she never had. Gabriella is one of a kind; her sexuality won't change that."

As usual, Martin put everything into context, getting to the bottom of what mattered the most.

"I agree! Ignore what I just said. You know me; I'm incapable of keeping my thoughts to myself. I'm sorry I upset you." Changing the subject, Kajsa asked, "Please tell us what happened with Mike. I can't believe the two of you are divorced! Last time I met him was before you moved to London."

"I wish I knew myself. Mike ended our marriage on our twentieth wedding anniversary. Since then I've sold our home in Barnes, rented a flat in Fulham, got a dog and moved to Malmö. Everything happened so fast I've barely come to terms with it." Louise omitted saying she'd taken an overdose of sleeping tablets and had been rescued by her best friend's teenage son.

"We'd have been there for you if we'd known what happened. You've been through so much! No wonder you can't decide what you want to do now. The Studio must be something you wish you could have brought with you! Nevertheless, you made the right decision to leave everything behind. Mike should be punished for what he put you through. Who in their right mind ends a marriage on their wedding anniversary? I hope he gets what's coming to him!" Kajsa had yet to meet someone she wanted to commit to. The majority of her friends were either divorced or contented with casual affairs that didn't involve emotional input. She belonged in the latter category.

"I'd have wrung his neck if I'd known what he did to you," Martin added. Louise was one of the kindest people he knew. In particular he recalled how she had stood by him after he told her he was gay. "What happened to that nice young man you used to date . . . Nicklas?" He asked in a casual voice.

"Nicklas? I've no idea. Trine keeps mentioning him too." Turning to look at Kajsa, Louise asked if she'd met someone special.

"Not yet! I'm a 'no strings attached' kind of girl. As soon as I let someone into my heart and bed, they take advantage of me. I've lost count of the number of guys I've ended up supporting financially. There must be an invisible sign on my forehead that says 'mug'!" Kajsa laughed, yet inwardly it still hurt that she'd failed to meet that special man. "Perhaps you ought to take a lover? Someone who's great in bed but won't impinge on your life."

"That's not for me. I'm an incurable romantic at heart. The idea of entering into a casual relationship isn't something I'd remotely consider!" Louise was outraged that Kajsa even suggested it.

"I agree. Casual flings don't lead to anything but heartbreak since one party usually feels more than the other. Anyway, there's something I need to bring to your attention." Martin turned around to see if anyone was eavesdropping on them.

"Please don't dampen her mood, she's not been in Malmö for long," Kajsa interrupted, glaring at him.

"That's of no significance. Louise needs to be made aware. What I need you to know, Louise, is that Malmö's changed in more ways than capture the eye. There's been an increase in racism and anti-Semitism. At first I refused to admit it. Sweden's normally renowned for its liberal and democratic approach and views. Sadly, many residents who've lived here for generations are now being persecuted due to their culture and religion. Particularly Jews and other ethnic groups feel harassed and frightened in their own country. Most of the victims don't report it to the authorities. I never thought this sort of thing would be part of daily life in 2015." Martin shook his head.

Kajsa sat forward in her chair. "Speaking of Nicklas, you mustn't forget to mention how badly Black people are being treated. Sweden's by no means worse than the rest of the world, though. Several cafés were banned from selling cakes that carry offensive names. Particularly women are reporting how men address them and view them as less of a human being due to the colour of their skin." An advocate for women's rights, Kajsa's voice was full of contempt.

"I'm sure these things take place everywhere, but since Malmö's a small city compared to, for example, London, the situation is highlighted and much more obvious than in a larger city where people are more anonymous. It's a dangerous and worrying problem." Martin signalled for a waitress to bring the bill. "This is on me. I'll invite you both and Gabriella out to dinner next time," he said, forcing a smile. Malmö was his native city; he loved it with all of his heart yet found it increasingly difficult and painful that some of his friends were assaulted because of their backgrounds.

"I never knew Malmö changed so much but I must admit I'm not surprised," Louise said. "This sort of thing happens everywhere. Narrow-minded people always find excuses to attack people who are different. The only difference is that we're confronted with them on and off the internet, unlike in the past, when they didn't dare to express offensive views for fear of being prosecuted." Louise had lived in London for too long not to have experienced the sort of people to whom Martin and Kajsa referred. Whether in a big or small city, prejudice existed everywhere.

But at that moment, Louise knew exactly what she wanted. Malmö, for all its pros and cons, was the city where she wanted to spend the rest of her life. The time had come to move on. She resolved to sell her share of The Studio to Trine and open her own ladies' boutique.

"I'm so pleased we finally had the chance to catch up. I enjoyed the lovely chat and *fika* and look forward to the party next Friday," she said, kissing her friends' cheeks and watching them walk off arm-in-arm in the opposite direction.

It was cold outside and passers-by wore extra layers of clothing to protect them from the chilly air. Looking up at the blue sky above, Louise noticed the sun was trying to break through the clouds. It struck her that it was a sign she was heading in the right direction.

All she had to do now was find somewhere to live and premises for her up-and-coming boutique. She had recently cycled passed her parents' old building in Fridhem. Fashioned from blue and yellow bricks it still resembled a boathouse, the old nickname they used when she was growing up and until they moved into a house in central Limhamn. Louise recalled how wonderful it felt to move from a flat into a house with a garden. Reflecting on it now, she made a mental note to get in touch with an estate agent to view available flats up for rent. The money she'd received from the sale of her house would come in handy if she decided to invest in premises for her boutique. Only time would tell.

★

"Did the three of you have a nice time yesterday?" Gabriella enquired over breakfast in the enormous sunny kitchen. Bare-footed and wearing a fluffy white robe, the older woman looked young for her age.

Suppressing the urge to ask why she had never married, Louise replied, "We had a great time. I didn't mention you want to invite them to dinner since Martin wants us to join him and Nils cele-brating their engagement at Limhamn's Smoke House next Friday at six. Don't you think it's wonderful they're getting married?" She decided now wasn't the best time to interrogate her aunt about her personal life.

Shrugging her shoulders, Gabriella smiled. "I'm not sure if I know what's best. As long as they're happy, I am as well. I've no objections whatsoever. You and Kajsa are yet to follow their example." Gabriella had never rated Mike as husband material. She topped up their cups with the kind of strong black coffee she knew Louise missed out on in London. "Would you like some more rye bread?"

"No, thanks. Did you change your hair? It suits you to have a parting on one side. I like the red lipstick you put on the other day. Silver grey hair and red lipstick become you. And you've managed to stay so slim!"

"Thank you, dear. Before you and Rufus arrived, I didn't exer-cise as much as I do now. He's a gorgeous little dog yet keeps me on the go all the time! Did I mention he sneaked into my bed-room in the early hours of the morning while you had a shower? We had a lovely cuddle."

Lying on the floor at Louise's feet, Rufus reacted to the men-tion of his name, raised himself and trotted up to Gabriella and licked her ankles. Bending to stroke his head, Gabriella remarked,

"I never thought I'd approve of having a dog inside my flat. Rufus truly is the exception to the rule!"

Laughing, Louise changed her mind and decided to confront her aunt. "Is there something you wish to tell me?"

"What do you mean? My life's an open book. There really isn't much to tell that you don't already know."

"It was something Kajsa and Martin said that got me thinking you're keeping something from me . . ." There. She'd said it. The words had come out of her mouth.

Looking into her niece's eyes, the same blue shade as her own, Gabriella replied, "Repeat their exact words." Her voice was suddenly ice cold. In her world people didn't talk behind someone's back, only directly to them.

Louise instantly regretted her indiscretion. "Let's forget I asked. It's none of my business. I must have got the wrong impression."

"Don't you dare not finish what you've started!" Gabriella snapped, her blue eyes dark with anger. If people she trusted engaged in idle gossip about her, she deserved to know why.

"Please . . . I never meant to upset you; neither did Kajsa and Martin! I just got the impression you have a secret life." Louise had the distinct feeling she'd gone too far. Gabriella's life was nothing to do with anyone but her. "Please don't take any notice of me. Just forget I asked," she said, looking down on her hands. The room was so quiet she couldn't hear anything except the distant sound of church bells further down the street.

"You're entitled to ask me anything you want. I'd just prefer it comes from you, not your friends." Louise's aunt sounded strangely muted.

"Okay . . . how come you never got married?"

"Who's asking, you or your friends?" Brushing off Louise's hand on her sleeve, Gabriella continued, "You didn't confide in me about Mike yet you're of the opinion it's my duty to tell you everything that goes on in my life. Some things are simply too personal to talk about."

Flustered and uncomfortable, the pair stared at each other in silence for a moment before Gabriella suddenly had a change of heart.

"Oh, sweetheart, you're still so naïve! The only person I confided in was your father. Simon always knew and eventually your mother. They'd worked it out for themselves. Please don't press me for more details, now isn't the right time." Her eyes begged Louise to drop the subject for now.

"That's fine! We'll discuss it another time if that's what you want." Louise started to clear the table, thinking something wasn't right.

Watching her from behind, Gabriella knew she couldn't keep her secret indefinitely. *Louise is getting too close for comfort. I'm not ready yet; I don't think I'll ever be able to tell her the truth . . .*

CHAPTER THIRTEEN

January 2016

"WILL YOU BE home in time for dinner?" Abby asked the minute Mike walked in the door. "I'll prepare something nice to eat." She'd decided to not aggravate him further and keep a low profile a while longer, in the event he started to trust her and tell her about what happened to his laptop, assuming he managed to find out its whereabouts. If Mike started to suspect it was she who stole that money, Abby knew she and Timmy would be at risk.

"I don't answer to you or anyone," came the unpleasant response. "Keep your damn thoughts to yourself."

"Suit yourself! I've no desire to pick up from where we left off the other day," Abby retaliated.

"Well, I've no desire to discuss my private affairs with you! I've got to ensure my son is safe. God alone knows what the future holds for him." Mike brushed past her and uncorked the bottle of red wine on the kitchen sink.

"*Your* son? Did you forget I'm his mother? Don't I have any say in matters that concern *our* son? For Christ's sake, Mike, you can't ignore my feelings!" Abby was furious he dared to shut her out of anything that involved their son. She was still hopeful Mike was the father; the other possibility was much too complicated to even consider. *I've got to find out what Mike's planning to do,* she thought, hell-bent on being one step ahead of him.

She'd made the effort to look her best, opting for a skimpy skirt, transparent top and stilettos. "I look like Camilla!" she'd said out loud when she saw her own reflection in the bedroom mirror. Heavy makeup and recently fitted hair extensions perfected the image of a woman who always got what she wanted.

Taking his hand in hers, Abby tried again. "Please stay a while longer, Mike. Call Steve and tell him to hold the fort until you arrive."

Taking in her sexy appearance and bedroom eyes, Mike was overcome with lust. "I'm late as it is . . . yet the way you look, I can't leave just yet," he said in a thick voice, wishing he could reject her proposition. Abby had mastered the skill to reduce a man to putty in her hands.

"Good. What have you got in mind?" she teased, steering him towards the black leather couch in the living room. Watching as she removed her clothes drove him crazy; everything she did to him, the sensation of her body beneath his, turned him on.

He was obsessed with her yet detested her. Afterwards, lying there next to her on the couch, clothes scattered on the floor, Mike fumbled in the semi darkness for his watch. *Shit! Steve's bound to wonder what happened to me. We've a meeting to attend in twenty minutes. I'll send him a text and say I can't make it. It's that bloody minicab firm we've signed an agreement with. Well, it serves him right after he went behind my back!* Five minutes later, sharing a cigarette, Mike puffed on it and blew the smoke in Abby's face.

"Stop it!" she protested. "Let's go upstairs and check on Timmy, then go to bed. Open a window, I don't want him to inhale the smoke."

Ignoring her, Mike lit another cigarette. "Don't be so bloody stupid! It'll only let the draft in. We'll do it in the morning instead, before you bring him downstairs. Now, where were we? I've got another erection, we'd better make the most of it." Putting his hand between her legs, Mike spread her thighs and pushed deep inside of her, oblivious to the fact Abby closed her eyes and thought of all the money she'd have when she figured out the number to Timmy's new bank account.

Several hours later, Abby tiptoed upstairs to check on her son. Timmy was fast asleep in his cot. Looking down on him, Abby felt tears well up in her eyes. Bending to kiss his little face and forehead, she knew she couldn't leave him behind.

What started as a means to get Mike to marry her had resulted in Abby becoming attached to her own child. *I've got to plan ahead and ensure both of us will be safe*, she thought. *Mike's not the man I thought he was. He's got anger issues I never noticed before. We've got to get out of here soon.* Looking at her son's chubby face, his long, dark eyelashes and his dear bald head, save a few strands of blond hair, Abby knew that if something happened to them she'd protect him with every bit of strength she had.

Returning to the living room, she found Mike seated on the couch, his eyes following her every move. "You should have told me you went upstairs to check on our son," he said, grabbing her arm. "Sit down! I've got something to tell you."

Too scared to not do as he asked, Abby seated herself next to him, heart racing inside her chest.

"Do you remember I told you I want to open an account in our son's name? It won't be a trust fund but an account that he will gain access to when he turns twenty-one."

"Sure. Can't it wait a while longer, though? He's too young to have a bank account. Why don't you deposit the money into your own account until he's older?" Abby was desperate for Mike to pay the sum into the account she already had details of in case she was unable to find Timmy's PIN and account numbers.

"Why on earth would I be that stupid? The missing laptop contains a file with the details. If it ends up in the wrong hands, everything I've accumulated will be lost. I'll not risk it!" Mike watched her nervously bite her lower lip. *She's no inkling I'm on to her. If only I can get her to confess it was she who hacked into my account . . .*

He'd received a phone call from Robert a couple of weeks after Mike went round to his and Natasha's house and requested their assistance in locating the laptop. Scared Mike would incur more stress on them, Natasha told her husband about 'Lis'. Both agreed it must have been Abby who called, pretending to be someone who was helping a former client to locate a missing file.

"Paige and Trine agree. There's only one person who may have had access to Mike's account details," Natasha said, persuading her husband to inform Mike about it.

"What about the baby?" Robert asked her. "If you're right, what will happen to him? Mike's not stable."

"It's better Mike shows his true colours now, before she agrees to become his wife. Mike loves that baby. He won't let him come to any harm." Natasha had spent many sleepless nights thinking it through. "Mike must have abandoned Louise because she didn't want a family. He won't do anything to jeopardise his son's life."

In her opinion Abby wasn't fit to be a mother. Camilla told Paige that the reason Abby never became emotionally attached to anyone was because her father had molested her. "Abby's been through too much to bond with her own child. It's the baby I feel sorry for; what if he ends up the same way? Steve has no idea he may be the father. Those two continued to carry on behind Mike's back."

Registering what she'd told her, Natasha was convinced Steve wouldn't find out Abby got pregnant around the same time she and Steve split up and Mike arrived on the scene.

"It's Abby we need to worry about. Camilla told me she's concerned that what her father did to her may affect the baby." Taking everything Natasha told him into account, Robert decided to make one final call to Mike, praying they'd not hear from him again. He had to put his family first; Natasha was a nervous wreck after Mike came round that evening.

"We'll apply for a place at a private school," Mike continued, pleased Abby seemed upset.

"No way! I'll not consent to send him away to some private boarding school."

"That's not what I meant. It takes years to get a place in a private day school. My son's not missing out on a good education!" He enjoyed tormenting her. Recently Abby seemed to have turned into quite the caring mother, but Mike wasn't fooled. It was obvious she did it to impress him.

Abby's only wish was to steal more money from him and her son. "Are you saying I've no say in my son's future?"

"I wasn't aware you cared."

"Don't you ever speak to me like that again! Unless you start to treat me with respect I'll leave and take my son with me!"

Realising he'd gone too far, Mike put his hands up. "Alright, alright, I hear you. You've got to control that temper of yours."

"Me? You're the one with a temper! First you accuse me of stealing from you, then you insinuate I'm a lousy mother! Timmy's not attending some posh school. As his mother I know what's best for him."

"Touchy, touchy. Is it perhaps because I'm not his real father that you're suddenly so protective of him? If that's the case, I've been screwed in more ways than one." Until he had sufficient proof she stole his money, Mike knew he had to keep his suspicions to himself. He'd already said more than he intended. "I've got to get in touch with the Larsens. They're Louise's best friends and bound to know what happened to my laptop."

Glaring at him, Abby put on her underwear and clothes. "You're sleeping in the box room tonight! Don't wake us up when you get up in the morning." Storming out of there, Mike knew she'd been warned to not take him for a fool. For her part, Abby's heart was in her throat. This was the first time Mike voiced concern that Timmy wasn't his.

If only I'd got her to marry me! Mike thought. As things stood, Abby was likely to gain custody of Timmy unless Mike was able to prove she hacked into his account. The only snag was Steve. If it became evident Mike paid a client's money into his secret account without splitting the profit between them, Steve would never let him get away with it. *That bitch will slip up sooner or later and I'll be there when she does!* All he had to do was to make sure Steve didn't sniff around and meddle in his affairs. With a bit of luck, Mike would recover his laptop and after Abby was caught out stealing from him, Mike would apply for custody of his son. Steve and Abby may have fooled around behind his back yet it was obvious Timmy wasn't Steve's son. *The baby is the spitting image of me at the same age.* He'd conveniently overlooked the fact there were no photos of him as a baby, only a few when he was in his teens.

"You look great!" Liam said after they'd finished the meal he cooked earlier. They'd decided to ignore the solicitor's advice to not meet up until the divorce came through and were in his flat where Paige would be staying the night.

"Mr Pollock can go to hell! I've done nothing wrong. I wish you and I met years ago." Paige snuggled up to him on the living room settee.

Since going into partnership with Camilla, Paige had discovered how well they complemented each other. Camilla was in charge of the development of the website, whereas Paige put together the Amazon page whose purpose was to get people aged forty-plus to sign up with their service. They'd handed out leaflets in local shops, schools and libraries, and as a direct result had been inundated with phone calls from people who'd given up on finding love. With almost five hundred applicants before they launched the website, both women were confident that their new venture was off to a good start.

"I already told you there's not much point in dwelling on the past. Everything happens for a reason. The main thing is that we've found each other now." Paige had restored his faith in life and women.

"Steve's keeping something from me, Liam. Camilla is certain he and Mike stashed away money somewhere. She thinks Abby may be in on it. Judging by her past, Abby's quite good at hacking into people's accounts. She and Camilla used to work for Kershaw & Matthews Limousine Service."

"If I were you I wouldn't listen to Camilla. The two of you get along and are business partners but I wouldn't trust her after what she did to you."

"You're wrong. Camilla genuinely regrets what she did. She's the only friend Abby's got. They've known each other for years."

"Still, promise me you won't get involved where Abby and

Steve are concerned. I know you're concerned about the baby but there's not much you can do."

Reaching for his hand, Paige put it on her thigh. "I don't know how I got so lucky. Meeting you is the best thing that ever happened to me."

Justin Pollock couldn't prevent them from seeing each other. Paige and Liam realised they couldn't bear to be apart any longer. As long as they didn't go out in public, Steve wouldn't find out about them.

But unknown to Paige, Steve already knew Liam's identity. The initial pain of losing her to another man was sharp yet slightly easier to cope with than the suspicion Abby and Mike's baby was conceived the night he and Abby made love in a motel the same week she and Mike became lovers.

CHAPTER FOURTEEN

THERE WAS A chill in the air as Louise made her way to Martin and Nils' party. Wearing an off the shoulder black dress with a leather belt and ankle boots, her hair blowing in the wind, she climbed into the cab that was parked outside Gabriella's flat. At the last minute Gabriella had declined Martin and Nils' invitation to attend their party. She'd come down with a bug and wanted to rest at home. Louise had decided to not pick up from where they'd left off the other night. Gabriella's personal life was nothing to do with her.

After signing up with a couple of estate agents, Louise was invited to view a few flats that were up for sale in Fridhem and Limhamn. The estate agent advised she'd be better off purchasing a flat in Fridhem as opposed to Limhamn as the flats on offer in the latter location generally required more work and were positioned near the harbour and quite a distance from local shops.

In the event, Louise had made an offer on one in Fridhem. Situated close to the Boathouse, it comprised two large bedrooms, a bathroom with a heated floor, an open-plan kitchen and living room, and a balcony with a view of the city and West Harbour.

Unless the vendor received a higher offer, Louise was confident they'd be able to draw up a contract in the near future.

Louise recalled only too well how wonderful Limhamn was during the summer yet not as convenient during the rest of the year. On the other hand, Fridhem was an affluent area within walking distance to central Malmö, Limhamn and the beaches. It was particularly popular with people who wanted a calm environment with plenty of quaint cafés, bars and restaurants in the vicinity.

For Louise it meant she'd come full circle. All she had left to do was find a nice location for her boutique. Until now she'd kept it to herself and came up with a name. La Femme was easy to remember and translated well into *Kvinnan* in Swedish.

The concept was aimed at women who were comfortable in their own skin and proud to be of a certain age. Louise intended to seek out international designers and keep an eye on up-and-coming talent that would appeal to her clients. So far she hadn't confided in Trine and intended to travel to London in the spring to shop around for new designers with whom to place orders.

Louise requested Trine and Jasper stored the rest of her belongings and gave notice on her flat in London. As soon as she finalised the purchase of the flat in Fridhem, she'd arrange for everything to be shipped to her. The final piece of the puzzle was to sell her share of The Studio to Trine and Jasper. Just thinking about it brought a lump to her throat.

Now, queuing up outside Limhamn's Smoke House, Louise looked around her. The guests were of all ages, ranging from twenty to eighty. She recognised a few male models with whom she'd worked on shoots in Milan and London. Waving at them, she recalled all the fun she'd had travelling the world and modelling on catwalks in Paris and Stockholm. It had been the perfect antidote to losing her parents and the pain she'd endured.

I wish Kajsa were here to keep me company. I wonder where she is, Louise thought, just as the hosts approached her on their way from Limhamn's Harbour.

"You look stunning! Only you can get away with wearing such subtle makeup," Nils said, bending to kiss her cheek. Both men wore white suits and looked delighted with the number of guests who'd turned up for the occasion.

Louise was about to say something to Martin, when she heard Kajsa's voice behind her. As she turned to greet her friend, she couldn't believe her eyes.

"Hi everyone, I've brought along a friend!"

The tall, dark Mediterranean-looking man standing next to Kajsa looked as if he was in his twenties. "I'm Milo," he introduced himself and kissed Louise's hand. It was easy to see why Kajsa was attracted to him. Articulate and handsome, Milo had a nice personality and injected excitement and vibrancy into her life. With her hair in a knot on her head, big hoop earrings and wearing a Lurex jump suit, Kajsa seemed happy and relaxed. It wasn't until she turned to talk to her latest boyfriend that Louise noticed the tattoos on her left upper arm.

"I never knew you're into that sort of thing," Louise whispered in her ear.

"There's a lot we don't know about one another. We'll catch up later!" Taking Milo's arm, Kajsa disappeared in the crowd inside Limhamn's Smoke House. At almost 7.00 pm on a Friday evening it was heaving with guests. Seating herself at one of the numerous round tables in the centre of the premises, Louise gazed over at the mouth-watering delicacies laid out on the buffet table at the entrance. She always preferred fish to meat and fondly recalled all the times her parents used to buy food and bring it home to the house in Limhamn. She stood and joined the queue at the buffet, the delicious aroma of marinated herrings, gravad lax, prawns, lobster and many other delicacies making her aware of how hungry she was, when out of nowhere a familiar figure caught her eye.

It can't be . . . surely not, she thought, feeling butterflies at the pit of her stomach. Suddenly her appetite vanished. *He's hardly changed. That midnight blue suit looks great on him . . .*

The young boy Nicklas Roxén once was had turned into a handsome man. Turning her back, Louise piled some food on her plate in the vain hope he wouldn't spot her. But she was wrong. He'd seen her talking to Martin and Nils. His eyes were glued on the tall, slim woman standing so close to him yet not close enough; her big blue eyes and blonde hair bringing back memories he'd suppressed for a long time.

They'd been so young back then and deeply in love. But everything changed when she moved away and he'd lost everything that mattered to him.

Willing himself not to call out her name, he slowly walked up to her, struggling with a flood of emotions he'd tried so hard to forget yet failed miserably. "Louise! It's really you. The world's truly a small place, especially Malmö and Limhamn. You're even more beautiful than I recall."

Eyes locking, both felt the same intense attraction that brought them together when they were young. The only difference was that they were adults now, not kids who tried so hard to find their special place in a world full of sadness. There and then everything around them ceased to exist, both overwhelmed by a feeling of déjà vu.

Except for a few lines on his forehead, around the eyes and mouth, Nicklas had hardly aged. Gazing into his blue eyes, juxtaposed with caramel skin and more than a passing resemblance to Denzel Washington, the faint scent of his aftershave still made

Louise weak at the knees. No other man made her feel this way, not even Mike.

"Where did you spring from?" he asked in a deep, sensual voice, eyes not letting go of hers. "I never thought we'd see each other again," he added, his heart melting at the sight of her.

"I've returned to Malmö to live here permanently," Louise whispered, acutely aware of how much his presence affected her.

"I've missed you," Nicklas said, leaning forward to kiss her cheek. They hadn't seen each other for almost a quarter of a century yet it was as if time stood still as they picked up from where they'd left off all those years ago. "Please forgive me if what I'm about to ask is too personal, but why did you decide to return?" Nicklas searched her eyes.

"My ex-husband and I were divorced not so long ago. We were married for twenty years. I've lived in London for longer than that. But Malmö's less stressful and I've missed Gabriella. She's the only family I've got." The words tumbled out of her mouth.

Feeling his hand on hers, Louise almost started to cry. Nicklas was always there for her in the past. Averting her eyes, she swallowed and looked down at their hands, lightly touching.

"I wish I'd known what you went through. If I did, I'd have been there for you. I'm so sorry things didn't work out between you and your husband. You seemed so sure he was the right man for you."

Louise detected an undertone of sadness in his voice. "I was young and naïve. Mamma and Pappa died . . . all I wanted was to get away from everything and everyone."

"I know the feeling. Not a day went by when I didn't think of you. I missed you so much . . . I still do, more than I'm able to express."

Louise knew for certain Nicklas meant what he said. Looking

into his eyes, she felt the same bond between them as the first time they met.

"Let's sit down. We're blocking the queue behind us," Nicklas said, gently steering her in the direction of an empty table near the entrance, his hand on her shoulder. Pulling out a chair for her, Nicklas fetched their plates and glasses, then returned, seating himself next to her. "This looks nice. I've not eaten here for a while."

Louise was almost at a loss for words. "How about you?" she murmured. "Are you in a relationship, kids?" She'd always wondered what became of him.

"No on both counts. I split up from my ex-wife almost ten years ago. Sofia is a wonderful woman but not for me. I divide my time between Malmö, Copenhagen and Paris where I've apartments and own art galleries. Perhaps you can recall I always wanted to paint? As it turned out, I never did. Instead I sponsor up-and-coming artists and exhibit their work with those who are established. It makes for a hell of a mix! I love my job and did well compared to how I thought my life would map out. At least professionally if not personally." His eyes were as warm and compassionate as she recalled.

"How did you and your ex-wife meet? I met Mike at a party in London when I was working as a model." One part of her wanted to tell him everything that had happened since they parted; another part held back for fear he'd not be interested.

"I see . . . Sofia and I met at an art exhibition in Paris. She's an art dealer. Before I knew it, we started to date and things developed from there. Eventually both of us realised we weren't compatible. Fortunately, we're still friends but not as close as we used to be." Louise sensed his reluctance to elaborate on the reasons, yet he continued speaking. "I was incapable of giving her what she deserved because I was still in love with someone else." He paused, considering his words carefully, then decided to open his heart. "You're the only woman I've ever loved, Louise. I never managed to get over what happened between us. Sofia never stood a chance."

Louise gasped. This was the last thing she had expected and her mind was whirling. They'd been apart for such a long time yet both were single and bruised by life.

"I'm genuinely sorry your life turned out different to what you expected it to be," Nicklas continued. "Please tell me why you and your husband were divorced."

For a moment, Louise was speechless. "I . . . I forgot you're so direct! Well . . . where do I start? Mike entered my life after my parents died. By then my modelling career had really taken off, I had Gabriella, my friends in London and you . . . Mike and I were happy for a long time. I was deeply in love, or so I thought. Looking back I can see we weren't as compatible and in love as I imagined." She sipped her wine and nibbled on a piece of bread. Seeing Nicklas again made her aware of how lonely and unhappy she'd been without him in her life. She laughed nervously. "It's funny, I was starving when I arrived, but now I've not got much of an appetite. It feels so surreal to be telling you all this," she said, wiping a tear from her cheek.

"I'm sorry, I've no right to meddle in your life. I never meant to upset you."

Nicklas put his hand back on hers. "Sofia remarried last year. They're expecting their first child," he told her.

"Aren't you upset she moved on so quickly?"

"Not at all. Had I not initiated the divorce, she'd not be as happy as she is now."

"What about you, are you dating someone?" Louise instantly regretted the question. His personal life was none of her business.

"No, I'm quite comfortable being single. Unless I can be with the only woman I love, relationships are off the agenda."

The sentiment was aimed squarely at her. Nicklas never tried to hide his feelings for her in the past and wasn't going to do it now. She recalled the first time they'd made love. It was in her parent's back garden when they and Gabriella travelled to Greece. They'd been so young and shy. Blushing at the memory of how inseparable they'd been, Louise's thoughts turned to the time she told him she wanted to model.

She had been discovered in the street by an agent who wanted to sign her on the spot. She and Nicklas had fallen out with each other when she informed him she'd signed the contract without asking his advice. Her parents were upset at first yet gave in when she told them she was eighteen and didn't require their permission. Then all too soon, her cosy, secure life changed overnight when she lost them and Trine suggested they accepted the offer to model all over Europe. When Louise met Mike she'd already closed the door to her previous life. She and Nicklas parted due to circumstances in both their lives and Louise's wish to become a model. She was young and in love yet also wanted to see the world. When Mike entered her life it seemed as if she was heading for a happy future, leaving all the sadness of the past behind.

Returning to the present, she heard him ask, "What were you thinking about, just now?", his hand still on hers.

"We had so many dreams back then," she answered wistfully. "I know I wasn't there for you as much as I ought to have been. I never deserved you, Nicklas, you were too good to me, despite your own problems."

"You mustn't think like that. Both of us went through a hard time. Oh, I've so much to tell you, Louise." His eyes bore into hers.

Raising herself from the chair, Louise looked around at the other guests, wondering if Kajsa, Martin and Nils were watching. Martin and Nicklas knew each other since school and bumped into one another at social gatherings from time to time. "How come Martin didn't tell me you were invited tonight?" she asked, concerned her friend had set them up.

"You know as well as I do he'd never interfere in our lives. I'm here because he and Nils commissioned one of my artists to paint a portrait of them. I wasn't aware you'd be here and was genuinely surprised you'd been invited."

"I'm sorry . . . I really must go. Gabriella's been so good to my dog and me. She invited us to stay with her until I get a place of our own. I must go back and check she's okay." Reluctant to leave him after they'd just met again, Louise whispered, "Please don't persuade me to stay, I've got to leave before we take another trip down memory lane. It's been so long since we last saw each other, I didn't expect to see you again."

"You can't just leave! Please say you'll come with me to a bistro in Limhamn where we can have a private conversation. We owe each other that much," Nicklas pleaded with her, the darkness of his hand on hers reminding her of what he'd been through after his father left him all those years before.

Together Louise and Nicklas managed to manoeuvre themselves through the crowd of guests who were engrossed in the celebration of Martin and Nils' engagement. Kajsa and Martin walked up to them, waving and smiling.

"I don't believe my eyes! The two of you must have such a lot to talk about." Kajsa blinked at Louise, as if to say, "Fate's giving you a helping hand here."

"We have, indeed. I don't mean to be rude and leave the party early, but would you mind very much if Louise and I go somewhere quiet to talk?" Nicklas was desperate to have her to himself, away from there.

"Not at all," said Martin. "Just promise you will take good care of her. Louise has been through a lot." Inwardly, Martin was delighted Nicklas had accepted the party invitation. He and Nils had deliberately postponed the celebration until Nicklas returned from an exhibition in Paris yet not let on Louise was back in Malmö.

"Can I speak to you in private?" Kajsa asked, not waiting for Nicklas to respond, as she pulled Louise aside and whispered in her ear, "I'm thrilled the two of you are reunited! You must give me a call later." Equal parts embarrassed and elated, Louise promised she would.

Seeing Nicklas waiting for her outside, she felt the same chemistry between them.

"We must celebrate we've met again in style," Nicklas said, taking her hand. "My car's parked in a side street not far from here."

Feeling his hand on hers, the scent of his aftershave and the knowledge she still had feelings for him caused Louise to tremble inside. They walked in silence for a few minutes before they reached the quiet street.

"That's mine." Nicklas said, gesturing to a black Ferrari, parked further down the street.

"Wow! You must be very successful, judging by your car." The young boy she'd known could barely afford to take her to McDonald's.

"I'll not deny it. Yet money can't buy happiness and fulfilment. Sadly, I've not had much luck with either." He wanted to add, "since you disappeared from my life."

"I'll not lie to you. Mike and I were happy for a while; I guess nothing lasts forever," Louise replied in a sad voice.

Nicklas opened the door for her, and she slid into the passenger seat, admiring the car's luxurious interior. "I thought we'd drive to the West Harbour and eat in a restaurant I frequently visit. The food's great and it's not as noisy as some of the other places."

"That sounds nice. Last time I visited Malmö it wasn't as developed as it is now."

"You won't be able to see it in the dark. I'll take you here in daylight, if you like?"

"I'd like that very much."

It felt odd, attempting to find the right things to say to each other. Nicklas wished she wanted to spend as much time with him as he did with her. "There's the restaurant I told you about," he said. "It's a Friday night but they'll sort out a table for us."

As they parked at the front of the venue, Louise noticed the patio where people were sitting at candlelit tables, music playing from the jukebox in the corner. "It seems very continental," she said, watching him open the door and help her out of the car.

"It's one of the best restaurants in Malmö. If you don't like it, I'll take you somewhere else." Nicklas still couldn't get his head around the fact they'd met again and was eager to please her, well aware she was used to London where the options outweighed most of what Malmö offered. Stepping inside the magnificent foyer, with its dim lighting, white washed walls and further into the restaurant where the tables were evenly positioned in the cosy room with candelabras in the corner, Louise instantly warmed to the quaint surroundings.

"Mr Roxén, how nice to see you again!" the headwaiter exclaimed, helping Louise take off her coat and adding, "How lovely you've brought a friend." He immediately found them a table in the back of the room, pulled out a chair for Louise and handed them the menus. "I'll return when you're ready to order."

Half an hour later, Louise looked at the plate in front of her and sighed. "It's delicious. I love salmon with new potatoes and asparagus with Hollandaise sauce but it's too much! Fortunate for me I didn't eat anything at Martin and Nils do. Limhamn's Smoke House is lovely; I'll have to return there soon."

"That's my fault for whisking you away to the West Harbour! Please say you'll forgive me." Nicklas had ordered cannelloni with mushroom and ricotta filling and a side salad with balsamic dressing, asking the waiter to bring them a bottle of white wine. Filling their glasses, he leaned across the table and reached for her hand. "I can't tell you how happy I am to see you again. Are you starting to settle in Malmö?" His strong hands and handsome face were distracting her from paying attention to what he asked.

"I'm gradually getting used to living here again. It helps I've got Gabriella and Rufus, my dog. Martin and Kajsa check up on me at least twice a week." Louise smiled. She'd almost forgotten how effortless it felt to talk and spend time together. "London's my past, not my future," she said, her voice faltering.

Squeezing her hand, Nicklas looked deep into her eyes. "Nothing lasts forever. We've got to make the most of what we have. You and I know that only too well. What's it like to live in a small town after all the time you spent in London? Surely, it must have been very stimulating?"

"It was . . . Mike and I were okay for a long time. Things changed between us. It was subtle at first, then obvious we had issues that required addressing. I used to think we had the same outlook on life. Turns out Mike wanted a family. I just wanted him. When Mamma and Pappa died I was lost and confused. Mike's presence prompted me to move on and look forward to the future." No sooner were the words out of her mouth, Louise wished she'd kept her feelings to herself. They'd only just met each other again. Nicklas would think she needed a shoulder to cry on.

"When Sofia and I first met I'd just emerged from my self-inflicted refusal to move on after you disappeared," he said, surprising her again with his direct manner. "I kept everyone at arm's length and wanted nothing to do with the world outside. When I lost my mother, it's an understatement to say I couldn't cope. Sofia became my confidante and saviour. Yet neither were sufficient to make the relationship last. I'm grateful for her support during a difficult time and that we've managed to maintain our friendship." Nicklas let out a sigh, taking a closer look at the woman seated opposite him. "You ought to eat more. What's wrong? I can see you've got a lot on your mind." He'd always noticed whenever she felt upset.

Picking at her food, Louise attempted to smile. "You're as perceptive as I recall. Don't concern yourself with me. I'll have more wine, it tastes great." She picked up the bottle and poured herself another glass just as he was about to.

Watching her drink it in no time, Nicklas asked, "Have you found a place to live? I assume you'll not continue living with Gabriella indefinitely."

His voice was so gentle it brought tears to her eyes. Seeing him again reminded her of what life used to be and how much they'd meant to each other. Composing herself, Louise raised her empty glass. "Here's a toast to us and the people we've lost. Yes, I've put in an offer on a two-bedroom flat in Fridhem. It's not far from where I was born."

"You're referring to the 'Boathouse'?"

"Yes, it's been refurbished yet looks just the same on the outside. Do you have a home in Malmö?"

"Of course, how could I not? It's where I was born and where Mamma used to live. Despite everything, she loved this city." It was Nicklas' turn to look forlorn. "I've got a flat not far away from here and another in Copenhagen. When I'm in Paris I always stay in a small bedsit on the outskirts of the city. It's a lovely place, you would approve of it."

"That sounds wonderful. You must be very proud of everything you've achieved. I cycled to Ribersborg the other day. As soon as the temperature's higher I'll return for a swim at the open-air bath. I've missed taking a dip in the sea." Visualising all the fun she'd had on the beach with her parents, Louise lost her train of thought.

Seeing her like that, so vulnerable and struggling to keep it together, caused Nicklas to open up. "You're so special in every way. I was a fool to let you disappear from my life," he said, his voice full of remorse.

Letting go of his hand, Louise shook her head. "Please don't talk like that. We were different people back then with problems of our own." She hesitated for a minute, then decided to bite the bullet and just come out with it. "Have you reconciled with the past?"

"No one else would get away with asking me that . . . I never even fully talked about it with Sofia, although she was a great support to me. She and Mamma never got the chance to meet. I simply can't relate to anyone the way I can with you." He was about to continue when Paul McCartney's voice echoed in the room. 'My Love Does It Well' had been their favourite song. "It feels as if we're back to where we were back then, just the two of us spending time together, talking, laughing and setting the world to rights," Nicklas said, reaching once more for her hand. As usual the world was a better place when he was around.

"Let's leave. Gabriella must wonder where I got to. I've had a wonderful time." Louise gently broke free from his clasp and stood up. After Nicklas signalled for the bill, he said, "I don't want us to lose touch again. Please say you want to meet up with me soon. There's a place I want to show you; the food's even better than here."

He looked so excited at the prospect of seeing her again that Louise couldn't help but nod. "Okay, it sounds intriguing. I guess it won't impose on our respective lives." She instantly regretted the unfortunate wording. "You know what I mean. Our lives are so different from what they were then." Looking into his eyes, she asked, "You were about to tell me about your mother . . . Mimmi." She felt awkward asking him something so personal. Perhaps he didn't wish to confide in her.

Nicklas stood up as well. Ignoring her question, he said, "I can't tell you how pleased I am you're back. Malmö is where you've got your roots. We'll talk more when we see each other next time. I'll give you a call on Wednesday. Here's my card with all my contact details." Nicklas handed it to her and smiled when she returned the favour. He'd have loved to meet up with her the following day but was scheduled for a conference in Copenhagen over the weekend and early part of the following week. "I'll think of you while I'm away," he said as the waiter returned with the bill and Louise's coat. Helping her put it on, he stood so close to her she could hear the beat of his heart.

Hand in hand, they walked out of the restaurant and onto the pavement.

"Thank you for agreeing to spend the evening with me," Nicklas said. "Next time I'll make sure you eat more and order dessert! You're just as slim as you used to be."

Listening to him and feeling him so close to her, Louise knew she'd never stopped loving him. However much Mike had meant to her, her feelings for him didn't come close to what she'd felt for Nicklas. "I'm so pleased I decided to return to Malmö," she said, smiling. "Rufus loves it here. What with all the parks and beaches, it's a canine paradise as far as he's concerned!"

"I bet it is. I recall your mother always kept at least three dogs at the same time. Elin and Simon loved nature and the sea. Those days were the best." His sentiment brought tears to her eyes.

"Oh, Nicklas, I so wish they were still alive! I miss them just as much now as I did when they died."

"I know the feeling . . . hey, cheer up! Life's not all bad." Nicklas wanted to tell her it wasn't as far as he was concerned, not now she was back in his life. "Let's get you home. I gather the old girl's still living at the same address?" he joked, lightening the mood.

Touching his face, Louise replied tenderly, "I sense you're unwilling to talk about the past . . . it's alright, there's no rush."

Unlocking his car, Nicklas opened the door and helped her get inside. Louise was right. He'd faced his demons yet wasn't keen to discuss it. Not even with her. Sitting quietly next to each other in the car, it wasn't long before he parked outside Gabriella's block of flats.

"Tell her I've been thinking of her. Gabriella is part of my history almost as much as yours. I've enjoyed tonight more than I can say. Stay safe until we see each other and get a good night's sleep. I'm missing you already." He couldn't wait to call her the following week. Watching her unlock the main entrance to the building, Nicklas knew without doubt he'd never willingly let her disappear from his life again.

Louise Berg had her own demons to deal with and all he wanted was to make her happy and spend the remainder of their lives together.

CHAPTER FIFTEEN

A T PRECISELY 10.00 am the following Wednesday, Gabriella called Louise's name, saying Nicklas wanted to talk to her. Holding her hand on the mouthpiece, she whispered, "He sounds exactly like he used to," then handed over the receiver. Gabriella insisted on holding on to her landline. As far as she was concerned, mobiles were a complete nuisance and social inconvenience that were surplus to requirement. She was incensed people hardly ever met face to face and texted one another instead. In her opinion it wasn't surprising everyone was lonely and starved of human compassion.

"How are you feeling? I kept thinking about you and had to call as soon as I walked in the door," Nicklas said, waiting for her response.

"I'm pleased to hear from you," Louise replied, uncertain of what else to tell him. She'd spent every day since they met at Martin and Nils' party thinking of him, wondering how she'd feel when he called.

"Are you still there? I didn't mean to put you on the spot . . . it's just that I miss you." He sounded so unsure of himself.

Louise felt awful she wasn't as receptive as he wanted her to be.

"We've only just met again. Let's take one day at the time. No unrealistic expectations, okay? I've had a lot to cope with recently."

"I agree. You're still willing to meet up tonight?"

She detected the apprehension in his voice and decided the best approach was to be completely honest. "I'd love to, Nicklas, but on the condition we meet up as friends. It's too soon to read more into it . . . I had a wonderful time last week but we're both conscious of the fact that sometimes past events can cause confusion and conflict of feelings."

There. She'd said it. The last thing she wanted right now was to go out on a date. Louise knew they meant more to each other than just friends yet for the time being friendship was the only thing she was prepared to settle for.

"That's fine by me. I'll pick you up at seven o'clock. Tell Gabriella I enjoyed talking to her." He hung up before Louise had the opportunity to thank him for calling.

Sitting in the kitchen reading the daily newspaper, enjoying a late breakfast of porridge and toast with cheese and jam, Gabriella poured Louise another cup of strong black coffee. "You never told me you and Nicklas are seeing each other. Kajsa called the other day and told me the two of you met at Martin and Nils' engagement party. The world's truly a small place!"

"We're not dating, Gabriella. Nicklas is just a friend. We've a history."

"I'm perfectly aware of that. Wouldn't it be great if you and he could pick up from where you left off? Your parents would be so pleased!"

"It's not what I want, haven't you listened to a word I said? I told you I've no intention of getting romantically involved with anyone anymore. My marriage was a complete mistake. I'd never willingly put myself through another failure. Nicklas and I didn't work out then and we won't now!" Louise picked up a magazine from the table and hid her teary eyes behind it, pretending to read.

Pushing the paper aside, Gabriella shook her head. "You can't hide behind what happened between you and Mike. Mike's your past but Nicklas is your future."

"Don't you get it? Mike never loved me. Doesn't it bother you my life with him was a lie?"

"Not in the least. I saw through him the first time you introduced us. You wouldn't listen since you were determined to marry him! But it's not your fault you fell in love with a man who never knew the meaning of the word. You've noticed I refer to him in the past tense? Mike's history – you can't permit him to ruin the rest of your life."

"You're wrong! Mike loved me enough to want us to have a family. It was I who rejected him! I know what he did was wrong but it's unfair to blame him for everything."

"Here we go again. Stop making excuses for him! Mike's an adult. He knew the score and still asked you to marry him. You were always adamant to not have children. There's nothing wrong with that. Not every woman wants to procreate. I'm the same as you. My career is more than sufficient for me. Nicklas was very supportive when your parents died, despite what he was enduring at the time. That man would go to the ends of earth to make you happy."

"Listen to yourself! You can hardly compare an adolescent fling with a twenty-year marriage."

"Can't I? Give me one reason you stayed for as long as you did and please don't say it was because you couldn't stand to not be with him. Mike entered your life at a time when you were at your most vulnerable. He used you for his own needs, then left when there was nothing more to take. I'm sorry if what I tell you isn't what you want to hear, yet it's the truth and deep down you know I'm right."

"No! Mike loved me. Why else would he marry me?" Louise mumbled, deep down acutely conscious of how immature he could be when she refused whatever it was he wanted at the time. Mike was a boy, not a man. He'd showered her with attention when it suited him, then treated her like she never mattered to him. She told her aunt as much.

Gabriella put down her toast, and made her way around the table to give her niece a hug. "And you let that poor excuse for a man walk all over you, yet you'll not give Nicklas the opportunity to come near you! Nicklas would never treat you like that. I'm sure he would understand your reluctance to get emotionally involved with him or any man just yet." Gabriella knew it wasn't just what happened with Mike that made Louise unhappy. Losing her parents when she was so young made her insecure and worried that everyone she loved and cared about would sooner or later leave her. "Elin and Simon would have hated to see you like this. They loved life and thought it was a privilege to be alive. I envied the love they felt for each other and for you. You owe it to yourself and their memory to move on."

"I've booked a table at Qui Osteria close to Fridhem Square. They're casual yet serve the most wonderful pasta dishes you've ever tasted!" Nicklas declared when he picked Louise up at Gabriella's flat that evening. He'd decided to play the part of not wanting more from her than to be her friend. Deep down Nicklas hoped that if he stayed patient a while longer, Louise would want more from him than just friendship. Seeing her looking so beautiful in a short black evening dress with slits on each side that showed off her long, shapely legs, he could hardly take his eyes off her. Mike Kershaw must have been an idiot for treating her the way he did. Martin had told him Louise blamed herself for the breakup since she didn't want a family, and advised him to give her time to heal.

"Mmm, if I wasn't invited to a friend's house for dinner, I'd join you!" Gabriella commented. She looked extremely smart too in a black and white suit, styled short hair and red lipstick.

"You never told me you're invited to dinner. Who's invited you?" Louise asked, curious to find out more about her aunt's personal life. Up till now she'd not seen or heard of anyone in particular. Her mind kept drifting back to what Kajsa and Martin said when they'd met up shortly after Louise moved to Malmö.

"No one special. Just someone I've known for years. A colleague."

Louise detected her aunt was reluctant to talk about it.

"Right, we're off. It's great to see you again, Gabriella. Enjoy your evening. I'll bring Louise back to you at a decent hour." Nicklas winked at her, almost as if they shared a special code.

They were halfway through their meal when he reminded her of the time he'd saved up enough money to take her out for dinner. "It was shortly before you signed up with the agency. I lived on hot dogs and canned soup for weeks after that!" Nicklas laughed.

"How could I forget? It was the sweetest thing a man ever did for me." Talking to him felt like the most natural thing in the world.

"That's what friends do for one another, right?" He emphasised the word 'friends' to reinforce that she needn't worry he'd trespass on what they'd agreed.

"You're right, we're old friends. You were also right about this place. The pasta is great!" She'd ordered linguini with olives and pesto sauce and Nicklas opted for the rigatoni with meatballs. For dessert they shared a large portion of tiramisu with black coffee.

Louise declined to have wine and watched him polish off his plate and pour himself another glass.

"Don't look so worried. I'm leaving the car in the parking lot until tomorrow and will book us a cab to take you home." Nicklas sipped his wine. "Do you want my advice?"

"No matter what I want you'll give it to me anyway. Everyone else does!"

Leaning closer to her across the table, he weighed his words carefully. "I think you're very unkind and unfair to yourself. What is it you miss from your life with your ex-husband?"

"Nothing in particular. Only the small things . . . The way we were in the beginning. I'll not lie to you. It wasn't all bad; we had our moments, albeit short-lived. Ours was a passionate marriage; Mike made me feel incredibly happy yet also very low."

"When did he make you sad?"

"We drifted apart. Mike had his job and I had mine. In the end our careers came before anything else, especially our marriage. Mike kept pushing himself to be on top in his field. Unless he felt good about himself and the business, he took it out on me. He made it up to me eventually. Yet he found it hard to accept I had a job and business I loved." Louise realised how pathetic she must seem to Nicklas. "It takes two to make a relationship work."

"I agree yet in your case it was he who called the shots, not you. He broke your heart, Louise. In my book that's not how you treat someone you love. You must stop making excuses for him."

"You make it sound so simple."

"That's because it is. The longer you hold on to the past, the harder it will be to move on."

"If what you say is true, that I sacrificed myself for someone who never loved me, how come you and I didn't last?" Louise asked, interested in what he had to say.

"I know what you're referring to. I was a mess. Mamma was a mess after my father left us and moved back to New York. I became the person she turned to for support, her rock. No child should have to go through what I did. I never had the chance to express how I felt when Dad left us, me. You'd lost your parents around the same time. I had to stay strong and cope by myself."

Hearing him pour his heart out made Louise feel terrible she hadn't been there for him, and she said as much.

"I don't blame you for our breakup," Nicklas was at pains to say. "You had your own grief to deal with."

"You know what? I've changed my mind and will have that glass of wine." Louise was fighting back the urge to cry. "The truth is, Nicklas, you reminded me of what I'd lost. I couldn't continue like that. It seemed so much easier to start afresh with someone else." She watched him pour the wine.

"Was it, really? Were you able to put everything behind you?" Nicklas asked in a kind voice.

"I thought I did yet it stayed with me in here." Louise put her hand on her heart. "Life goes on, it always does no matter what. I had my new life, marriage and career. The Studio took up most of my time, as did living in London, the house and friends. Ultimately, I simply refused to dwell on the past. It's partly the reason I rarely visited Malmö. Returning gave me nightmares and reminded me of everything I lost. I felt as if all of it took place so far away in another era and place . . ."

"The rest is history, as they say." Nicklas filled in the gap.

"Something like that. But please continue with what you told me earlier. About your mother. Did you really put it behind you or are you just putting on a brave front for everyone's benefit?" She intuitively didn't believe him when he said he'd moved on. It was evident how much he still hurt just listening to him talk about his mother.

Taking a deep breath, Nicklas shrugged his shoulders. "Doesn't everyone now and then? I'm not the same person as I was then, Louise. Let's stop pretending and address what really happened. I'm biracial — the outcome of a liaison between a white woman and a black man. My so-called father lived with us until I was a teenager, then left just when I needed him most. I'll not deny how hard it was at the time and in some ways still is to be looked upon as the odd person whose skin is different from everyone else's. I stuck out like a sore thumb. The other kids at school called me a freak. Being of mixed race back then I'd not wish on anyone. It wasn't until years later when I encountered others like me that I realised I wasn't on my own. It's partly the reason I never want to have a child. I'd never put them through what I've had to endure." Nicklas' eyes clouded over at the memory of it.

Reaching for his hand on the table, Louise asked, "Are you sure you've managed to come to terms with everything now?"

"I'm not that insecure, scared kid any more. As an adult I can be rational yet if someone gives me a hard time, the old wounds are ripped open. It is of no relevance whether you're black, Jewish or Muslim. You name it; the list goes on. Bigotry comes in many disguises. Prejudice will prevail. You feel attacked and become defensive. What I've learned is that I have to live my life to my best ability. Everyone does. But life's not worth much without that special person to share it with. It saddens me you've not had much happiness in your life."

It was typical of him that despite his own misfortunes, Nicklas thought of her.

"I've come to realise that due to my parents passing, I don't want a child of my own," Louise admitted. "Losing someone you love leaves you with not only a sense of loss but also the worry that history will repeat itself. Like you but for a different reason, I couldn't put anyone through the same ordeal. I know now that Mike wasn't the sort of man I thought he was. I've known it for a long time. When he got his way, life was good. When he didn't, I was the person he'd vent his frustration and anger on." It felt good to finally speak her mind. Up till now she'd only admitted it to herself.

"You're the only person I can be completely upfront with. You always saw behind the colour of my skin. The boy and eventually, the man. A human being with a heart, flesh and bones just like everyone else with his own views and flaws. I've not met anyone with such integrity and compassion as you. Your parents were the same." He kissed the palm of her hand. "I was too young and immature to realise how much you were hurting. You meant everything to me yet I couldn't get past my own pain and feelings of rejection. I'll never forgive myself for not being there for you." His voice faltered.

"You not being there for me? I've never heard such nonsense in my entire life. Everything you did was for me! Instead of dealing with everything you went through, you kept worrying about me. Can't you see? I was too young to commit to you. You meant just as much to me but I had my own dreams and aspirations. Gabriella's warnings about Mike fell on deaf ears. You were the best thing that happened to me. I just didn't appreciate you as much as I ought to have done at the time." Louise felt strangely unburdened as she made her admission.

"Deep down I always knew how you felt towards me. You and your parents always accepted me for who I am. It was I who didn't accept who I was. How is that even remotely possible when your own father rejects you? Oh, I know how much Mamma loved me. It just wasn't sufficient when there was so much I had to deal with. Not only the fallout at school but also that I didn't look like her or anyone else. It was as if I was a different species, yet I couldn't let her down when she relied on me for everything. I had to take care of her, a woman who spread sunshine wherever she went. An alcoholic who drowned her sorrow in a bottle. According to her doctor, Mamma died from sclerosis of the liver. She and I knew she died due to a broken heart. I was twenty-one when I found her on the kitchen floor, a bottle of whisky next to her body. She used to be so beautiful and full of life. Her blue eyes, compassion and zest for life are the only proof she and I are related. To die like she did, with no resemblance of the kind of person she really was . . . Mamma gradually vanished and turned into someone I no longer recognised. Like a flower that's never given water. Her own family and peer group cast her aside. And for what? Because she had the audacity to fall in love with a black man and bear his child. It took years to come to terms with my family's betrayal. A big part of me never will." Nicklas eyes clouded over once more.

"Are you finally able to see past the prejudice? Just look at what you've achieved despite it! You should be very proud of yourself. I am," Louise persisted, holding his gaze. She'd admitted to her own feelings of despair and rejection. It was his turn to follow suit.

"Honestly? Yes, I believe I've come to terms with it but I'll never accept it. Hell will freeze over first." Leaning across the table, Nicklas cupped her face in his hands. "Yes, I was wrong to think everyone hated me. You and your parents were always there for me. My only regret is that I never appreciated it as much as I should have at the time and that, for all my efforts, Mamma was beyond saving. Her life would have turned out so much better if she'd not met my father and had me."

"Don't say that! Mimmi loved you so much. She'd be so upset if she could hear you now. It wasn't either of your faults she fell in love with the wrong man. The colour of his skin had nothing to do with it! No one can predict who's worthy of our love. I ought to know."

"I don't pass judgement on anyone. It's just that at times it's so damn hard to be judged by the colour of my skin. Always expecting someone to scrutinise and offend me. In those days, women like my mother were viewed as cheap trash." Nicklas put Louise's hand on his heart. "Mamma loved spending time with your parents and Gabriella. Apart from the love she felt for me, those were the happiest times of her life. She always used to tell me how much she looked forward to us getting married. Mamma thought we were made for each other . . ." He sighed. "Whatever life throws at us, I will always be here for you, Louise. Through thick and thin."

"You told me you found her body on the kitchen floor. Would you mind telling me what led up to it?" Louise gently removed her hand from his chest.

"Mamma's parents wanted nothing more to do with her. Each time she turned up at their house on the outskirts of Limhamn, they threw her out. To them it didn't matter she gave birth to their only grandchild. I was persona non grata as well. Mamma became heavily dependent on alcohol and when my father left us in the rundown flat in Möllevång Square, her health deteriorated and there wasn't much anyone could do to reverse it. She literally drank herself into oblivion when my father didn't return. We never saw or heard from him again. I've lost count of the times your kind parents took me out looking for her only to discover she'd been drinking in some sleazy bar all night. But whatever people thought of her, she will always be my beloved mother. Nothing will ever change that. I'll stand up for her until the day I die," Nicklas said with conviction.

"Did you find out what became of your father?" Louise asked, holding her breath.

"No. I buried him along with my mother. People like him have no place in my life." His voice was hard and unforgiving.

"Then we're both orphans. I lost my parents in an accident. You lost your mother due to prejudice. We're the only thing that's left of them."

"Which makes it all the more significant we get on with our lives and find happiness," Nicklas replied, eyes locking with hers. "I'm so glad we got the opportunity to meet again."

"I really enjoyed tonight. Thank you for persevering with me." Louise loved the way they'd opened up their hearts to each other. As an afterthought she added, "Don't give up on me just yet." Her voice was a mere whisper.

"Take all the time you need. I'll still be here."

That night Louise started to put what happened between her and Mike behind her. She'd already sacrificed too much and now all she wanted was to get on with her life and move into a place of her own with Rufus. After Nicklas dropped her off outside Gabriella's block of flats, she was ever more determined to find the appropriate location for La Femme.

Tomorrow would be the perfect time to start looking.

Chapter Sixteen

Increasingly concerned for Abby and Timmy, Camilla decided to confide in Paige. They were in the study, designing the finishing touches to the Forever Yours website when Camilla said, "Did I mention Abby was abused by her father?"

"I can't remember. I guess you didn't. It's not something I'd forget," Paige replied, not overly concerned about a woman who willingly got entangled with any man who propositioned her.

"It's something Abby said when we last saw each other. Trine Larsen thinks Mike's mentally ill."

"What's that supposed to mean? Trine's overreacting. She and Jasper never approved of him. Can't say I do either after the stunt he pulled on Louise."

"Perhaps you're right, yet I've a feeling that bank account has a lot to do with it."

"You've got a lot to learn about married men. Many keep their wives in the dark – I'm living proof of that."

"Abby's not dependent on a man. In fact it's the furthest thing from her mind! Having affairs and engaging with dubious dealers and taking risks, sure. She positively thrives on it, yet that's as far as it goes. I know how you feel about her and won't mention her again." Camilla's voice was subdued. Ever since she'd moved in with Paige, both women got on well and enjoyed working together on the strategy of Forever Yours.

"I've no doubt Abby looks after number one. She's the kind of woman who loves a challenge and getting the upper hand. I wouldn't put it past her to steal from Mike's account. What Abby wants Abby gets, including my soon to be ex-husband." Paige frowned. She'd already decided she wouldn't allow that brash woman to come between her and a happy future, but there was one detail concerning her. "Do you suppose it was she who stole Mike's money?"

"If she did, Mike will find out. It's only a matter of time. Abby and the baby will be at risk." Camilla paced the room. She and Abby weren't as close as they used to be yet Camilla didn't wish her or the baby any harm.

"I ought to get in touch with her, seeing as she may hold the key to my problem. If Mike and Steve are trying to trick me out of my share of that account, Abby's got no option but to confess to her part in it. Either that or I'll make sure the three of them are prosecuted!" Paige went up to the side table and poured herself another mug of herbal tea. She'd vowed to cut down on her intake of sweets, coffee and biscuits, hoping to shed half a stone so she could fit into the new dress Liam had chosen for her when they visited Harrods a few weeks ago. He said she ought to get used to receiving gifts from time to time. It was Liam's way of reassuring her she needn't go without anything since, unlike Steve, he would always put her needs before his own.

If Steve and Mike had conspired to trick her, Paige knew she'd find out via her attorney. Excusing herself, she told Camilla she had to prepare dinner. "Josh and Alec are coming round later but

I've got to buy the ingredients for lasagne as it's their favourite dish. Please hold the fort if anyone calls," she lied, not willing to let on she and Natasha had arranged to meet in a café on Richmond Hill.

Putting on the new coat Liam had insisted on buying her, Paige rushed out the front door and drove to Richmond. Exactly on time, she spotted Natasha sitting in the café, reading a daily paper.

"You sounded so frantic over the phone I came as quickly as I could," Natasha said. You must fill me in on what Camilla said Abby told her." She was constantly worried that Mike would turn up when she and Robert least expected it.

"I know someone hacked into Mike's secret account," Paige replied. "Wait till you hear this. Camilla thinks it's Abby!"

"Does she have any proof?"

"Not really, only what Abby told her about how skilled she is when it comes to hacking into someone's account. It takes someone as inhuman as her to do something like that."

"Have you talked to Trine Larsen?" Natasha didn't like what she heard. Soon Mike would accuse all of them of tampering with his laptop. "It's got nothing to do with us. I've got to leave. Robert's picking me up. We're attending a charity ball in the West End in aid of children with autism. Robert sponsors them whenever he can find the time."

"I've not found the time to call Trine. Besides, she won't admit anything seeing as she and Jasper are Louise's friends. We'll have to stay patient and see how things unravel. I don't think that baby is at risk. Mike wouldn't harm his own child . . ." Yet as Paige thought of it, it dawned on her it may be Steve who was the baby's father, in which case he'd not only lied to her but also to his best friend.

Waving goodbye, Paige decided to get in touch with Trine. It was high time she got some answers and Louise was bound to have confided details of Mike's laptop to her closest friend.

Hours later, Paige excused herself from her family, stating she was tired and in need of a good night's sleep. It was fortunate that Josh and Alec approved of her partnership with Camilla. The only person they blamed for the breakup of their parent's marriage was Steve. From the privacy of her bedroom, Paige dialled Trine's familiar mobile number, mouth dry as sand paper.

"It's me, Paige. Can we talk? There is something I need to ask you."

Tired after a hard day's work at The Studio, Trine let out a sigh. "I'm in bed so can't talk for long. What is it you want to know?"

"Did Louise discover the whereabouts of Mike's laptop? Please don't hide anything from me. If Steve and Mike opened up an account behind my back I've the right to know!"

"I've no idea what you are talking about." Although the Larsens had agreed to store the laptop, Trine was adamant she didn't want to get involved. "All I know for sure is what Louise told me. Mike opened an account in his own name, no one else. If you don't believe her, I suggest that you request your solicitor investigates it. Who knows? It may be the only way to get the answers you want." Before Paige could put forward more questions, Jasper joined his wife in the bedroom. "Take my advice, Paige," Trine said before she hung up. "Steve's many things but he'd never trick you out of money that he and Mike earned. Personally, I believe Steve ought to be informed of the secret account. It'll speed up the legal process and give you both closure."

★

At the end of that week Paige requested that her solicitor interrogate Mike and Steve about their respective and joint accounts. It wasn't long before they had to hand in PIN numbers and statements. Concerned that they were on to him, Mike decided to visit Trine and Jasper, and demand they hand over his laptop. If they didn't, he knew Paige's attorney would request a warrant to search his house.

He'd lose everything he owned: money, house, cars and the business. Steve would prosecute him for withholding funds. Mike had made a hefty profit and managed to dupe Louise into clearing the company's debt and if he was found out, he was liable to serve a prison sentence for fraud and money laundering.

Driving home late one evening after he'd spent the entire day attempting to find a solution to his problem, Mike knew it was only a matter of time before he was arrested.

I've got to locate that damn laptop! Abby is the only person who could have discovered my file. I scribbled down the details and put them in a drawer in my office. She or Camilla must have come across them when they worked in the office. If only I could set a trap for them. I know, I'll pretend I already deposited a large amount, say £10k, into Timmy's account, which will be transferred into a trust fund when he's ten. If Abby's the one who hacked into my account, she'll be desperate to pull one more stunt. Her kind can't resist the challenge.

Mike turned into the quiet side street, parked at the front of the house and got out. With a bit of luck he'd soon locate the laptop and wipe the content before it was confiscated by the police. *If I'm wrong and Abby's not the one who outsmarted me, I'll make sure she never finds out about it.*

As he entered the spacious foyer, Mike could hear her singing a lullaby to Timmy upstairs. Taking two steps at the time, he shouted her name from the landing and opened the nursery door.

"There you are. Some jerk solicitor demands I give him access to my accounts. They are adamant I hand over my PIN number and recent statements. Trouble is, I've either lost or mislaid the file where I kept the details and the PIN number, which I wrote down on a piece of paper and put in a drawer in my office. You and Camilla are the only people who were permitted to enter that room."

Abby's breath caught. She leaned over Timmy and pulled the cover over his tiny body. "Why are you telling me this? All of it is nothing to do with me."

"I agree. This has nothing to do with either of us. I've not seen Steve since last week. We argued and decided it was best he takes his annual leave, then return when he's in a better mood," Mike lied, fully aware Steve still resented him for saying the business belonged to Mike despite the two of them owning an equal share.

Picking up the baby from the cot, Abby buried her face in his soft neck. "I still don't understand why you involve me in this. You must tell Steve and demand he returns from wherever he is!" *I'll change my bank details in the event the police are able to trace me*, she thought, fully aware Mike wouldn't let her get away with what she did to him. "What about Camilla? After all, she's always indebted to someone and offers sex in return for money."

Thinking she may have a point, Mike shook his head. "A huge amount of money went missing from my account. Just you wait until I get my hands on whoever stole it from me!" His fists were clenched.

Scared he'd sussed her out, Abby began to shake. "No wonder you're upset . . . I'd feel the same if it was me who lost all that money!"

Mike moved through the darkness of the nursery to stand next to her. He reached out to touch her face. "Are you planning on leaving and taking my son with you? Is that the reason you tremble so much?"

Face still buried in Timmy's neck, Abby forced herself to stand up to Mike. "Are you accusing me of betraying you? First you make a decision about some bloody trust fund behind my back, now this! Next you'll accuse me of hacking into your precious account," she hissed.

Abby's mind worked overtime as she attempted to make a plan for her and the baby. They belonged together. She had no option but to ensure his safety. Irrelevant of whether it was Mike or Steve who turned out to be the father, the time had come when Steve had to step up and take action. She and Timmy had no one else to turn to.

Furious she dared to cross him, Mike put a hand over her mouth. "Are you telling me I'm not good enough for you, is that it?" he shouted in her ear, his hand wandering to her neck, then her spine.

"Of course not. Stop it, Mike. Can't you see you're scaring Timmy? I know you're under a lot of pressure but please don't take it out on us." Timmy had begun to wail at the commotion and she held him so close she could feel his little heart pounding in his chest. If she carried a knife, Mike would be dead by now.

"I left Louise so I could have what she denied me! A family and new life. You've ruined everything with your constant demands of me. First a flat, then a house . . . I work my arse off while you sit at home, playing with our son and gossiping with your bloody friend!" He'd worked himself up to a crescendo of accusations. "You don't love me – hell, you don't even respect me!"

Fed up with his ranting and raving, Abby managed to calm the baby down and settled him in the cot where he instantly fell asleep. "You can tell me whatever you like but don't you dare involve our son! If you're not careful I *will* leave you and take him with me. Your worst nightmare will materialise." Thinking she may have said too much Abby added, "You're your own worst enemy, Mike. Of course I love you. Who else would be willing to put up with you? Go to bed and sleep off your anger. For all you know, that laptop will materialise. Meanwhile get yourself back to work in the morning and call Steve. He'll know what to do."

This was the final straw. Now she couldn't wait to get away from him. *I've enough money to last us forever,* she thought. *Why was I so greedy? It's too late to hack into the account Mike opened in Timmy's name. I've got to get out of here!* The problem was she had nowhere to go except Camilla yet Paige would never allow them to stay with her. *Steve's our best bet! I hope he found somewhere to live after he and Camilla broke up? Damn Mike! It wasn't supposed to end this way . . .* She'd made plans to rob him of everything he had.

"Let me get you a drink," she said aloud. "It'll calm you down. G&T okay with you?"

"Why not, but only if you join me." Mike's eyes held her gaze.

"You know I can't. What if Timmy wakes up and I'm too drunk to hear him?"

"Fair enough. Bring me the entire bottle of gin!" They went downstairs and Mike's eyes fixated on her as she opened the drinks cupboard in the living room and returned with the bottle he demanded she hand over to him. "Sure you don't want to join me?" he asked, opening the bottle and downing half the content.

Realising she and Timmy would be in danger if she didn't act fast, Abby whispered, "I'm going to bed. Please try not to wake us up when you've finished the bottle."

As she moved to walk past him, Mike grabbed her hair with one hand, the bottle firmly in his other hand. "Don't tell me what

I can and can't do in my own home!" he screamed, throwing the bottle on the floor.

Planning to run upstairs and lock herself in the nursery where she'd left her mobile and call Steve, Abby felt Mike's hands around her neck. He squeezed until she couldn't breathe, and she began to see stars at the edge of her vision. Just as she began to pass out, Abby reached for the bottle and managed to grab it with one hand. Aiming for Mike's skull, she smashed it onto his head until he let go of her neck and collapsed in a heap on the floor, too drunk to realise what had happened.

Abby stood there a moment, shaking, and making sure Mike wasn't about to get up again. Eventually she bent down, picked up what was left of the bottle and wiped it with her sleeve, just in case someone entered the house, discovered Mike lying on the floor and called the police. She didn't want her fingerprints to incriminate her. "Just so you know, I never gave a damn about you," she told the motionless body. "Nor the baby at first. Well, I've come to love him and I'm going to make sure you never get to see him ever again! One more thing: it was I who stole that money. It was child's play to discover the details in your office drawer. £1.2 million should see us through for a little while." She leaned closer to him and spat in his face.

Unbeknown to Abby, Mike was still partly conscious and heard everything she told him. He lay there, listening to the sounds of her packing up her and Timmy's belongings, his gin-drenched brain trying to make sense of it all. Finally he heard the door slam shut and the sound of keys dropping through the letterbox in the hall.

After that everything became hazy until he fell into a deep sleep, haunted by demons coming after him in the bottomless darkness.

CHAPTER SEVENTEEN

February 2016

"I HARDLY GET to see you nowadays. The flat and La Femme take up most of your time," Gabriella complained, missing Louise and Rufus, and all the fun they'd had when they stayed at her flat. She'd persuaded Louise to join her for lunch at ZinZino, not far from her new flat in Fridhem Square.

Louise and Rufus had only lived there for a couple of weeks and loved their new home. The familiar area, shops and parks were to die for, not forgetting Ribersborg and Limhamn with the parks, coastline and beaches in the vicinity. From her balcony Louise had a spectacular view of the West Harbour and Öresund strait.

Louise decorated her new home in soft pastel colours and furnished it with a mix of modern pieces she'd purchased in local shops and items she'd inherited from her late parents. It felt wonderful to have a place that belonged solely to her and the small dog, who preferred to sleep in his basket on the kitchen floor. When Louise invited her aunt, Nicklas and friends to her housewarming party, everyone agreed the flat was the best investment she'd ever made. Serving a buffet of Swedish delicatessen, herrings, cucumber salad, gravad lax, meatballs and potato salad, the guests had a wonderful time and toasted Louise's future. After she filled up her guests' glasses with wine and lingonberry squash, Louise stood on the balcony that overlooked the people, shops and commons below on the ground, celebrating with a little moment to herself. *I did it! I got divorced, relocated to Malmö and bought this flat.*

Recently, Louise also sold her share of The Studio to Trine and Jasper. It felt strange at first to give up on everything she and Trine worked so hard to achieve. Even stranger that their partnership came to an end. The two friends called and texted each other almost every day. Trine and Jasper told her they missed her very much but were happy she'd taken a leap of faith and settled in Malmö. What they omitted to tell her was that Abby had left Mike and moved into a small flat with the baby.

"I almost pity him. He abandoned Louise to have a family and then lost everything," Trine said to her husband.

Mike had been hospitalised for two weeks after a neighbour found him lying unconscious on the living room floor; a nasty, deep cut in his head and the remnants of a bottle of gin soaked in blood next to him. It was hard to feel sorry for him after everything he did to Louise. At least now that Abby had left him, Trine and Jasper didn't worry about Timmy anymore in the event it turned out Mike wasn't the father.

Abby clearly doted on her son and was a good mother, according to Camilla, who helped find her friend and the baby a place to live in Hampton Court where both knew Mike wouldn't be able to locate her as easily as Richmond.

Nevertheless, Mike didn't give up on finding them and applying for custody of his son, and only kept a low profile until he found his laptop. He and Steve stayed out of each other's way to avoid heated discussions and arguments. Steve had too much on his mind to challenge Mike about his account; most significantly if Abby's baby was his. As soon as the divorce between him and Paige was finalised he'd persuade her to agree to a paternity test.

By early February Louise found suitable premises for La Femme in Little Square, only a short walk from where she and Rufus lived in Fridhem Square and even closer to Gabriella's flat in central Malmö. She'd been looking at surrounding areas yet preferred the quaint, picturesque environment, cobbled streets and old buildings mixed with new architecture to the buzzing trade of Möllevång Square, which was inundated with boutiques, restaurants and cosmopolitan food markets.

Little Square was the perfect location for a boutique aimed at mature women, stocking international designers and labels, unlike The Studio that catered to women of all ages and stocked Scandinavian labels. It cost a fortune in rent for just a tiny room, stock room at the back and small pantry and toilet. Yet, in Louise's mind, La Femme was a dream come true. She was planning to open her boutique in the summer, and told Trine she'd visit London in late spring and place orders with established and up-and-coming designers. It felt wonderful to know she and Trine would finally meet again after nearly six months.

"You've accomplished a lot since you moved to Malmö," Gabriella commented after they ordered from the menu. ZinZino was hugely popular with the locals and served delicious Italian food that Louise couldn't resist.

"You're right, I have so far. Yet not as much as you have. Will you soon retire all together from work?"

"Definitely. I want to leave the hospital before I'm too old and infirm. It's time to give way to someone who's younger and eager to establish themselves. It'll benefit the patients and staff. New blood needs to be injected from time to time." Gabriella wasn't in the least upset or sentimental. She'd worked as clinical Neurological Director at Malmö's large hospital for nearly forty-five years and couldn't wait to retire and spend more time with her friends, read books and travel.

"Don't you wish you had someone special to share your life with?" Louise asked, repeating what they'd discussed before. "I know you don't want to talk about it but you mentioned Mamma and Pappa were the only ones who knew. What did you mean by that?"

Gabriella was the only family she had left and vice versa. Louise felt she had the right to know if her aunt had a secret only her parents had shared.

Sighing, Gabriella replied, "You're not willing to let it go, are you?"

Shaking her head, Louise looked deep into her aunt's eyes. "Why are you so determined to keep whatever it is to yourself? I've told you about Mike."

"That's true but I'm much more interested in you and Nicklas getting together. Friendship's a good foundation yet it'd be a great pity if the two of you can't move on from there."

"Don't change the subject. Please tell me what it is you've been keeping from me for so long."

"I'm sure you can figure it out for yourself." Gabriella frowned, looking flustered. Kajsa and Martin are right. I've been in a relationship with a colleague who is ten years younger than I am."

"But that's wonderful news! How come you never told me you've got a partner and why aren't the two of you living together?" A million thoughts entered Louise's mind.

"I've not told you everything. Simon was the first person I confided in. The second was your mother. They were so understanding and open-minded. I'm gay, Louise, and they were the only people who knew. Apart from them and you, I've not told anyone about it. Åsa is a wonderful woman. We're in love, very happy and have shared twenty years together. The only time we're able to come out in the open is when we travel abroad where no one knows us. So now you know why I was reluctant to tell you. I was scared you'd view me in a different way. I couldn't cope if you turned your back on me."

Stunned at the revelation and hurt Gabriella didn't think she was capable of being tolerant, Louise swallowed hard. "I wish you told me years ago. I'm so happy for the two of you. When will you introduce me to your partner? I'm dying to get to know her."

Walking round the table, Louise held her aunt close, thinking how extraordinary it was that she'd known Gabriella all her life yet never knew the secret she carried inside of her until now or the woman she'd loved for so long. Gabriella's generation didn't automatically come out to their nearest and dearest the way Louise's friends Martin and Nils did. Despite being modern in many ways, Gabriella was as averse to discussing matters of a personal nature as she was to technology.

The following week, Gabriella invited Louise, Kajsa and Martin to dinner. Nils was at a shoot in Brussels, supervising his and Martin's top model.

Louise didn't tell Kajsa and Martin what Gabriella had confided in her. It felt wrong to convey something so personal and sensitive.

"Do you want me to bring something?" she'd asked her aunt, when Gabriella called early that morning.

"Only yourself and Rufus. Oh, and don't forget his toys. Last time you did, he chewed on my shoes in the hall!" As much as she missed their company, while Louise and Rufus were staying, Gabriella never got the opportunity to see Åsa. Now they had all the time in the world to meet up and spend the night and odd weekends at either of their places.

Just like her partner, Åsa was a highly respected neurologist who at sixty had some time left before retirement. They'd met at a conference in New York nearly twenty years ago. A divorcée, Åsa always suspected she was gay, although she married her childhood sweetheart who persuaded her to have a child. Sadly, Åsa miscarried twice and eventually had the courage to end the marriage when she realised she was no longer able to pretend everything was alright and lie about who she really was: a reputed consultant who'd fallen in love with her equally highly qualified colleague.

The age gap didn't bother them, only that they felt they couldn't go out together in public and announce their love and commitment. They'd been together for almost ten years, when out of the blue, Åsa's brother saw them walk hand in hand on the beach. Unknown to them, he'd been so disgusted he called the hospital, asked to talk to the registrar and revealed they were an item. Shocked that someone had seen them, especially Åsa's conservative brother, Gabriella threatened to leave unless the registrar apologised for allowing Åsa's brother to badmouth them. "Our sexuality is our business and not reflective of our work!" she'd said, refusing to accept that anyone would have the right to question their professionalism due to their sexual preference. Since then, both women decided to keep a low profile and accepted it was for the best if neither of them accepted joint invitations until they retired.

Sitting at Gabriella's candlelit table, Louise wondered if her aunt would tell Kajsa and Martin she was gay. At that moment, Gabriella raised her glass in a toast. "It's great to see you. I've made gravad lax and potato salad. Please bring your plates into the kitchen and pile up the food! There's plenty of wine to go round."

Returning to their seats, Louise realised her aunt had laid the table for yet another person. "Are you expecting someone else?" she asked.

Gabriella was about to respond when the front door opened and a tall, slim woman with mousy hair and green eyes entered the dining room.

"You ought to have locked the door to prevent strangers trespassing," Kajsa said, curious to find out who it was that joined them.

Putting her jacket on the settee, the woman said, "Gabriella's invited me to dinner. She wants to introduce me to you." Walking up to her, Gabriella put her arm around the other woman and surveyed her guests.

"This is Åsa, Åsa Lundberg. She's my colleague and my partner. It's high time all of you were introduced to each other."

Staring at them, Martin put down his knife and fork, asking, "Is this your way of telling us that the two of you are a couple?" He got up from his chair, went up to them and gave both women a big hug, then returned to his seat.

"Well, I'll be damned . . . how did you manage to keep it from us?" Kajsa asked.

"It wasn't intentional." Gabriella turned to look at her niece, hoping she'd say something, anything.

"I think it's wonderful the two of you found each other," Louise said, her head buzzing with questions.

Watching the newcomer and their hostess, Martin thought they looked great together irrelevant of age and gender. "Seat yourselves while I pour each of you a glass of wine," he told them, pulling out a chair for the guest and hostess. Half an hour later, everyone was talking and laughing. Åsa was kind and sweet and it was evident she and Gabriella were in love.

"Will you retire as well?" Kajsa asked her.

"Not yet. I've another few years to work. Gabriella and I plan to travel the world when both of us are retired."

The evening passed too quickly. By the time Kajsa and Martin left and Åsa excused herself, saying she had an early start in the morning, it was almost time to go to bed.

"Stay a while longer," Gabriella told Louise. "Åsa and I are too old to continue like we were. I feel so liberated you and your friends got to meet her."

"You seem to have a lot in common apart from work. I want you to know I'm delighted for you both."

Sitting next to each other on the couch in the living room, Gabriella asked, "If Åsa and I can sort out our lives, you and Nicklas can as well. Don't worry about me. I've had a wonderful life. Having you here in Malmö where you belong is a dream come true." She kissed Louise's cheek and sipped her wine, adding, "Mike had no backbone! I'm so pleased you and Nicklas met each other again. He's turned his life around. What happened to Mimmi was a tragedy."

"Do you think he's put everything behind him? Nicklas claims he has yet I don't believe him. I'm not saying he's a liar. Only that old wounds never heal."

"It's irrelevant if he has or not. Nicklas loves you; you ought to trust what he tells you."

"I do. It's myself I don't trust to yet again get it wrong. Oh, I know Nicklas is nothing like Mike, but I've a tendency to ignore my intuition and it's telling me Nicklas hasn't dealt with his demons. However much I care about him, I've got to listen to my gut instinct. I also need more time to myself and La Femme."

Louise could tell by the expression in her aunt's eyes that she didn't believe her.

"Nonsense! You can have a personal life *and* a career. Don't project your insecurity on him. If you're not ready to take things further between you, at least tell him! Nicklas assumes you need more time to get over Mike. You and I know that's not completely true. You are scared to be intimate with a man, in case you'll get hurt. It's so much simpler to avoid it altogether."

"How would you know? You've not endured what I did," Louise said sharply. She'd had enough of everyone dispensing advice on her personal life.

"No, I don't. But I've spent almost half of my life denying my own sexuality. It took someone as wonderful as Åsa to bring me out of my self-imposed prison. On the outside I had everything. Money in the bank, a lovely flat, stimulating job and friends. On the inside I was a mess. I pretended I was someone I'm not, just like a lot of people of my generation. Please don't make my mistake and bury your head in the sand. Face up to your fears and don't worry so much about Nicklas. He's not that lost young boy he used to be anymore."

"I know. We're friends and I want it to stay that way a while longer."

"That's fine as long as you don't waste too much time. Life's too short and precious for that. You deserve to be happy and so does Nicklas. Take my advice: you and Nicklas are meant for each other. Everything will sort itself out one way or the other."

★

When Nicklas called the following evening, asking if she wanted to have dinner with him in yet another of Malmö's trendy restaurants, Louise immediately accepted.

"You're absolutely certain? Epicuré is a lovely place to eat. It's situated close to Fridhem."

"I'll look forward to it."

"Great! I'll pick you up at seven." Nicklas made a mental note to reserve a table in the morning.

Over the next few months they spent a lot of time in each other's company, meeting up for dinner or a drink in Malmö's numerous restaurants and wine bars. He'd pick her up and take her home yet never expected anything of her, except her friendship.

In early spring Louise at long last opened her boutique in Little Square.

Trine recommended several designers who were promoting their brands in Portobello Road. True to her word, Trine made the effort to visit each designer's outlet and emailed details of everyone to Louise. Ultimately, two designers stood out from the rest. One was Spanish, the other British. When she received the small collections, Louise knew she'd made the right choice. The bias cut dresses and palazzo trousers would suit most women regardless of age or size. In addition, Louise found a local jeweller who offered to design a special range of costume jewellery exclusively for La Femme.

Eventually, the boutique would stock more brands but not until Louise calculated if the expenditure was justifiable and reflective of what her clients wanted.

As time passed by it became evident La Femme was more successful than the numerous shopping centres that popped up in almost every part of Malmö. Although people preferred to shop in big supermarkets that offered everything from food to furniture, most women of a certain age wanted to stick out from the crowd and were prepared to pay more for the privilege. They also didn't want to queue up for hours on end, surrounded by customers whose only wish was to get a bargain as opposed to paying more for a quality garment.

By March Louise had made a small profit, mainly because she didn't employ someone to work part time in the boutique. Instead she worked all hours, including weekends and national holidays. Around the same time, Nicklas opened up a new gallery in the Old City, close to The Central Railway Station. Frequently attending exhibitions and dinners in Epicuré, ZinZino and Oui Osteria, the two of them became even closer than ever.

Six feet tall and handsome, Nicklas was completely immune to women's admiring glances when he and Louise were out together. He didn't belong to the type of men who flashed their assets, cars and money. What Nicklas accumulated stemmed purely from hard work. Perhaps Gabriella was right, saying Louise should let him get closer to her. As it was, neither of them wanted to rock the boat and redefine the friendship that meant so much to both of them.

That was, until one evening in late spring.

Gabriella was in the middle of planning her and Åsa's summer vacation when Åsa collapsed in Gabriella's flat. Taken by ambulance to the emergency unit in Malmö's main hospital, the duty consultant informed Gabriella that her partner was in danger of having a stroke due to extremely high blood pressure.

"Your friend is very fortunate to be alive. Had you not been present and called for an ambulance, she'd be dead," the consultant told them.

Lying in the hospital bed, attached to a drip and with an oxygen mask on her face, Åsa blamed herself for missing the signs.

211

She'd felt lethargic and short of breath for some time and blamed it on the stress of working all hours. Unless she decreased her workload, she wouldn't survive and all their plans for the future would be in vain.

Gabriella was so shaken up by the incident that she nearly had a nervous breakdown. She'd always assumed Åsa would survive her since she was ten years younger.

Louise was at Nicklas' art gallery when Gabriella called, too upset to make any sense. "Where are you, is Åsa with you? Tell her I want to talk to her!" Louise cried, petrified something terrible had happened to her aunt.

"There's nothing wrong with me. It's Åsa! She was rushed into hospital by ambulance earlier tonight. We're in the A&E. She has to stay here until she's improved. The consultant told me she's at risk of having a heart attack or stroke! I'm at my wits' end." As Gabriella dissolved in tears, Louise promised she and Nicklas would leave immediately for the hospital.

Seeing her so distressed, Nicklas excused himself from a client. "What's wrong? You look as if you're about to faint!"

Louise realised her legs were shaking. "Gabriella called to say that Åsa's been admitted to hospital. I told her we're on our way."

"My car's parked outside Palace Park. I'll return and collect it in the morning. We'll get a cab instead." Fortunately, they were close to a taxi rank and succeeded in finding a taxi that wasn't reeking of booze that time of night. Seated next to each other in the back seat, Louise suddenly burst into tears.

"What will I do if something happens to her? Gabriella's my only family; I've not got anyone else," she cried, her face buried in his neck.

Tilting her chin so that he could look into her eyes, Nicklas held her close. "You will always have me."

"You're too nice to me," Louise whispered. "I don't deserve it."

"Yes, you do. We'll talk about it later." Now wasn't the time to do anything except get to the hospital.

The driver dropped them off outside the main building, watching them get out of the taxi and run towards the A&E entrance.

"I hope we're not too late," Louise said over her shoulder, "there's always a risk at their age."

Gabriella was sitting on the bed next to Åsa, who was asleep. She looked in a bad way. The nurse had given Åsa a sleeping tablet to relax and calm her down, but Louise could tell she was gravely ill from the pallor of her face.

Never letting go of Louise's hand, Nicklas said, "I'll get you something to drink, your face is as white as a sheet." He helped find a chair for her to sit on and went out into the corridor to ask a nurse where he could get something to drink.

Hours later the same doctor entered Åsa's room. "She's sufficiently stable to move into the ward upstairs. We'll keep her in until we're satisfied she's recovered." Too tired, dizzy and weak to talk, Åsa lay back against the pillows of the hospital bed with her eyes shut.

Seeing how close she and Gabriella were, faces touching as the latter snuggled up to her partner, Louise realised how frail life was and that at any time the people she loved may be taken from her, just like her parents were all those years ago. Turning to look at Nicklas, she said, "Do you recall what I said to you when you told me life's too precious to waste?"

"I do." Nicklas gave her a wan smile. "You told me I have to stay patient a while longer."

"Will you?"

"You already know the answer. I'll always be here for you."

Nicklas pulled her into his arms and reassured her everything would sort itself out. Reassured that Åsa was out of danger, they ordered a cab to take them back to their respective homes. Dropping Gabriella off first, they helped her inside and promised to call in the morning. It wasn't until she was standing on the pavement outside her building in Fridhem, that Louise said, "Please stay patient until I return from London."

She'd booked a flight in May and was invited to stay at the Larsens'. She and Trine were planning on spending time together to locate other designers whose collections may prove successful for La Femme.

"I'll hold you to it," Nicklas replied, waiting until she'd safely stepped inside the front door of the building, then returned to the cab and gave the driver his home address.

CHAPTER EIGHTEEN

April 2016

*W*HAT DOES MIKE *want from us now? We've told him we don't want anything more to do with him.* Natasha was busy preparing dinner when she noticed his car pull into the driveway. Her heart began racing. Mike wasn't the kind of man who took no for an answer.

As he walked up the path and pushed the doorbell, Natasha dried her hands on her apron and called her husband on his mobile.

"Mike's returned! He's outside on the porch. I don't know what to do!" She was trembling all over.

"I told that bastard to never bother us again. Don't let him in. I'll drive home as quickly as I can. Just sit tight." Robert was furious Mike had ignored his warning to leave them alone.

Pushing the doorbell once more, Mike took a step back and banged on the window until Natasha shouted, "Go away, I'll call the police!"

Anger building up inside of him, Mike banged on the door. "You and Robert will not fob me off again! Unless you tell me who stole my laptop, I'll get my solicitor involved. Is that understood?"

Wringing her hands, Natasha prayed her husband would turn

up soon. "It's got nothing to do with us! Go pester Steve or Abby instead of us. We'll take action against you if you continue to harass us!"

Mike smiled nastily. "Oh, I'm shaking in my boots! Tell that idiot husband of yours I don't take kindly to people stealing from me. I demand Robert tells me where my laptop is! All of you are conspiring behind my back. It's Louise's way of getting back at me for dumping her!" Mike had become increasingly irrational and paranoid ever since he discovered Abby had hacked into his secret account. Eyes narrowing, he kicked the door with his shoe. "You'll regret treating me like this!" he shouted and walked back to his car.

Fed up with his threats, Natasha unlocked the door and came after him, screaming. "How dare you suggest Robert and I conspired to steal your bloody laptop? Louise is well rid of you. She's moved on with her life. No one wants to have anything to do with you, Mike! If I were in Louise's shoes, I'd have set fire to that laptop. Everyone's figured you out and seen you for who you really are – nothing but a vicious bully and a cheat!"

Incensed she had the nerve to talk to him in such a derogatory manner, Mike took a few steps closer to her. "You'll pay for this, Natasha! No one talks to me like you just did."

"Is that it? Are you quite finished or do you have something else up your sleeve? Louise was the best thing that ever happened to you. She always covered your back and you repaid her kindness and generosity by sticking a knife in her back. Just leave, Mike, and don't come back. If you do, I'll pay you back for what you did to my friend!" Natasha was shaking with anger. As she slammed the door behind her, she saw the shocked expression on his face.

Mike never knew she had it in her to stand up to him. "Go to hell!" he shouted and walked sheepishly towards his car.

"Ditto! Good riddance to you." Natasha was so upset she couldn't care less what the neighbours must think of them, shouting and arguing in the quiet residential street. As far as she was concerned, Mike could rot in hell.

Standing just inside the door, Natasha started to laugh, the tension slowly evaporating inside of her. It suddenly dawned on her that Mike might go after Trine and Jasper in the same way he'd harassed her and Robert. Dialling Trine's number, Natasha sighed when she heard the familiar voice. "Mike's just left. He came here twice to interrogate us about some missing laptop. The mood he's in, I need to warn you he may turn up at your house next, or The Studio. Please be on your guard – he's not right in the head."

"I appreciate your concern," Trine replied, thinking quickly. "The truth is, Louise asked us to store Mike's laptop. He'd opened an account in his own name and withheld it from Steve to cover his back. Apparently, a file was discovered on Mike's old laptop, containing details Steve has no knowledge of."

"Louise must have found it when she packed up her things in the house?"

"That's right. Mike left his laptop behind and Louise initially put it in a drawer. As soon as she realised it contained confidential documents, she managed to gain access to his password and discover the file."

"Promise me you'll be careful. Mike's completely deranged. I think he's mentally ill. You must ask Jasper to pick you up from The Studio."

"Don't worry about me, I'll be fine. Besides, I've parked my car in a side street only a five-minute walk from here. I appreciate your concern and am very sorry Mike caused you and Robert such a lot of hassle. He'll get what's coming to him. People like him always do. Say hello to Robert from me." Trine switched off her mobile and returned to what she was doing before Natasha called.

Busy sorting out the new collections, Trine was pleased The Studio attracted lots of media attention, especially after she decided to add the popular designer label, Mint Velvet. Lately Trine had been busy preparing for the fashion show and spent nearly every night at The Studio. The idea of combining a sense of comfort in daily events, such as shopping, reading and style of clothing was initially a Danish concept that turned into a world-wide trend. Scandinavians in particular loved to read a good book by an open fire and wear casual clothing that was trendy yet also kept them warm during the long, dark winters. It became a way of living life to its full potential without compromising on quality and style.

Mike's getting increasingly frantic someone will find out what he did, Trine thought, debating whether or not to call Louise and tell her he'd pestered the Sturgess family twice in recent months. *Nah, I'll work on the latest preparations for the fashion show. That way I'll get the time off to spend with Louise when she visits London in May.*

Putting Natasha's warning at the back of her mind, Trine concentrated on her work and it wasn't until she'd completed the task in hand that she looked at her watch. *Shit! It's nearly six o'clock. Time's passed me by too quickly. I'd better call Jasper and tell him I'm on my way home or he'll get worried.* Five minutes later, pleased with what she'd achieved so far, Trine remembered she hadn't told her husband about Natasha's concern Mike may come after them. She was just thinking that she'd tell Jasper when she saw him when she heard a knock on the front door.

Worried whoever it was would cause her more delay, Trine glanced out the window to see Mike standing outside on the pavement. *Damn him! Natasha was right in saying he'd not give up so*

easily and come after us! I'm an idiot, why on earth didn't I ask Jasper to
pick me up?

Ignoring the knock and hastily pulling on her coat, Trine opted to leave via the back entrance just in case Mike was waiting for her at the front of the building. He continued banging on the front door, shouting, "I know you're inside! You'd better let me in. If you don't, I'll make sure you'll regret it!"

Mike was slurring his words. After he'd left Natasha he'd had a couple of drinks in a pub on his way to Fulham. Listening to him, Trine was desperate to call Jasper yet was too scared to use her mobile in case Mike could hear her. When he began to shout obscenities at passers-by in the street, Trine decided to come out from where she was hiding at the back of the property.

"Get the hell away from me or I'll call the police!" she shouted, thinking he looked awful with a big, ugly bruise still on his forehead, dating from when Abby acted in self-defence.

"You and Jasper stole my laptop! The two of you are nothing but a pair of thieves! As for Louise . . . how dare she involve herself in my affairs? I'll wring her neck if she messes with me again!" Mike was shouting so loudly people were staring at them. Oblivious, he went up to Trine and grabbed her arm. "If you scream, I'll kill you. It's up to you what will happen next if you don't return my laptop to me." In his stupor he'd forgotten the laptop was probably hidden in Trine and Jasper's home, not The Studio.

Petrified Mike would hurt her more than he already did, Trine attempted to break free from his hold on her arm. Wincing in pain, she started to cry.

"Shut your mouth!" Mike warned her, dragging her to the side of the pavement, where she stumbled and fell at his feet. She was ready to surrender to him, saying she'd put the laptop inside her office – anything as long as he left her alone – when out of nowhere two passers-by came to her rescue.

"Stop what you're doing or we'll call the police," the older man said, striding straight up to Mike. Letting go of Trine's arm, Mike ran towards his car across the street, swearing. As the younger man helped her to stand up, the older man asked if she was okay.

"I'm alright . . . b-but if you h-hadn't come along when you did . . ." She was shaking so much they thought she would have a fit.

"Is there someone you want us to call?" the older man asked in a kind voice. *Whoever assaulted her deserves to be punished,* he thought, a grim expression in his eyes.

"P-pl-please call my h-husband. The num-ber's in my m-mobile." Trine gestured at her bag. Half an hour later Jasper arrived on the scene, his van parked outside The Studio. He ran up to her and wrapped his arms around her.

"Shh, I'm here now. You're perfectly safe. Nothing more will happen to you, I give you my word." When he'd received the call from the older of the two men telling him his wife was attacked in the street, Jasper immediately thought of Mike. "I'm indebted to you both," he said, turning to the men. "If you hadn't come to her rescue . . ." His voice faltered. *I'll kill Mike if he comes near her again! He's damn lucky I wasn't here or I'd have beaten him and taken him with me to the nearest police station.* Internally Jasper swore there and then to destroy Mike and inform Steve of the secret account the following morning. "Thank you both so much. How can I repay you?"

The younger man shook his head. "No way. We'd do it again. If something like that happened to my girlfriend I'd never let the guy get away with it!"

Shaking their hands, Jasper helped Trine to get up from where she sat on the pavement, still too numb to move. Later that night, in the safety of their home, he held her close to him in bed, both of them too shaken to talk and dreading to think how far Mike would go to retrieve his laptop.

"Please try to sleep. I'll pick up your car in the morning; you're taking a couple of days off work," Jasper said, pulling her closer.

In his drunken rage, Mike cursed the men who interfered with him and Trine. He'd been so close to finding his laptop, and was now certain she'd stored it in her office.

As he drove on to his and Steve's meeting with the minicab company, Mike ignored the traffic lights and tried to come up with a reason to get rid of the deal that in his opinion lowered the standard of his business. The more he thought about it, the angrier he became.

Mike parked in the lot outside the premises, attempting to calm down sufficiently to handle Steve without losing his temper. *I've got to put up a façade were he's concerned or risk that he finds out I opened an account with his money,* he thought.

Now he knew Abby had stolen £1.2 million, Mike wasn't prepared to let her off the hook and lose the rest to Steve. *Paige knows I've got a secret account and thinks Steve's aware of it. If she instructs her solicitor to look into it I will be found out and Steve will sue me for everything I've got.* Willing himself to put on a front, Mike got out of the car and steeled himself for his encounter with Steve and the minicab firm.

"Where the hell have you been?" Steve said the minute he entered the office. "I've waited for at least an hour and the meeting's already in full swing. I had to tell the representative to delay part of the agenda."

"That's fine by me. You're the one who got us into this mess, you'll bloody well get us out of it!"

Taking a closer look at him, Steve could tell he'd been up to something. He could smell the alcohol on his breath.

Mike had inherited his vicious temper from his father. The fact he managed to control it when he was married to Louise never ceased to amaze Steve. If someone or something didn't agree with him, Mike didn't bother to work it out, instead he'd use his fists to bring home the message he wasn't taking any bullshit. It didn't matter who was wrong: unless Mike got what he wanted, he'd not let his opponent forget it. Louise was a calming influence on Mike, even to the extent that Steve believed he'd changed for the better and at long last dealt with the conflicting feelings he had for his father. In his heyday, Mike Kershaw Snr was a formidable man with an enviable life, wife, son and business. Yet when he died, he was a broken man due to gambling away his money and never missed an opportunity to beat his wife and son.

Mike's a carbon copy of his father, Steve thought, *down to the same bullish behaviour and undermining everyone around him.* "Have you got something you want to get off your chest?"

"Meaning? Are you suggesting I'm hiding something from you? Is that it? How long have we known each other?" Mike asked, not meeting Steve's eyes.

"You're lying to me! I know you and Abby are over. Camilla told Paige."

"Paige? I thought you'll soon be divorced . . . perhaps she's let you back in the bedroom – is that the reason you're against me all of a sudden? Are sexual favours worth more to you than my friendship?" Mike still refused to look into Steve's eyes for fear that Steve would see through him and his lies.

"Did you commit fraud, Mike? Jasper Larsen reported you to the police, claiming you attacked his wife. He told me you're looking for a laptop that stores information of an account. I will get to the bottom of it. You can be certain of that!" He didn't give a damn about missing the meeting, only that they'd clear the air between them once and for all. Steve had had enough of Mike's infantile behaviour and their constant arguing.

"Don't be so bloody melodramatic," Mike replied. "Have you lost your mind?"

"Go on, put the blame on me. It's what you've done for as long as I care to remember. I've concluded Paige and I are better off apart. I let her down too many times. The time has come to cut my losses." Steve had reconciled himself with the past and all the hurt he'd inflicted on her.

"My heart bleeds for you! Abby and I are over, yet unlike you I've got a son who loves me. Your sons don't care whether you're alive or dead."

"Say that again and I'll beat you until you beg for mercy!" Steve was about to punch Mike in the face when their recently appointed PA entered the room, a stern expression on her face.

"I apologise for interrupting but everyone's waiting for you. The meeting will soon be over." She looked at them and wondered if they'd fallen out over something serious or if they were just having a laugh. In her mind, the former seemed more appropriate. Stunned neither of them addressed her, she left them to it and decided to inform the chairman neither of them had the time to take part.

"Great! At least now everything will get back to normal, right, Steve? I've no intention to cater to that poxy firm's requirements!

Unless you agree, you are welcome to go and apply for a job with them, in which case I'll instruct our solicitor to sell your share of the company and the title will reverse to Kershaw Limousine Services." Walking up to him, Mike spat in his face.

Furious and disgusted, Steve grabbed Mike's arm then cried out in pain when Mike put his hands around his neck and squeezed. It wasn't until Steve was almost blue in the face and summoned the strength to kick him in the groin that both men stopped fighting.

"I know what you did," Steve choked. "Trine found out from Louise that you've accepted money from a client behind my back. Unless you pay back the money I'm owed, I'll see to it you're locked up for a very long time. I've nothing else to say to you except we're through. Now get the hell out of my life!" Steve snarled at him and left the building. Mike meant nothing to him anymore.

The only thing he cared about now was whether Timmy was his. Steve vowed to demand a paternity test. The sooner he knew where he stood, the sooner he'd be able to get on with his life.

When Louise found out Mike had attacked Trine, she felt sick.

"Trine didn't want me to tell you but you'd have found out about it sooner or later," Jasper told her. "Mike's threatened Natasha and Robert that unless they tell him the whereabouts of his laptop, he'll continue to harass them. Abby left Mike and took the baby with her. Mike's mentally ill, Louise. You had a lucky escape."

"He actually hit her?"

"He twisted her arm and threatened to kill her. He scared her so much, she still has nightmares. Had it not been for some men who were passing and rescued her . . . suffice to say Trine may not be alive. I've reported the incident and handed in the laptop to the police. Mike's ruined, Louise. He's lost everything, yet he still thinks he'll get custody of the baby . . . talk about being deranged."

Listening to him, Louise held the receiver so tight, her hand hurt. "All of this is my fault! If I didn't get involved with that damned laptop – oh, Jasper, do you suppose Trine will ever forgive me?" she cried.

"There's nothing to forgive! What I can't understand is why we didn't suss him out earlier. Trine wants to talk to you. Take very good care of yourself until we meet."

Talking to Trine reassured Louise that she was on the mend yet still in shock after what happened. "I'd never have forgiven myself if something had happened to you! I ought never to have asked you to store that laptop; I'm pleased Jasper handed it over to the police and hope Mike gets what he deserves."

No matter how much Trine reassured her she was fine, Louise couldn't get her head around what Mike did to her and knew she never would. *What if her best friend hadn't survived the assault?* Louise knew she'd never have coped if Trine had died.

Suddenly the trip to London and La Femme weren't important. Had it not been for the grace of God sending those men to rescue her, her best friend wouldn't be alive to tell the tale. It was a sobering thought and made Louise realise how fortunate she was to be rid of such a violent and unpredictable man.

CHAPTER NINETEEN

"WHAT DO YOU want?" Paige asked when Steve called to ask if he could come over later that afternoon.

"I just want to talk to you. Is that really so strange after all the years and history we've shared?" It was his biggest regret that he'd caused irreparable damage and it was too late to change it; their divorce was imminent.

"Alright, but only on the condition you don't upset Camilla. She and I are friends now and we run a business together."

Listening to her, Steve almost laughed. Not so long ago Paige detested every woman he'd engaged with, in particular Camilla and Abby. It proved how much she'd changed. While Steve had finally accepted the marriage was over, he hoped they could still be friends. "I've no intention of getting into an argument with anyone. You may not believe it, but I've changed. Gone are the days when I could stay up late and still work in the morning. It doesn't suit me anymore."

He sounded sad, yet Paige no longer cared. She and Liam had got engaged at Easter and hadn't told anyone since the divorce wasn't finalised yet. "You can come round at 3.00 pm. Camilla is seeing a friend and won't return until late. I'd prefer the two of you don't see one another." Paige didn't give a reason; her only concern was that in the event her sons came round, it'd be unethical if Steve and his former mistress were there at the same time.

Pleased they'd not argued, Paige called Liam. "I miss you so much! It's a drag that we can't be seen together in public," she said, debating inwardly as to whether she ought to mention Steve was coming over later.

"Are you doing something special today?" Liam asked. It still seemed unreal to him that he'd met and fallen in love with a woman with whom he wanted to spend the rest of his life. After everything he'd endured, Liam was finally beginning to put the past behind him. His physical wounds may have healed a lot sooner but the mental scars would never leave him, much like a soldier returning home after years in a warzone. Paige was a vital part of his healing process. "I've no particular plan. How about you?"

She hated she couldn't be honest with him where Steve was concerned. But Liam detested him because of all the pain and heartbreak he'd caused. "I'm invited to a friend's birthday party," she lied. "He and I used to work at the same café in Hammersmith years ago. I've hardly seen him since then." Wishing each other a nice day, Paige told him she'd call the next day. "We'll get tickets for that matinee you told me about in the West End. I've been looking forward to it for quite some time."

It was wonderful that Liam shared her interests; Steve's only pastime was to sit in a pub and drink. In her mind, it was odd they'd lasted as long as they did. Now she and Liam alternated between the house and Liam's flat, Paige decided to sell the former. The boys both had places of their own; Josh with a girlfriend he'd met at college, and when he wasn't travelling, Alec rented a one-bedroom flat in Kingston not far from Liam.

Paige and Liam enjoyed spending time with the boys and it

didn't take long for her sons to accept him as a permanent fixture in their mother's life. Lately, Alec spent the odd weekend with Steve, but Josh needed more time to decide if he wanted a relationship with his womanising father.

Indeed, apart from Steve, everyone had moved on with their lives.

As she waited for her ex to arrive, Paige considered how she no longer felt the burden of dressing nicely for him. Since Liam turned up in her life, she had no desire to make an impression on her ex. Steve made her feel insecure and unwanted, causing her to suppress her feelings of inadequacy behind a mask of heavy makeup.

Arriving on time, Steve handed her a bouquet of lilies of the valley, which he recalled were her favourites.

"You needn't buy me flowers," she said, breathing in the rich scent. Steve used to bring her flowers when they were dating and he picked her up outside her parent's house. Yet as soon as they married and Josh was born, the floral offerings stopped as he started having affairs.

Just thinking about that made her sad, even now when they were getting divorced.

"Come into the kitchen; I've made us sandwiches," she said, leading the way.

Counting down the hours until she would next see Liam, Paige couldn't help thinking how fortunate she was to have met a man who was honest and wouldn't dream of betraying her. Compared with Liam, Steve looked haggard and shabby in a pair of tight blue jeans that would be more becoming on a younger man.

"Are you okay?" she asked, then was instantly sorry she'd taken an interest. What Steve did and whom he saw was nothing to do with her anymore.

"I guess so. Did you know Mike and Abby split up?"

"Camilla mentioned it. She and Abby aren't as close as they used to be. I'll not pretend I'm the slightest bit interested in Abby. Her kind usually doesn't give a damn about anyone but themselves."

In comparison, Camilla had changed so much for the better. Recently, she'd met someone online with whom she had much in common. Brian was a retired police officer who at sixty was a lot older than Camilla, yet the two of them hit it off from the start. Tall, fair-haired and with the kindest blue eyes Paige had ever seen, Brian treated Camilla with respect and made her feel good about herself in a way no other man did. She still wore skirts that were too short and tight, yet Brian accepted her just the way she was and told her how much he loved her all the time until she eventually started to believe she was loveable and worthy of someone as decent as him. The woman who'd spent her entire life having casual sex in return for money so she could pay her bills and keep a roof over her head turned into a person who didn't permit men to exploit her.

Paige was immensely proud of Camilla's ability to take control of her life and not succumb to the life that ultimately destroyed her mother. The social heritage Camilla endured for so long had finally came to an end. After Paige sold the house, Camilla and Brian planned to live together in his small flat in Twickenham.

Returning to the present, Paige heard Steve say, "I'm sorry I behaved so badly towards you. If I could turn back the clock, I'd never have cheated on you."

"Oh, Steve, you and I both know that's a lie. You can't help the way you are. It's water under the bridge now."

"Yeah . . . I guess you're right. I'm only deluding myself I've changed. My old man had affairs left, right and centre. Mum, bless her soul, was the sweetest and most understanding person. She kept telling me it didn't matter as long as he always came home to her. I swore that I'd never be like him. But look at me! I've lived my life just the way he used to, betraying the people I love. And for what? To have sex with women I don't even care about. You know what that says about me, don't you? No wonder you don't love me anymore. I'm a pathetic liar and a cheat."

"Perhaps. But I think there's more behind it than that. Your mother was always so submissive and accepting. It probably contributed to the way you view women. That's no excuse for what you've done, merely an explanation."

"You really believe that?"

"I do, but I also think you're addicted to sex, in the same way an alcoholic is addicted to alcohol and a drug addict to drugs."

"I suspected as much yet I refused to admit it to myself until now. The bottom line is I don't know what I can do to change it." Steve looked so upset, Paige wanted to put her arms around him but knew that wouldn't be wise.

"Only you can do something about it. If there's a will there's always a way."

Registering what she told him, Steve finished his coffee in one gulp. "I'm fed up with Mike," he announced, changing the subject abruptly. "He went behind my back and accepted money from one of our clients. Mike deliberately tricked me: instead of splitting the profit equally between us, he deposited it into his own account. Now that would have been fine if it was his own money he was using, but it wasn't, it belonged to both of us. What's more, he physically attacked Trine Larsen when she refused to return his laptop, which Louise asked Trine and Jasper to store in their home."

"I thought as much. Mike's a very sick and dangerous man.

The man all of us used to view as a friend is a manipulative and selfish person capable of doing whatever it takes to get his own way." Paige was still reeling after Trine told her about the night Mike attacked her outside The Studio.

"I've come to realise I never knew him at all. We were friends for a long time. At least that's what I believed. I trusted him with my life and invested a substantial sum of money in his father's business. Look at me now: I'll never get back what I invested! I'll be lucky if I get a fraction of what I put in. Mike will have to declare himself bankrupt. Either way you view it, no one's going to invest in us now. Jasper and Robert told everyone they know what Mike did to Trine and me. I ought to be angrier than I am, but what's the point? It won't change what happened." Steve looked as if he was about to burst into tears.

"I used to think the two of you were scheming to withhold that money from me. Are you saying you had no inkling what Mike was up to?" Paige asked in a shaky voice.

"I've done many things I'm deeply ashamed of yet I'd never rob you of what's yours. Never! You're the woman I love and mother to our sons. Do you really think that badly of me?" Steve's eyes were moist.

"But you led me to believe you weren't willing to give me anything!" Paige snapped at him in frustration.

"I did nothing of the sort. I was upset you didn't love me anymore and said things I didn't mean."

"You really didn't have a clue about that money?"

"Of course not!"

Paige believed him. Steve was capable of a lot of things but he'd never withhold money from her. Face crumpling, she raised herself from her chair and went round to him. "I'm sorry I doubted you," she said, looking into his eyes.

"I'd never do something like that to you, we've got a history and kids for Christ's sake."

Overwhelmed by the enormity of what he'd told her, Paige kissed his cheek. "I'm pleased we've made up. It'll enable us to end our marriage with dignity."

"We'll always be part of each other's lives because of the kids," Steve told her. He paused. "What if I was to tell you I'll do whatever it takes to be the kind of man you deserve? We had it all. We can again."

Shaking her head, Paige sighed. "It's too late, Steve. I'm in love with another man. He's my soul mate and I wish to spend the rest of my life with him."

Nodding, Steve stood up and said, "I know. And that's what you deserve. Someone who loves and treats you with respect. Say hello to our sons from me." Walking towards the entrance, Steve turned to look at her one last time. "I'm sorry I failed you, you'll never know how much . . ."

As he left, Paige suppressed the urge to cry. She and Steve had finally put their grievances behind them and she couldn't wait to see the man she loved the following day.

Abby was in a bad mood. She'd managed to find a one bedroom flat for her and Timmy and furnished it with cheap furniture she'd bought in IKEA. Rumour had it Mike was still looking for them, yet was somewhat preoccupied since Louise discovered he'd committed fraud and Jasper handed in Mike's laptop to the police.

Camilla rarely spoke to her anymore. She'd met some man on a dating site and they were planning to live together in his flat.

Irrelevant of what Mike had put her through, Abby wished she had someone to lean on, yet relished living in her own place with her son. Timmy was now five months old and he meant everything to her. It was so unexpected, but her love for him had grown despite herself. She'd never wanted to be a mother after what her father put her through and her mother turned a blind eye to his abuse. The memory of it still caused her to get angry at life for giving her such a lousy deal.

Now Abby knew she would never have been able to forgive herself if she'd put Timmy up for adoption. He was a part of her and the only family she had. Watching him, fast asleep in the crib, Abby suddenly wished Steve was the father, not Mike. *Sooner or later Mike will find us,* she thought, fear curling in her belly. *It's only a matter of time. I've got to call Steve and ask for help.*

If only Abby hadn't admitted it was she who'd hacked into his account and stole £1.2 million when Mike lay motionless on the floor. Surely he was too incoherent to register what she'd said? Yet as long as there was even the smallest risk he'd remember it, Abby was petrified he would come after them and hurt her. After all, he had nothing more to lose.

It was the end of April and Abby knew she had sufficient funds to sustain the two of them for the rest of their lives. *Money won't keep us safe. Steve was adamant about having a paternity test. The time has come when our lives may depend on it,* she thought, dialling the familiar number on her mobile.

"Hi, it's me . . . I was wondering if you've got the time to come over? There's something I need to discuss with you."

"What is it that's so important it can't wait until the morning?" The last thing Steve needed right now was someone as manipulative as Abby to further add to his problems. His GP had referred him to a therapist who offered counselling to sex addicts. Unable to go through with it, Steve had turned down an appointment the following week.

"I'm just so worried that Mike will find us!" Abby's breath caught.

"He won't. Mike's not been arrested and charged with anything yet but it's only a matter of time. He won't risk further charges. Committing fraud and assaulting a woman are enough to put him in prison for quite some time."

"Will you come over if I change my mind about the paternity test?" When there was no reply at the other end of the line, Abby assumed Steve wasn't interested in finding out if Timmy was his.

"You're serious? You'll agree to a test?" Steve murmured, uncertain if she was stringing him along for her own purposes.

"Yes, I am. I'll rustle up something to eat. Bring a bottle of wine with you." She gave him the address and turned off her mobile, wondering what would happen if the test was positive. *I don't want to be the only one that Timmy relies on! No man is an island. Even someone as independent as I am needs security and love.*

Just like any other devoted parent, in the event something happened to her, Abby wanted her son to be safe and loved.

Chapter Twenty

"You're here, finally!" Abby stood aside and let Steve in. "I thought you might have changed your mind. Timmy's asleep. Would you like to see him?"

"Of course I came. You sounded so . . . strange; I had to come over. This place looks nice. You've made it look cosy with those bright curtains and couch. I never knew you liked strong colours." Steve took off his jacket and put it on the armchair in the corner of the living room.

"There's a lot you never knew about me. Can I get you something to drink?" she asked, thinking he'd changed somehow.

"No thanks, I'm fine. Let's cut to the chase. I want a paternity test. You said yes. It's the reason I came. Well, that and how off you sounded over the phone. It was almost as if you were scared of something. What's up?" Steve began to pace the room, distracted. Ever since he and Paige were divorced, he'd isolated himself in his bedsit and rarely showed up at work. Mike had betrayed him, their friendship was over and Steve's solicitor was dealing with the outcome. Now that he knew what Mike was capable of, Steve wanted nothing more to do with him, only his share of the business.

"You know what's wrong. I'm petrified Mike will find us." Abby sounded cagey.

"No, you're lying to me! Something must have happened between you . . . unless you level with me, Abby, I'll leave and you'll be hearing from my solicitor about the paternity test!" He'd turned over a new leaf in his life and didn't want her to ruin it with her lies and deception. She'd done it too many times and he'd repeatedly fallen for it. So much so, he'd lost his wife. Yet, out of all the women he'd been involved with, Abby was the only one he returned to, time after time. Why was that? "Right, I'm leaving!" Steve announced and grabbed his jacket from the chair.

Running after him, Abby begged him to stay. "Please don't leave! I will be straight with you. Let's go to the kitchen and talk." She stalled for time, yet again offering him something to drink.

"Tell me now or you'll not see me for dust!" Steve thought she looked different to her normal self. The hair extensions were gone and she wore loose-fitting slacks and an oversize T-shirt.

"Sit down. You're in for a shock."

Doing what she asked, Steve waited for her to say something.

Standing with her back to him, Abby covered her face with her hands. "I discovered Mike's PIN number in a drawer in the office. I was the one who hacked into his account. Mike figured it out and soon he'll find out where we live and punish me!"

Speechless, Steve shook his head and started to laugh. "You're pulling my leg, right? You're not a thief!" He'd known about her father and everything she'd been through, but this? But the longer it took for her to reply, the more Steve realised she was telling the truth.

"I've done it for years; hacking into men's accounts are my speciality. I learned from the best."

236

"But why? Surely, there's no reason to do something like that?" Steve was amazed she'd got away with it for so long.

"Don't look so concerned, I never stole from you."

"That's because you know I've not much in my account! If there was, would you have done it?" he asked, thinking she'd succeeded in duping both him and Mike, manipulating them with her seductive appearance and brash personality. Although deep down he suspected Abby was just as vulnerable as everyone else and had adopted a tough exterior to camouflage her insecurities.

"Of course not! I only stole from rich men who don't need all the money they've accumulated. Oh, don't look at me like that; I got a raw deal! My father was a paedophile and my mother turned a blind eye to what he did to me. For years he used to come into my room and force me to have sex with him, his own daughter! Ever since I escaped, I vowed to never let anyone hurt me again! I'm the one who's in control of my body and life now, not some man. The tables have turned. I never told anyone except Camilla. You only knew a fraction of what I went through. But please know I don't steal from people I care about and who can't afford it." As her confession came to an end, Abby felt an unexpected sense of relief.

Steve's eyes widened. "I wish I'd known . . . Oh, Abby, how come you never confided in me? We were pretty close."

"You think it's easy to talk about it? I spent years trying to come to terms with it! I know now that I never will. Besides, you got exactly what you wanted: a casual affair with no strings attached. I used to believe I never wanted to be a mother. Well, I was wrong. Timmy's everything to me and I'd die for him!" She began to pace the room. "Mike's coming after me, Steve! He's adamant about getting custody. If Mike takes Timmy from me, I've got nothing left!"

Seeing her so scared and distraught, Steve walked up to her and pulled her close to him. "I'm sorry I shouted at you. While I'm around, Mike will never hurt you again. But the state he's in, I wouldn't put it past him to try. To stoop so low as to assault a woman . . . You obviously heard what he did to Trine?"

"Yes and the awful thing is it could have been prevented if I'd only told the truth! When Camilla called and said Mike attacked Trine, I wanted to come clean. Yet if I had, Timmy wouldn't have his mother because I'd be arrested! God alone knows what might have happened to my son. Social Services would probably have taken him away from me." By now Abby was sobbing. Steve handed her a tissue from the box on the table, and watched as she wiped her eyes and nose. "Why didn't the police arrest Mike for what he did to Trine? What's taking them so long?"

Pulling her even closer to him, Steve replied, "Leave Mike to me. I'll make sure he never comes near you and Timmy! He's fortunate to have such a loving mother as you," he whispered in her hair.

"Mike's got it into his head Timmy looks like him when he was a baby!" Abby continued to cry even harder, imagining how awful she'd feel if Mike turned out to be the father.

"Are you saying you wish someone else was his father?" Steve tilted her face and looked into her eyes. She'd been crying so hard they were red and puffy.

"What do you think? Of course I am! You and I were always so careful . . . except that one night when we forgot to use protection. Everything happened so fast. One minute we were back together, the next Mike and I were dating . . ."

"So Timmy really could be mine, then?" Steve had been a lousy father to his own sons. If the baby turned out to be his,

Steve thought he deserved much better than having him as his father.

"No, oh, I don't know! Mike's probably the father; I stopped taking the pill so we'd conceive a child. But the timing . . . I thought it'd get me what I wanted: financial security for the rest of my life. Trusting Mike was the biggest mistake I ever made!"

"You can't be one hundred per cent certain Mike's the father. The only way to know for sure is to have a paternity test. It's what I've wanted since Timmy was born."

Sighing, Abby disentangled herself from him. "You and me . . . we had a fling. It ended a while ago. Timmy's my son, irrespective of who is the father. All I ask of you is that you help me to protect him from Mike. Can you do that for me, Steve?"

She wasn't sure if she wanted more from him than friendship. For the first time in her life, Abby had someone who belonged to her and she wasn't keen to share.

Eyes narrowing, Steve shook his head. "No. You can't do this to me, Abby. You can't just request I'm here for you both only as a friend. I need to know if he's mine! If he is, I want to be part of his life. Take it or leave it."

He looked so determined, Abby had no choice but to nod. "If that's what it takes for you to help us . . . so be it."

"Good. Now, try to get some sleep. I'll sleep on the couch."

"Mike Kershaw, I'm arresting you for the assault of Mrs Trine Larsen and for withholding money from your business partner," said the young police officer. He and another officer had turned up at Kershaw & Matthews' offices one weekday morning in early May.

"You can't arrest me without sufficient evidence!" Mike was outraged. "Trine Larsen stole my laptop. It's her you should be giving a hard time, not me! My ex-wife put her up to it. Ever since I dumped her, Louise's hell-bent on revenge!" Ignoring the outburst, one police officer proceeded to handcuff Mike, while the other warned him that everything he said may be used against him in a court of law.

Forming a semi-circle outside in the corridor, members of staff eavesdropped on the conversation and could hardly believe what they'd heard. They'd never seen their boss as incensed. Rumour had it Steve was cutting his losses and wanted to sell his share of the business to Mike.

Handcuffed and humiliated in full view of his staff, Mike was seething with anger.

"Mind your head," one of the officers warned as they shoved him into the car taking him to the station.

Hours later, surrounded by his legal team, Mike was released on bail until the prosecutor had compiled sufficient evidence against him to substantiate a court hearing. Taking a cab home, Mike was furious with Louise and Abby for causing him to spend hours in a filthy police cell. *If Louise had only handed over that bloody laptop to me instead of the Larsens, today's events would never have occurred*, he thought. *And as for that slut, Abby . . . she'll never succeed in taking my son away from me. I'll apply for custody.*

Within a week, Kershaw & Matthews Limousine Service lost most of their clients. The minicab firm with which they'd recently extended their agreement immediately asked their legal adviser to terminate the contract since the limousine service ceased to deliver on what they'd promised. The news was a devastating blow during a period that saw one client after another take their custom elsewhere, putting their trust in the competition.

In addition, Mike feared he would lose all his savings and risk not having sufficient funds to raise for his bail. In the event he was found guilty of fraud, the amount that was left after Abby stole £1.2 million would go straight towards paying Trine for the injury he'd inflicted on her arm.

All that remained was Steve's share of the company and Mike had neither the means nor the intention of buying it from him.

The following weeks were the hardest Steve had ever experienced as he and Abby awaited the outcome of the paternity test. Concerned about what Mike might do to them if he found them, Steve volunteered to temporarily move in with the little family for their protection, and together they located a bigger flat for them all. The new flat was situated in Kew, not far from the shops and station, and with a bit of luck, Mike wouldn't find out where they lived as it wasn't an area he normally visited. Furnishing it with a mixture of Steve and Abby's belongings, they moved in shortly after they'd signed the tenancy agreement and made sure the locksmith installed a safety lock that would prevent anyone from breaking in.

Working all hours to get the flat organised and ready to move into, it dawned on Steve how much he'd turned his life around in a relatively short period of time since he and Paige were divorced. She'd called shortly after, saying the boys were willing to meet up with him and that she and Liam had moved into a bigger flat after he sold his.

The weirdest development of all was that Camilla and her boyfriend, Brian, were now living in Paige and Steve's old home. Paige and Camilla's matchmaking service had gone from strength to strength, so much so they branched out with another online service, catering to people who were gay and bisexual. It was Camilla who suggested that they rent an office in the high street. In addition, she and Brian made an offer on the house. Delighted the property her father bestowed to her didn't have to be put up for sale and sold to a stranger, Paige immediately accepted.

Now, sitting in his new, possibly permanent, home, Steve too stood on the brink of a new life. He'd already furnished the bedrooms and nursery to ensure Timmy would be comfortable, surrounded by his toys and sleeping in his old cot. One afternoon he took a few minutes' rest on the couch in the large living room. Surrounded by half-unpacked boxes, he reflected on how much his life changed.

I do hope Timmy's my son. Josh and Alec will be shocked yet eventually as happy as I'll be if the test proves I am the father. I'll get the chance to be the sort of father I should have been when they were young . . .

His thoughts were interrupted when Abby walked in.

"Camilla called earlier. Apparently, Mike was arrested and let out on bail until there's sufficient evidence against him." She couldn't believe the police hadn't kept him in custody. "Oh, Steve, Timmy and I have been through hell. Ever since that night when we had to escape from Mike, I've had nightmares!"

"Come and sit next to me on the couch." As she did so, he put his arm around her and couldn't help thinking how good it felt to have her next to him. "Abby, I gave you my word you would never have to worry about Mike. Please be honest with me. Do you think Timmy's my son?

"I honestly don't know. Why is that test result not back yet? What's taking so long?"

"We must stay patient. I'm sure it won't take much longer. We'll soon find out if I'm Timmy's dad." The alternative didn't bear thinking about. As far as Steve was concerned, he'd cut all ties with Mike and gained another son. It no longer seemed to matter as much whether he was Timmy's natural father.

"I genuinely hope Timmy's our son, not mine and Mike's," Abby whispered, leaning her head against his shoulder.

Stunned by her admission, Steve replied, "I don't deserve him. Just think of the pain I've caused everyone."

"Everyone deserve a second chance to put things right. You and Paige sorted out your grievances; we did as well. What I did to Mike was despicable yet nothing compared to what he did to Louise, Trine and you. Mike stole from you. It serves him right if he loses everything. Only then will he know how it feels to be shafted." She was determined to stop blaming herself for what she did. Abby's life so far had been inundated with men who abused her trust. First her father, then the countless men who attempted to control her. Mike pretended he loved and cared about her yet all along the only thing he wanted and what Louise denied him, was a child.

"I'll make a deal with him. If Mike agrees to buy me out for a fair sum, I won't press charges against him for going behind my back and cheating on me. If he refuses I'll make a statement, saying he attacked you and Timmy in his home that night. Either way, Mike will not press charges against you for hacking into his account. My lips are sealed."

Abby's eyes lit up at the prospect of Mike ending up destitute unless he agreed to Steve's conditions.

Pulling her closer to him, Steve said, "It's odd but I'm not in love with Paige any more. Don't get me wrong, she was the love of my life for a long time and it was I who ruined everything. Paige and I met and married when we were too young. Kids, really. When the boys came along I felt trapped. I've no excuse for my behaviour. I'm addicted to sex, Abby. Just like an alcoholic is to booze and a drug addict is to drugs. But it's too late for regrets. I've got to sort myself out. I will go and see that therapist after all. I'll not give up. It's evident to me that my father's womanising caused me to be like him. Kids don't take any notice of what they're told; only what you do. Actions speak louder than words."

"You're not in love with Paige?" It was as if Abby hadn't heard his latter admission as she stared at him in disbelief. Every single time they'd argued and split up in the past, Steve had told her Paige was the only woman for him.

"That's right." Steve paused. "I've got feelings for you, Abby. I always felt that way about you. It's funny, really. The sex addict and the victim of sexual abuse, wouldn't you agree? I'm not referring to the abuse as such – that's despicable and people like your father deserve to be severely punished – what I mean is that I think I'm falling in love with a woman who was subjected to the most horrific abuse. You must, quite rightly, detest any form of intimacy with a man. Especially a sex maniac like me."

"Actually, Steve, you're wrong. I've got feelings for you as well. I always felt there was something between us . . . it just happened gradually, I've tried to deny it, but I can't. The way that you've stepped up to the mark, ensuring Timmy and I are okay – I've been so touched by everything you've done for us. Steve, I . . . I think I want us to give it another go . . . how about you?"

Surprised she felt the same way, Steve smiled. "We're drawn to each other like magnets, aren't we? Yes, I do. Let's take things slowly." He was painfully aware of how difficult it must be for her to put her trust in any man.

"Make love to me," Abby whispered. "I need you to make me feel safe and loved." She'd never expressed herself like that before.

Taken aback by her request, Steve asked, "Are you sure that's what you want? I'll promise to protect you from Mike – we don't need to do this if you don't want to."

"No! That's just it: I'm not scared of Mike, or any man, anymore. I can't live my life that way any longer! For my sake as much as my son's. Mike will never be Timmy's father – you are, regardless of the outcome of that test." Abby raised herself from the couch and took his hand in hers. "How about we make sure that Timmy's okay and have an early night? It's high time we had some quality time to ourselves."

"I'd say that's an excellent idea!" Smiling broadly, Steve followed her upstairs, admiring her figure as she checked on the sleeping baby, then smiled and led him to the bedroom. "Come here!" He playfully pulled her down on the large bed and gently caressed her face and neck, exploring every part of her body until she placed his hand between her legs.

"You know how I like it. We've known each other for too long to not know what the other wants," she said, caressing him where he wanted to be touched the most.

As he watched her legs straddle around either side of his back, Steve whispered in her ear, "It never felt this good or special with anyone else." He reached for the condom on the bedside table and gave it to her to put on him.

Hours later, lying entwined in each other's arms, Abby said, "Yes. I think I'm falling in love with you too." Apart from her son, it was the first time she'd ever expressed feelings towards another human being.

They received the outcome of the paternity test the following day. To their utmost joy and immense relief, it proved without doubt that Steve was indeed Timmy's father.

From that moment onwards, Abby and Steve knew they'd been given a second chance to be happy and this time around they would do whatever it took to not destroy it.

CHAPTER TWENTY-ONE

May 2016

Louise was so busy with La Femme it wasn't until the end of May she managed to take a week off and travel to London. Exhausted with everything she had to undertake on her own, including the daily running of the boutique, plus the window display and the stocktake, Louise was pleased when her part-time assistant, a young girl on a gap year from university, volunteered to look after everything while she was away. Lina was accustomed to the daily routine, fiercely loyal and loved by all. She also had an uncanny talent for spotting which designer would be successful and didn't mind staying late in the event a customer called to say they were delayed in picking up a garment on their way home from work. Already La Femme was a roaring success among Malmö's discerning ladies and even extended to Danish customers frequently visiting the shop in their quest for unusual clothing and costume jewellery.

Louise and Nicklas met up at least twice a week, still shaken up by what happened to Åsa and conscious of how close she had been to dying that night. Now that she was on the mend, Åsa made the decision to semi-retire.

One evening shortly before Louise's departure, Nicklas invited her to have dinner with him in his flat in Ribersborg. An extremely affluent area close to shops, restaurants and coastline with a sandy beach and views over the Öresund strait, Louise hesitated for a minute then thought better of it and accepted his invitation. She'd visited in the recent past but only for a brief time to have a drink prior to eating in a restaurant.

Nicklas' flat was enormous, with a roof terrace that was nearly as big as Gabriella's. He'd decorated it by himself and Louise thought it was lovely with its large sash windows and excellent view of Turning Torso and the West Harbour. The furniture was bold and exclusive, most of it purchased abroad during Nicklas' extensive travels.

After Louise told Nicklas about her trip and explained Gabriella and Åsa would be looking after Rufus while she was in London, Nicklas asked, "Will you take some time to think in which direction you want us to go? I'm happy we're so close yet I cannot deny my feelings for you indefinitely." She meant too much to him. They'd lost decades in relationships with people who weren't right for them.

Not sure how to respond to his question, Louise whispered, "I'll think about it . . ." Nodding, Nicklas smiled, his eyes full of warmth and kindness.

Everywhere they went, everyone looked at them. At first Louise imagined it was because they had different colours of skin. That was probably true to an extent, but then it dawned on her they were simply a nice couple, both tall and good-looking.

Seating them in the open plan kitchen and living area, Nicklas laid the oval oak table with crystal plates and glasses. The centrepiece was a large oriental porcelain vase with red roses. He'd made the effort to shop and cook; normally a catering firm delivered pre-ordered food but tonight was special and he wanted to lovingly prepare dishes she'd enjoy. For their starter they had avocado mousse with smoked salmon; the main course was porter steak with gravy and pommes duchesse; and dessert was Louise's favourite: crêpes suzette with lemon sorbet. Everything tasted delicious, just like the expensive wine. Filling up her glass between dishes, Louise started to feel slightly drunk and relaxed.

"Thank you for serving such a wonderful meal. I've not eaten as much as I've done tonight! Gabriella is a great cook but your cooking is on par with a haute cuisine chef in a Michelin-starred restaurant." She smiled happily at him.

Nicklas thought Louise looked exquisite in a loose-fitting dress, flat shoes and her hair in a knot, strands falling down her ears and neck. He'd put on a blue suit, starched white shirt and looked extremely sexy in a laid-back kind of way. They'd finished eating when he suggested they retire to the roof terrace. "We'll get a great view of the West Harbour up there." Saying he'd clear up in the morning, Nicklas put an arm around Louise's shoulder and pushed the button of the recently installed lift that took them upstairs to the roof terrace.

Standing so close together in the confined space, Louise looked down at her feet. She'd visited his flat several times yet had never had quite as much to drink. Tonight was the first time he'd suggested they spend time on his roof terrace.

Taking her hand in his, Nicklas led Louise out of the elevator and onto the terrace that looked as if it came straight out of a fairy tale, with large windows and a water fountain on one side and black and white sculptures on the other. The chrome table in the centre and white leather sofa were the icing on the cake.

"Wow! It's beautiful up here. Did you design it yourself?" she asked, admiring the breathtaking view.

"Yes, I did. I wanted to put my own personal stamp on it."

He wanted to tell her he'd been thinking of her. Louise used to love to decorate her parent's house in Limhamn, yet to their chagrin she'd lost interest in becoming an interior designer and signed up with the modelling agency instead.

Standing there, admiring the view of the blue sky above them, Louise didn't know what to say. He'd gone out of his way to please her and was now telling her about his involvement with children in need and animal welfare.

"I don't wish to come across as vulgar and boasting," he said. "My chosen charities are subsidised through my galleries, not directly in my name. I've recently become patron of a governmental body whose main aim is to initiate a deeper understanding and dialogue between the residents and immigrants of other cultures." Nicklas wished he could kiss her. She looked so beautiful in that dress, her eyes matching the colour of the sky.

"You must love this place," she said, wondering if he wanted to kiss her as much as she wanted him to.

"I do but not remotely as much as I love you." He'd had enough of keeping his feelings to himself. "Do you recall the poet Karin Boye? She wrote a poem I used to recite to you when we were young. It's as poignant now as it was then."

Smiling, Louise replied, "Mamma and Pappa loved her poems too. You're referring to *The Best*?"

"That's the one."

"I used to know it by heart." Louise felt warm inside at the memory.

"I still recall the first verse. It reads: 'The best that we possess we cannot give away. We can not write it either and neither can we say.'"

Listening to him, Louise's eyes welled up. Nicklas had an uncanny way of pulling at her heartstrings.

"Why won't you let me into your heart?" he asked, eyes locking with hers.

She tried so hard to maintain a respectful distance between them. He wasn't sure if it was because she was still in love with her ex-husband or scared of admitting she still had feelings for him. Perhaps it was a combination of both. Looking down at the panorama beneath them, Louise moved closer to him and said, "I never stopped loving you, Nicklas. We were so young and innocent back then. Things happened that neither of us was mature enough to handle. That's life. I'm sorry I wasn't around to support you when Mimmi died."

Tears streamed down her face. He was such a big part of her youth. They'd been deeply in love and when tragedy struck, neither of them had the tools to deal with it. She buried herself in her modelling career, then put her faith in a man who never loved her and adjusted to a life that wasn't what she imagined it to be. He was left to pick up the pieces of a shattered life, then married a friend, hoping it would restore everything he'd lost . . . which it didn't. No wonder neither of them was happy. Each of them had lived in a bubble of pretence.

Still, it wasn't all bad. Far from it.

"You're avoiding my question. What's the answer, Louise? Are you afraid I'll hurt you, because he did?"

"Not at all. Mike meant a lot to me but nothing compared to how I feel for you. I know you would never let me down."

"Then what is it that prevents you from loving me? Is it the colour of my skin?" He sounded confused and hurt.

Outraged he'd even ask her something like that, Louise looked him in the eyes. "I'll pretend you never said that. I'm not racist as you're well aware! The reason I don't want us to be more than friends is because I'm scared that if we don't work out I'll lose your friendship and that is hugely important to me. We lost each other once. I don't think I could cope if it happened again."

"But that's ridiculous! You'll never lose me again. I'll always be your friend. That will never change. We're adults now. A man and woman who love each other. Take all the time you need to decide where we go from here. But while you're in London, ask yourself if you miss me. I miss you all the time. Before we met at that party, I'd resigned myself to never seeing you again. Now I refuse to give up on the chance of a life together! I love you, Louise."

It was dark outside when he drove her back to Fridhem. As he helped her out of the car, Nicklas kissed the palm of her hand, the scent of his aftershave lingering in the air. "Please return to me soon. We'll meet up when you get back." It was his way of telling her he thought it was best they kept a distance until she knew what she wanted.

"I will think about it. Please don't give up on me just yet," she whispered, in turmoil.

Waiting for her to unlock the main door of the building and step inside, Nicklas waved goodbye and drove off into the darkness of the night.

When Louise arrived at Heathrow she realised how much she'd missed London's buzz and cosmopolitan pulse. Everywhere she looked, travellers wore casual summer clothes and carried suitcases. They were either departing somewhere or returning to London, like her.

After she collected her suitcase and went through passport control, Louise walked into the arrival lounge where Jasper and Zack awaited her.

Embracing her warmly, Jasper informed her Trine was waiting

for her at home. "She spent the morning preparing for the forthcoming fashion show. I honestly don't know how she copes! You always kept a cool head; we're thrilled you've opened your own boutique. Trine's been in contact with several designers and can't wait to tell you about them."

"I missed all of you so much. Malmö's a great city and cultural hub yet there are times when I ask myself if it's where I want to spend the remainder of my life. Then all I have to do is visit Limhamn's Harbour and I know I made the right decision to move back."

"You look great! The life you've made for yourself clearly agrees with you. Mind you, you could do with putting on a few kilos. Why the hell are women so keen to appear too slim? Seriously, Louise, I'm so pleased you're here." Jasper turned to look at his son. "Just imagine how happy Mamma will be when she sees Louise again!"

Zack grinned in response. "We've all been looking forward to your visit. I made up your bed in the spare room." For a split second Louise and Zack's eyes locked, both recalling the night she'd taken an overdose.

"I'm fine, you needn't worry about me anymore. I was in a bad place back then," she whispered so as to not involve Jasper in their conversation.

"I know you were. Mamma told me what Mike did to you and her. He's not part of our lives anymore." Zack's eyes clouded over at the memory of what might have happened to both of them.

"Are you okay?" Louise asked, a concerned tone in her voice.

"Yeah, I've just finished college and can't decide what I want to do next. Perhaps I'll take a degree in economics."

Wearing faded blue jeans with holes in the knees and baggy T-shirt, Zack wore his hair in a ponytail and had grown a beard.

Looks aside, he reminded her of herself at his age. Being a teenager in the present era wasn't as easy as when she was young. There were so many distractions and the internet dominated everyone's lives.

As she sat in Jasper's old station wagon on the way towards the family home in Putney, Louise felt excited to see her best friend after months apart. So much had happened since she and Trine last saw each other.

They'd barely parked outside the front of the familiar property, when Louise heard a voice shout, "You're finally here! I can't believe we've not seen each other for so long!"

Jumping out of the car, Louise threw her arms around her friend, took a step back and said, "Your hair's longer. It suits you and you're wearing a skirt! What's happened to you while I've been away? Are you finally taking my advice to show your beautiful legs?"

Laughing, Trine shrugged her shoulders. "Maybe. I've ordered quite a lot from Filippa K's recent collection. My skirt comes from the latest delivery. They're selling like hot cakes." Trine did a twirl to show Louise how versatile it was, with deep pockets on either side and a high waistline that accentuated her slim figure and long, shapely legs.

"Mmm. I like it. Perhaps I ought to buy it as well."

"I'll give you one when we visit The Studio in the morning," Trine said, giving Louise another hug.

She and Trine went to The Studio the following day. As she browsed the latest collections, Louise thought the place looked exactly the same as when she left. "What's it like to run it on your own? La Femme's taking up most of my time. There are times when I wish we could work together again." Louise had a wistful expression on her face.

"I do as well. Not least having someone to talk to and brainstorm with. Jasper's great but he's not a woman! I keep telling him he's got to leave anything to do with styling to me. Jokes aside, we've had a great time, getting to know each other as partners, which is very different to being husband and wife." Trine peered closely at Louise. "So what's going on between you and Nicklas? Last time we spoke over the phone, I got the impression the two of you are just friends."

"I've told him I need more time to decide what I want. Oh, Trine, this is exactly what I referred to earlier! I so wish you could be there, talking some sense into me. Nicklas wants more than just friendship! What if I lose him again?" She looked so upset that Trine put her arms around her.

"It's less than a year since you met each other again and you've been divorced for nearly two years. If I were you, I'd think carefully about what you want. Sometimes meeting a person you had strong feelings for in the past plays tricks with your mind and heart. It's much too easy to confuse what you felt for him then with what you feel for him now. People change. Nicklas and you were kids back then. However, if you still love him, what's stopping you from giving it another go? Just make sure you're with him for the right reasons, not because you're sentimental and lonely."

As usual Trine's direct approach helped Louise to make sense of her feelings. "You're in the wrong line of work! You should be a counsellor instead," she joked with a hint of seriousness.

"Only you can decide what will happen between you and Nicklas. He's right, you've got to make up your mind to give it another go or just stay friends, even if it means you'll risk losing each other again. It's your life and only you can decide if you want more than just his friendship. I will give you one piece of advice: regretting what you didn't have the courage to do is worse than failing. At least be in the position to know you've tried."

"You're of the opinion I ought to enter into a relationship with him?" Louise asked in a subdued voice. "It's not that I don't have feelings for him – I do."

"Then what's stopping you? You're not as young as you used to be and God alone knows what you went through with Mike."

"I'm scared, Trine. I'm so scared Nicklas hasn't dealt with his past. I told him I don't want to lose our friendship if things don't work out between us . . . I know I should trust him when he says he's dealt with his demons, but his mother died of a broken heart. She drank herself to death when Nicklas' father left them. I used to believe Sweden wasn't as difficult to live in for people of mixed race. Nicklas got me to re-evaluate everything I believed and trusted. The question is, has he really faced his past demons or is he just pretending so that he can get on with his life?"

"I see what you mean. Listen to me, Louise, Nicklas was a young boy when his mother died. He's an adult now. Whichever way he worked through some of the issues in the past doesn't necessarily reflect who he is now. You've got to give him credit for everything he's achieved despite the raw deal he and his mother got. You've also got to believe him when he tells you he's come to terms with the past. That kind of pain never goes away. The memories will live with him forever. But that needn't affect your life together. Nicklas' memories aren't altogether bad. The two of you have your own happy memories as well.

"He and you were in love; I believe you still are. The way his mother dealt with what happened to them isn't how Nicklas would have dealt with it. Of course he resents what happened, in

255

particular the way they were treated as social outcasts. That's water under the bridge now and has been for a very long time. The guy loves you. If you love him too, you'll have to take a gamble just like everyone else or face being alone for the rest of your life." Trine gave Louise a hug.

"I hear you. The problem is, Nicklas isn't the only person with a past. I have as well. My parents died when I was too young to cope. I married Mike, whom everyone who met him told me was wrong for me. When he dumped me I nearly killed myself. Yet here I am, starting afresh in my native city, with a new business and my own flat. You're right, life *is* a gamble, and sometimes you lose. I lost out big time yet I found something better than what I had with Mike. I can't start all over again, Trine! I just can't brush myself off and go through what I went through when Mike left me. Nicklas is nothing like him yet I've got to be absolutely sure I don't make another mistake. As you so rightly put it, life's simply too short and precious to waste."

"So take the time you need to decide. You're forgetting one thing. In the past couple of years you've become much stronger and more resilient. Now you can either live like Gabriella and not live life to its full potential because you're too scared to live it on your own terms, or you can throw caution to the wind and live it as you please. When I found out about Gabriella and what happened to Åsa, all I could think was how sad it would be if after everything they went through they'd still continued to hide their feelings. Luckily, they've moved on and that's what you have to do as well. What better way than you and Nicklas doing it together?" Listening to her friend's advice, Louise felt much better.

Racism, prejudice and betrayal were part of life everywhere. She and Nicklas had endured so much yet never gave up. It would be a great shame if she gave up on them just because she was scared of what the future held. Her life would be lonely and empty without him in it.

Louise had spent three days in London when Trine introduced her to the new designers she'd researched before Louise arrived. "I know you will love them! One's a costume jewellery designer, another designs her own take on casual clothing, the third trained with Pucci and Cavalli. They've a unique style and approach to fashion."

"Sounds interesting. Which designer will we visit first?"

Hours later, returning to Putney in the early evening, Louise was so excited she could hardly wait for the items she'd ordered to be delivered to La Femme. "Wow! That costume jewellery designer was the weirdest yet most fun of the lot of them! I wish I'd placed more orders with her." She'd placed orders with everyone totalling a small fortune, yet was confident La Femme's clientele would snap everything up in no time.

"You were right to buy from them. Their designs will be the talk of the town! The Studio isn't as versatile as La Femme."

Louise and Trine spent most of the time gossiping until the early hours of the morning. They were on their own in the rustic kitchen, when Trine told her about what happened when Mike attacked her outside The Studio. Listening to her, Louise felt stricken with guilt that she'd asked her friends to store Mike's laptop in their home.

"He's got it into his head that it's your fault that damn laptop went missing," Trine said. "He's out on bail until the court hearing. He attacked Steve as well and Abby left him, taking the baby with her. She and Steve are in a relationship. Paige and her lover, Liam, are getting married. Oh, yes, I nearly forgot, Camilla met someone online! She and Paige started their own online matchmaking service for mature people. They've made a mint out of it so far! Gone are the days when Camilla relied on some man to pay her bills."

"Sounds like everyone is getting on with their lives, me included." Louise had almost decided what she wanted from Nicklas.

"How about you take a trip down memory lane and visit Barnes? I'll drive you. I've got to make an appearance at The Studio. We'll go out for a drink later. Just call me on my mobile when you want me to pick you up."

"What if I bump into someone I used to know? Oh, Trine, I don't think it's such a good idea to go there . . ." Deep down Louise wanted to see the house she and Mike lived in.

"You're referring to Mike, aren't you? He won't be there. He's got more important matters on his mind. He stands to lose everything if he's convicted of committing fraud and assaulting me."

"You're right, Mike's nothing to do with me anymore. I won't let him dictate where I go! You don't have to drive me. I'll catch a cab in the street."

"But I don't mind. Are you sure you'll be okay on your own? What if you feel awful when you see the house?"

"I'll be fine. We'll see each other later."

It was the first day in June and Louise had no idea what the day had in store for her.

CHAPTER TWENTY-TWO

June 2016

Louise asked the cab driver to drop her off outside Sainsbury's in Barnes High Street. As she climbed out, she looked around, her initial impression being that nothing had changed since she sold the house and rented a flat in Fulham. *Everything's the same as it was when I left*, she thought, recognising the quaint shops, estate agents and hairdressing salons. Totally Swedish was exactly where it used to be when she shopped there, buying the food and sweets she missed from home.

Walking further down the payment towards The Sun Inn, where she and Mike often had a drink and a snack at the weekend, Louise sat down on a bench by the pond opposite the pub. *I used to love living here. It reminded me of the nature and scenery in Malmö . . .* Suddenly she wasn't sure if she wanted to see the house in case it brought back too many bad memories, but something was drawing her onwards.

Eventually she passed her old house on a side street and liked what she saw. It was obvious it was well looked after, judging by the neatly mown lawn at the front, nice blue curtains and no waste bin or rubbish in sight. Taking a deep breath, she took one last look, said her goodbyes, and moved on to browse the shops and cafés on either side of the road.

Standing outside the greengrocer's where she regularly bought fruit and vegetables, ordering dill on a weekly basis to put in salads and garnish on food, Louise had the distinct feeling she was being watched. She looked around, but no one was there. She shook off the feeling; it must have been her imagination.

The weather was hot and sunny so she took off her jacket and put it under her arm. She was about to cross the street, when a voice called out her name.

"Louise? It is you! I thought as much. What the hell are you doing here?"

There was no mistaking that voice. It belonged to the man she had shared her life with for over twenty years. *It can't be! Trine told me he was recently released on bail . . . Oh, why didn't I listen to my intuition? If I did I wouldn't be in this situation...*

Louise's initial instinct was to turn around and march into a ladies' boutique next to a pharmacy further up the pavement, where she would feel safe. Seeing as it was a Saturday afternoon, lots of people were out walking their dogs and shopping. Families were having a coffee break in the cafés and the sun was shining from a clear blue sky. She stayed in the boutique for nearly ten minutes, then came out, hoping he'd realised she wanted nothing to do with him. There was no sign of him and she sighed with relief.

Walking back towards The Sun Inn, eager to have a quiet drink and call Trine, Louise was on the verge of changing her mind and calling for a cab to bring her back to Putney, when she felt a hand on her shoulder.

"You little bitch! I know you've been spreading lies about me. It's thanks to you that I've lost everything!" Mike grabbed her hand, causing her to grimace with pain. "Unless you keep your mouth shut I'll hurt you even more!" he hissed in her ear, froth appearing at either side of his mouth. Praying passers-by would notice her distress and come to her rescue, Louise thought, *What everyone's said about him is true. Mike's mentally unstable and dangerous. If he manages to get me away from here, anything could happen!* Her heart beat so fast she thought she would die.

"No one will come to your rescue. You'll never screw me over again." Mike whispered, eyes red and puffy from drinking himself into a stupor. "I've got you exactly where I want you. Poor, silly Louise! Did you really imagine you would get away with what you did to me? You couldn't let it go, you just had to involve the Larsens and the Sturgesses." With a firm grip on her arm, Mike dragged her to where he'd parked his Jaguar, on the corner of the side street adjacent to the pub.

If only I can talk him into having a drink with me. It's my one chance to call Trine and Jasper, she thought, smelling his sour breath and feeling his sweaty hand on hers.

"Get into the back and keep your head down!" Mike pushed her so hard fresh tears of pain seeped down her cheeks.

"Haven't you caused me enough misery?" she said in a loud voice, desperate for someone to hear her and wonder what was going on. "I gather this is how you treated Trine?" Inwardly she kept thinking what a fool she'd been to visit Barnes.

"That bitch and her idiot of a husband refused to hand over my laptop! Jasper even had the nerve to give it to the police! You denied me the family I always wanted. Now I've discovered Timmy's not mine. Steve's the father! My so-called best mate betrayed me, and Abby stole £1.2 million from my account. If it wasn't for you telling everyone about my laptop, I'd at least have my business, but thanks to you I've had to buy Steve out with what little money I had left in my account. You're the reason I've ended up with no son, no business and soon no roof over my head! I've got to pay my solicitor's fees." He was spitting in her face.

Hearing him blame her for everything that had gone wrong in his life, Louise finally understood that the man she was married to for twenty years was mentally disturbed. Unless her friends came to her rescue, she may never be able to return to the man she loved.

She wiped her face with the sleeve of her dress. "After everything you put me through, I'm not scared of you, only disgusted. You've got exactly what you deserve. I hope you get a long sentence and rot in prison." She was shouting at him now, completely oblivious as to what he had in store for her. She was the best friend he'd ever had, bailing him out time after time and he repaid her by dumping her on their wedding anniversary. Yet everything she said fell on deaf ears. Mike was too far gone to reason with. He'd long since lost the ability to differentiate between acceptable and unacceptable behaviour.

Unknown to her, earlier that day Mike had visited a café in Fulham where he and Louise had frequently met for coffee in the past. Passing The Studio on his way home, he'd nearly had a fit when he saw Louise step into a black cab. Following close behind, Mike was delighted to finally get the opportunity to punish her for everything she'd caused him. He'd dreamed of the day he'd get her to himself and teach her a lesson, and now that day had arrived.

"I've had enough to deal with where you and your friends are concerned. Louise wants this, Louise wants that!" he mimicked her. "It's all I ever had from you for over twenty years. You demanding I did what you wanted. Your bloody career, house and business. Not forgetting all the times I had to listen when you whinged about your parents. You want a trip down memory lane? I'll gladly accommodate you."

"Okay, why not? Let's go inside the pub and have a drink." Louise felt a glimmer of hope. "I don't want to argue with you, Mike. After you left me I tried so hard to get on with my life. At least have the guts to explain it to me calmly. We always used to enjoy a drink in The Sun Inn."

He turned off the engine. Perhaps she had got through to him?

"Alright. But only if you keep that damn mouth of yours shut."

Leaning over the front seat, Mike watched her open the door of the back seat and attempt to get out, then pulled her back inside and slammed the door shut. "Did you imagine I'd let you get away so easily?" he asked, mocking her.

As he put a hand on her thigh, Louise felt his fingernails dig into her skin until he drew blood. Gritting her teeth, she said, "I never knew you hated me so much. Please, let's go inside the pub and have a drink." Feeling his nails dig deeper, she cried out in pain.

"Silly, stupid Louise. I bet Aunty Gabriella's over the moon we're divorced. That bloody lesbian hates my guts! Now that you've returned to Malmö, perhaps you and that guy you used to date when you were young are reunited? The old bag couldn't stop talking about him every chance she got. What was his name ... got it! Nicklas." Mike was getting more incensed by the minute.

Ignoring his comment, Louise made a snap decision. If she pretended she cared, then maybe she could get rid of him "Why didn't you tell me I made you unhappy? Can't we talk about it in the pub?" There and then, she knew exactly how Trine must have felt when Mike attacked her.

Eyes narrowing, Mike replied, "Yes, why not? Let's pick up from where we left off. After all, we never got the opportunity to celebrate our 20th wedding anniversary. I'll drive to Barnes Common. No-one will bother us there seeing as everyone will be preoccupied with stupid games and football. I'll have you all to myself, Louise." He laughed nastily, an expression of pure evil in his eyes.

"You're going to rape me, aren't you?" Louise managed to whisper. She'd rather die than succumb to him.

"Why not? It serves you right for messing with my life!" Mike spat in her face, then grabbed her hair until she cried in pain.

Louise felt a wave of nausea grip her stomach. She'd never been this petrified in her life.

"And raping you is just the beginning, oh yes. Just you wait and see what I've got in store for you!" Mike tightened his grip on her hair.

Suddenly, as if someone or something gave her the strength to retaliate, Louise screamed, "You bastard! I wish you'd never entered my life! Gabriella's right: you're a vicious bully and the worst thing that ever happened to me!"

As Mike's face contorted in rage, he noticed a group of kids standing outside the car. With his free hand, Mike rolled down the window. "Get the hell away from us!" As they ran off, he laughed maniacally.

For a split second Louise had the opportunity to break free from his grip on her hair and managed to get out of the car. The pavement swam before her as she skidded and nearly tripped. Blood was dripping down her thigh and leg.

Not bothering to lock the car, Mike ran after her and seized her arm. "You say anything to incriminate me and I'll make you pay!" He shoved her towards the entrance. Unsteadily, she staggered into the back of the dark pub and slumped down on the wooden bench. With her sleeve she wiped Mike's spit from her face.

Louise was trembling at the shock of what Mike had just put her through and what she now knew he was capable of. *If I hadn't got out of the car when I did, God alone knows if I'd still be alive,* she thought. Imagining what he had in store for her made her shake all over.

Feeling the tension in the room as staff stared at them from behind the bar, she forced a smile. She was close to collapsing. If that happened, maybe she'd get the opportunity to tell them what Mike was doing to her? Perhaps someone would contact Trine and Jasper.

The jukebox at the front of the bar churned out tunes from the Sixties and Seventies, drowning out the noise from the few people who were there. A tall blonde came up to them and asked if they wanted something to drink.

"Are you two okay?" she asked, the question aimed directly at Louise.

"What's it got to do with you?" Mike snapped at her. "Get us a couple of glasses of red wine."

Livid he was shouting at her, the young barmaid replied curtly, "Don't you take that tone with me! Keep your voice down. You're not the only people in the pub."

"What bloody people?" Mike shouted at her, his eyes full of contempt. "There's only a couple of old farts here. You won't get busy until later!"

Ignoring his outburst, the girl looked at Louise and shook her head. Returning to the bar she uncorked a bottle of red wine, poured some into two glasses, returned and placed them on the table. Turning to look at Louise she said, "I'd never let a guy treat me like that. I'm not surprised you're upset. I'd give him a piece of my mind if I were you!"

Too scared to respond, Louise sipped her wine, the hand holding the glass shaking so much she spilled some of it on her dress.

Glaring at the barmaid who left them to it and returned to the bar, Mike mocked his ex-wife. "Isn't this cosy? Just you and me having a quiet drink in our favourite pub."

"What is it you want from me, Mike? We've not seen each other for nearly two years." She was desperate to get away from him and message her friends. They must be wondering what happened to her by now. While Mike downed his wine in a few gulps, she spoke quietly but firmly. "How dare you put the blame on me for what happened with Abby and Steve? Not forgetting you and me! You stole from me, pretending you didn't have the funds to clear your debts. I'm pleased Steve found out about the account!" She kept her voice steady and on the same level as before. The last thing she wanted was to attract the wrong attention and risk being thrown out of the pub. If they were, Mike would harm her even more than he already had.

"There you go again, feeling sorry for yourself! You deliberately handed over my laptop to your friends. Thanks to you I don't have a leg to stand on with Steve. He's got me by the balls. Unless I agreed to buy his share for an extortionate amount of money, he would have reported me to the police for attacking Abby! That bitch stole my money and completely got away with it. She hit me on the head and nearly killed me before she ran off!"

Mike's voice was so loud, the young barmaid and her stocky middle-aged supervisor came up to them, their eyes blazing. "Sir, you've been asked to not shout. Please be so good as to leave this establishment."

"That's fine with me, this place is a dump!" Mike replied, laughing in their faces.

"Please . . . I'm feeling unwell. We'll not shout anymore," Louise stammered, praying they'd let them stay a while longer.

"Continue the way you are and you leave me no option but to call the police," the supervisor warned, red in the face.

"Okay, mate. I'm sorry I raised my voice earlier. The missus and I were having a domestic!" Mike excused himself.

"This is your last warning. You'll be thrown out if you don't behave."

They'd barely left them and returned to the bar, when Mike hissed, "Shit! Some bloody traffic warden just put a ticket on the windscreen on my car. What the hell?"

"You must talk to him, try to make him change his mind. I feel as if I'm about to faint . . . Please can you get me a glass of water?"

Mike exploded. "Always the actress, aren't you? I'm not fooled by you anymore, Louise. You meant nothing to me! All you ever were was a meal ticket, especially after your parents died and left you all that money. You sure as hell fell for me, hook, line and sinker!" He relished seeing her looking so distressed.

"Please get me some water . . . I've not had anything to eat since breakfast . . ."

Ignoring her, Mike ran out into the street to check if he'd received a hefty fine. With shaking fingers, Louise reached for her phone and keyed in a text message. It was almost 6.00 pm and Trine and Jasper must be worried sick about her. They only had another couple of days left together before she travelled back to Malmö.

Approaching her again now she was alone, the young barmaid had a worried expression in her eyes. "Are you sick, Miss? I'll get you a glass of water, okay?"

"Thank you, that's very kind of you."

The room started to spin around her. Suddenly, Louise couldn't care less what happened to her. Mike was nothing but a bully and fraudster. She'd stopped loving him a long time ago.

As Mike came back in, swearing and clutching a parking ticket, she decided enough was enough.

"I curse the day I met you!" she cried. "You're nothing to me. You're dead to me, is that understood?" Tears streamed down her face and mouth.

Seeing her distress, the blonde girl and the manager ran up to them. "Right! That's enough, you bastard. I warned you to keep your mouth shut! If you continue to upset this lady, I'll call the police," the manager shouted at Mike.

"Here's your water, Miss. Is there something I can do for you? You're looking awfully pale . . ." The girl watched as Louise sipped her water.

"No...thank you for the water. I'll be fine once I've calmed down." Louise's voice was trembling so much she could hardly get the words out, praying her friends would turn up before she collapsed.

Seething with anger, Mike put his hand up. "All right, I hear you. We'll leave as soon as my wife's calmed down. Now go and tend to your punters." Daring to look into the manager's eyes, Mike sneered, "What's wrong? I don't take orders from a jerk like you."

"Is that right? We'll see what the police have to say about it, shall we? I'll call them straight away."

The manager was on the verge of calling them from his mobile when Mike's expression changed from one of menace to abject horror. The two people he hated almost as much as Louise had just entered the pub. His gaze swung accusingly from the newcomers to his ex-wife. "You must have texted them while I was outside in the street!"

Fortunately for her, Trine and Jasper received the message just as they were on their way to pick up Zack from a friend's birthday party. It had taken less than fifteen minutes to drive from Putney to Barnes High Street.

As her friends rushed up to her, Louise heard Jasper say, "You sorry excuse for a man!" Oblivious to everyone in the pub, he put a hand around Mike's neck and dragged him out onto the pavement and punched his face. "That's for what you did to my wife and Louise!" he said, swearing. "If you ever come near us again, I'll get my mates to teach you a lesson you'll never forget!"

Meanwhile, Trine put an arm around her friend and walked her slowly out to Jasper's van, where she held her close in the back seat. Her friend was shaking so much she could barely speak.

"Please say you're okay!"

"I will be in a while . . . Mike's beyond help. To think I actually loved him . . ."

She was close to collapse. Taking a sip of the bottle of water Trine gave her, Louise stared out of the van window, watching Mike attempting to break free from a police officer holding him in a firm grip, before the other officer handcuffed him and they pushed him inside the police car that was parked outside the pub. "I was married to a sociopath and I wasn't even aware of it," Louise said, surprisingly matter of factly. "There's only ever been one man I truly love and who feels the same about me."

They were on their way back to Putney when Jasper turned to look at her in the van. "Are you feeling better?" he asked, concern etched all over his kind face.

"I am now, thanks to you turning up when you did. Today's been the worst yet also the best day of my life. At least now I can get on with my life and not worry about getting the answers I needed. Mike's a dangerous and sick man. I'm pleased Abby and the baby are safe with Steve." Despite her terrifying ordeal, Louise felt more at peace with herself than she had in a long time.

They spent the next couple of days recovering at Trine and Jasper's house.

When they said goodbye at the airport, Trine whispered in Louise's ear, "Let Nicklas into your heart and life. I know the two of you will be perfect for each other."

Touched she always had her best interests at heart, Louise replied, "I already did all those years ago. Watch this space."

She gave Trine, Jasper and Zack a hug and walked towards the check-in desk. The moment had arrived when she had to focus on what mattered the most in her life.

After she returned to Malmö, Louise instinctively knew she needed to keep busy and spent the first week calling designers recommended by Trine. When the deliveries arrived from the new designers she'd placed orders with in London, Louise was even more impressed. They'd surpassed her wildest expectations and not only sent her what she ordered, but also samples from their forthcoming collections.

It was exciting to see proof of their talent and evidence they weren't limited in what they had to offer. The combination of new and established designers worked out way above expectations and enticed clients to return again and again.

While she was in London, Trine had suggested she offer accessories including scarves, belts and bags, in addition to costume jewellery, but that wasn't something Louise planned to do until later. All the same, Little Square was heaving with tourists who frequently shopped in La Femme and word of mouth soon spread about how versatile and chic the collections were. Louise's dream to open her own ladies' boutique in Malmö was not only a roaring success locally but also acknowledged in Stockholm, Copenhagen and abroad.

Louise had every intention of calling Nicklas on her return, but every spare moment seemed to be swamped with work for La Femme, and she needed a little headspace to come to terms with what had happened with Mike. Late one evening, just as she entered the flat and fed Rufus, the phone rang. It was him.

"You're back! I apologise if I woke you up. Gabriella said you'd returned from London a week ago. We bumped into each other at a friend's gallery in Copenhagen the other day. She looked great. Apparently, Åsa is on the mend. I'm pleased to hear they've decided to retire simultaneously."

"I am as well. It makes perfect sense, given the circumstances. Are you okay?" She wanted to tell him how much she'd missed him but decided to tell him in person when they met up instead.

"All the better for talking to you . . . did you have a good time with your friends?" Nicklas knew how difficult it must have been for her to return to a city she got married and divorced in. He wondered if she'd found the time to decide if she wanted them to be more than just friends, but couldn't bring himself to ask over the phone.

"Yes, I did. It was wonderful to spend time with Trine and Jasper. They're taking great care of The Studio. I've just received deliveries from the new designers I placed orders with when I was in London . . ." She trailed off. Jabbering on about her shop wasn't exactly what she'd had in mind when she talked to him.

"La Femme is great!" Nicklas said with enthusiasm. "You ought to be very proud of yourself. It requires a lot of perseverance to open your own shop and you've done it twice. Louise . . . is something wrong? I can tell by the tone of your voice you've something on your mind." *Perhaps she met someone who said or did something to upset her,* he thought.

"I visited Barnes while I was in London. I wanted to see the house we lived in for so long. Mike turned up unexpectedly. He's ill, Nicklas." Louise took a deep breath. "He assaulted me and we ended up in a pub on the high street. I thought it was the right thing to do. God only knows what would have happened to me had I not managed to text Trine and Jasper. Luckily they turned up shortly before the police arrived and took Mike away." Louise felt guilty she hadn't called Nicklas the minute she returned home.

Speechless she'd been through such an ordeal and that he wasn't there to protect her, Nicklas let out a big sigh. "Is that the reason you didn't call me?"

"Yes. I needed some time to myself to work through what happened...I was just about to call you when you beat me to it." The words came tumbling out of her mouth before she had time to think. It felt so good to be able to tell someone about it, other than Gabriella, who'd nearly had a fit when she found out what Mike did.

"I miss you . . . please let me know you're okay, even if you don't want us to meet just yet."

"But I *do* want to meet up with you! I've missed you so much. Please don't think I'm avoiding you, because I'm not."

"Louise, I can't imagine what you must be going through. I'd have killed the guy if I'd been there. I love you and I'm here for you. Take all the time you need. Meanwhile I'll be waiting for you to get in touch. Sleep tight." He hung up before she had time to respond. After what she'd confided in him, Nicklas also required time to get his head around what happened with Mike.

The following day, Louise finished early at the boutique and went straight home to feed Rufus and take him for a walk in Willow Park. It was a hot day and she stopped at a kiosk and bought an ice cream cone. Sitting on a wooden bench at the entrance with Rufus half asleep at her feet, Louise wished Nicklas was there with them. *I've got to call him and tell him I can't wait to see him*, she thought and got up from the bench, Rufus wagging his tail as if to say he agreed.

Suddenly she knew exactly what she had to do. Running all the way home, Louise and Rufus entered the apartment building just as Trine called to tell her that Robert had phoned, saying Mike had been found guilty of assault and fraud and sentenced to five years in prison. "It serves him right after what he did to us and Steve!"

Ecstatic he'd finally got his comeuppance, Louise replied, "That's wonderful. Thank you for letting me know. Now I'm ready to move on with my life."

"What about Nicklas? I hope he's not given up on you!"

Smiling to herself, Louise replied, "I do believe we're heading in the right direction."

Laughing, Trine exclaimed, "Hallelujah, you've finally come to your senses!"

With shaking hands Louise dialled Nicklas' number and almost gave up, when after eight rings she heard his voice at the other end of the line. "Hi, it's me . . . Louise. Are you free to talk?"

"Of course, it's wonderful to hear your voice. I was just on my way to Copenhagen to attend a meeting. Are you okay? You sound tense."

"I just found out my ex-husband's been sentenced to five years in prison. It sounds awful but I'm so pleased. Anyway, I didn't call about that. When will you return to Malmö?" Louise held her breath, praying he wouldn't be away for long. She was aching to see him.

"I'm back early evening. Someone's picking me up and I'll book a cab to drive me across the Öresund Bridge when the meeting's finished. Why do you want to know?" He sounded hopeful. Perhaps she was ready to meet him, after all.

"Will you let me take you out to dinner tonight?" Louise asked, heart in her throat. "I need to talk to you."

"Only if it's on me and please say yes. I'm dying to be with you."

"But it's only right I pay after all the times you've footed the bill."

"You did that plenty of times when we were young. Please don't argue – it's not up for discussion."

"Alright! How about we meet at ZinZino at seven o'clock?"

"I'll be there. Oh, Louise, I'm so happy you called."

"Have a good meeting in Copenhagen. I can't wait to see you." She was so excited to see him again she couldn't stop smiling.

The hours went by so slowly as she busied herself with getting ready to meet him. Wearing a blue organza dress, large hoop earrings and her hair loose, Louise applied more makeup than usual. Catching a glimpse of herself in the bedroom mirror, she smiled at her reflection. *I'll soon be with him,* she thought, feeling deliriously happy.

The restaurant was only a ten-minute walk from the flat, and as she approached, Louise saw Nicklas standing outside the entrance, waiting for her. His eyes lit up when she went up to him.

"You look beautiful . . . Your hair's grown. I haven't got the words to describe how I feel."

Putting a finger to his lips, Louise replied, "Me neither. You're looking very handsome tonight. I hope the meeting went well?"

He wore a dark grey suit and blue shirt and tie. She wanted to run her fingers through his thick, dark hair, the way she used to when they were kids. "Who cares? All I can think of is the present. I booked us a nice table further inside the restaurant; we need to talk. I've waited so long to tell you how I feel."

He cupped her face in his hands and kissed her mouth, making her melt inside.

Entering the restaurant hand in hand, Louise felt the other guests' eyes on them.

Sensing her apprehension, Nicklas pulled her close to him. "I'm fine. We're a nice couple, let's leave it at that." When a waiter walked up to them and took them to their table, Louise ignored the stares from the people at the table next to them.

"I don't understand how people can be so rude! Fortunately, this sort of thing doesn't happen often, yet when it does, I get so upset. I for one intend to ignore them. I suggest you do the same," she said, reaching for his hand across the table. The restaurant was as cosy as she recalled.

"Hey, we must put them out of our mind. I got used to that kind of behaviour years ago. The world's full of ignorant people."

After they'd ordered tagliatelle with salmon and spinach for her and lamb cutlets in brandy sauce for him, Nicklas asked her if she wanted white or red wine.

"I'll have the same as you. Red goes well with lamb."

"White goes well with salmon. Tell you what? We'll have both." He signalled for a waiter to place the order.

"Is this how it will be in the future? You ordering double of everything in order to prevent us from falling out?" she joked.

"As long as we're together, I don't mind," Nicklas replied with a twinkle in his eye.

Louise raised her glass in a toast. "I'm so pleased we met at Martin and Nils' party! I've never felt this happy before. You always make me feel loved and safe. I've thought about what you said when we last met. I'm not afraid anymore. Mike meant nothing to me compared to how I feel about you. I want us to be more than friends, Nicklas. Much, much more."

Nicklas' joy was written all over his face. "Oh, Louise! I never thought I'd hear you say that. I was prepared to wait indefinitely if that had been the case. You're the only woman I love and want to spend the rest of my life with. I'm madly in love with you and it's the best feeling in the whole world!"

They'd spent a lifetime apart, but that was about to end.

"This is our time to be happy. I never said goodbye to my parents or to you . . . We're so lucky we've got a second chance to be together." Louise had tears of happiness in her eyes. "Please come home with me . . . we've so much to catch up on," she whispered, her toe wandering up his leg under the table. She'd never desired anyone as much as him.

"I'll get the bill," Nicklas said in a hoarse voice. The food lay untouched on their plates. Suddenly all the years they were apart made him impatient to recapture what they'd once shared. Catching a cab in the street, they held each other close in the back seat.

It wasn't until they entered her flat, that Louise whispered, "I'll die if you don't kiss me now."

The passion she'd always felt for him hadn't diminished over the years; she'd just put it to the back of her mind. Bending to kiss her lips, neck and shoulders, Nicklas wondered how he'd survived for so long without her, the woman, lover and best friend.

Leading the way into the bedroom, Louise turned on the light on the bedside table. "Make love to me, I've spent too long in a life without love," she said, pulling him down on the bed. Feeling him so close to her, their faces and lips touching, Louise watched as he helped to remove her clothes, until she was naked. Returning the favour, Nicklas sighed contentedly as she unfastened his trouser belt and whispered, "I'm on the pill . . . in case you were wondering."

"I wasn't. But you're right. We're sufficient just as we are." He always knew she didn't want a family. It wasn't a big deal to him. Louise was all he wanted and needed. If he'd wanted kids, he could have had them with his ex-wife.

Moments later, feeling him push inside her, Louise murmured, "I never knew it could be like this; I'd forgotten how good we are together."

Afterwards, when they lay together, his arms wrapped around her, she heard him say, "I love you. Will you marry me?"

Blinking away the tears that welled up in her eyes, Louise replied, "I'd love to."

"Is that a yes?" he persisted, kissing the nape of her neck.

"I'll do whatever you want as long as it makes you happy." She'd gladly have settled for what they had yet also knew how much he wanted her to become his wife. "We will never lose each other again," she added softly, caressing his neck, shoulders and back. They didn't need anyone or anything to be happy and fulfilled apart from each other. Louise suddenly laughed. "I just thought of something. If Mike never left me I'd not have met you again. Do you realise how lucky I am that he did? Mamma always used to say that life has a way of sorting itself out."

"My mother used to say, 'Be careful what you wish for!' Wishes don't always turn out the way you expect them to. Mike's sure as hell didn't!" Nicklas felt the happiest he'd ever been. At long last, the only woman he'd ever loved was right there next to him.

"Our mothers were right. I lost my marriage yet gained more than I could ever have imagined – I found you again and returned to the place I left behind. I guess miracles do exist."

Louise snuggled up to the man she loved and fell asleep, a contented smile on her lips. She had finally come home.

ABOUT THE AUTHOR

Born into a bilingual family (Swedish/English) Hélene Fermont enjoyed an idyllic childhood on the outskirts of Malmö, Sweden's third largest city and major cultural hub. Growing up in the 1970's, she had a brief musical career on Swedish TV and radio prior to pursuing a career in teaching and eventually as a child therapist specialising in children with learning difficulties. Hélene has lived in London for over 20 years. She regularly returns to her native Sweden which further inspires the creative process. Hélene is currently hard at work on her next book.

Follow me @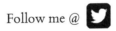

Meet me on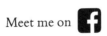

And visit my website www.helenefermont.com

24509704R00169

Printed in Great Britain
by Amazon